ALL for LOVE

ALL *for* LOVE

THREE HISTORICAL ROMANCE NOVELLAS *of* LOVE *and* LAUGHTER

The Boden Birthright
BY MARY CONNEALY

A Lady of Esteem
BY KRISTI ANN HUNTER

At Your Request
BY JEN TURANO

BETHANYHOUSE

a division of Baker Publishing Group
Minneapolis, Minnesota

The Boden Birthright © 2016 by Mary Connealy
A Lady of Esteem © 2015 by Kristi Ann Hunter
At Your Request © 2017 by Jennifer L. Turano

Published by Bethany House Publishers
11400 Hampshire Avenue South
Bloomington, Minnesota 55438
www.bethanyhouse.com

Bethany House Publishers is a division of
Baker Publishing Group, Grand Rapids, Michigan

Printed in the United States of America

ISBN 978-0-7642-3102-5 (trade paper)
ISBN 978-0-7642-3199-5 (cloth)

Library of Congress Control Number: 2017961162

These are works of fiction. The names, characters, incidents, and dialogues are products of the author's imagination and are not to be construed as real. Any resemblance to actual events or persons, living or dead, is entirely coincidental.

Cover design by Brand Navigation

Authors are represented by the Natasha Kern Literary Agency.

18 19 20 21 22 23 24   7 6 5 4 3 2 1

Contents

THE BODEN BIRTHRIGHT

A Cimarron Legacy Novella

MARY CONNEALY

1

BOSTON, MASSACHUSETTS
AUGUST 1852

"Bad boy!" Grandmama Bradford slapped Cole's wrist. "You've sloshed tea on the lace of your shirt."

Tea on the lace of his shirt? What? Chance Boden felt like he'd taken the slap himself—with a ten-day-old, ice-cold mackerel.

When had his son started wearing lace?

He woke up at that instant to realize he'd been in a daze ever since Abby died. He'd loved her so much. Abby, precious Abby, dying in his arms. He never should have let her have another child.

The grief almost dragged him back under. The guilt. The emptiness. The pain.

The lace.

His eyes focused on his son. He had on pastel blue velvet short pants. His dark hair was in . . . in . . . God have mercy, it was in ringlets.

There were high heels on his shining black boots.

Cole, four, flinched at the slap and said in a cultured, quiet voice, "I am sorry for my carelessness, Grandmama."

What four-year-old talked like that?

When Chance was four, he'd lived in Indiana on the frontier. He'd spent his time trying to grab his pa's shotgun to shoot squirrels. Pa

9

hadn't slapped him, either. He'd laughed and taught Chance how to fire the gun, then carefully hung it out of reach between lessons.

"I should hope so, young man. Your new shirt is ruined."

Chance opened his mouth to start yelling. To drag his son out of this room, and this house, and for heaven's sake out of that lacy shirt. He'd get the boy some proper trousers . . . and a haircut. The lace was bound for the fire.

Then he clamped his mouth shut, stood, excused himself and left the room. He knew his mother-in-law, Priscilla, too well. Nope, if he started yelling he'd lose this fight the minute he started it. He had to do something radical and he thought of exactly what as he marched out of the mansion.

He'd always been a man who faced things head on. Being clear-eyed and fast-thinking had helped him get very rich in Boston.

Now he faced the fact that his in-laws would fight him for control of the boy who would be their only heir. And even considering that Chance was very well-off, his wealth wasn't a patch on Priscilla and Davidson Bradford. They had enough money and connections in Boston to take his son from him.

So Chance didn't consider it an overreaction to decide to grab his boy and run. Take him somewhere the Bradfords couldn't influence lawmen and judges.

Indiana where Chance had grown up wasn't far enough.

He spent days making careful, quiet financial moves. He converted everything he had into gold. It was considerable because Abby was a wealthy woman in her own right, and Chance had done well working in business.

He found a wagon train leaving for the West. It was late in the year, so it was heading for St. Louis and staying to the south along the Santa Fe Trail.

Working through discreet agents, he bought three covered wagons, supplies to fill them all, mules to pull them, and tools to build a home when he decided where the trail would end. All under an assumed name.

Then he bought clothes for his son. Real clothes, not a stitch of lace or velvet anywhere. He packed the bulk of them, but kept one outfit along with a pair of scissors.

Chance hired good men to drive his wagons with his plans carefully explained. Chance didn't fool himself that Priscilla would make it easy. He knew her too well.

As he worked out the details, every evening Chance went home and ate supper like a good little boy, as obedient as Cole. When he made his move it had to be sudden, the break absolute. But the year was wearing down. By choice he stayed away when the wagon train headed out with his men and wagons.

Nearly two weeks went by before Chance's time came.

The wagon train was far down the trail. It could go about ten miles a day. He needed it to be a good distance from Boston before he joined it.

Priscilla and Davidson were leaving early in the morning for a weekend garden party with friends. There would be a buggy ride in the country to a big estate, and Cole wasn't invited.

Which was unusual.

Now that Chance's eyes were open, he realized Priscilla kept Cole at her side almost every minute.

The waiting had driven Chance half mad, and he'd avoided the house a good deal of the time to keep Priscilla from getting suspicious.

When Priscilla and Davidson left, Chance acted almost as soon as the dust settled behind them. He left a note saying he was taking Cole to the shore for two weeks.

Priscilla would assume he meant the Atlantic shore when in fact they'd be skirting Lake Erie.

No details beyond that. He sincerely hoped she didn't look for them until they'd caught up with the wagon train and were past St. Louis. Then if she hunted them, she'd be looking in the wrong place. With luck, by then he'd have well and truly lost himself on the Texas prairie. The woman had always been determined to control anyone who was within her reach, and her husband, Davidson Bradford, was worse.

They'd never had much luck controlling Chance. Abby had stood against them at Chance's side.

But they got Cole, because Chance was so buried in grief.

After the Bradfords left, Chance, not all that certain where his son's loyalties lay, said, "Cole, we're going for a ride in the park this morning."

The boy might tell the butler if Chance explained what was going on and then word could reach Priscilla within hours.

They rode out. Chance was careful to be on his own horses, not animals the Bradfords could accuse him of stealing.

Chance met a man in the park, who quickly traded horses with him, so that his own glossy, fine-boned thoroughbreds couldn't be described. Then Chance rented a room in a crowded boardinghouse. He only needed it to arrange a disguise. His and Cole's. He dressed them both in rugged wear fit for a long trip. Chance cut his son's hair and pulled a broad-brimmed western hat down low on his forehead.

"What do you think, son?" Chance held a very pretty brown curl up in front of Cole's eyes.

Those eyes gleamed in a way that gave Chance hope that his son wasn't hopelessly lost to the shallow ways of his grandparents.

"I like having short hair like you, Papa."

Chance hugged Cole close, and those small arms came around. Chance held him so tight he wondered if the boy would protest. But Cole nearly strangled him as he clung to his neck.

Finally, Chance pulled back, his throat feeling tight. "I love you, son. I have been bad to you."

"No, you haven't, Papa. You've just been sad."

"Call me Pa from now on, instead of Papa."

Cole tilted his head and a spark showed in his eyes. "Pa. All right."

Chance realized he hadn't seen such a lively expression since he'd begun planning their escape. It gave him hope that he could help Cole have a childhood again.

"I *have* been bad to you. I haven't spent time with you or talked to you like I should. It was sadness about your ma dying, but I have a fine son. I should have been spending time with you. You've needed me and I haven't been a good pa to you. That's going to change. You and I are going away where we can be a family again."

12

Cole blinked a few times, and Chance braced himself to be told by his son that the boy loved his grandparents more than he loved his pa. It was what Chance deserved.

"Can I stop wearing clothes that itch now, Pa?" The hope in the boy's eyes wrung a chuckle out of Chance.

"From now on you are going to wear clothes like these I just put on you. Clothes like the ones I've got on." They both wore brown trousers and a broadcloth shirt. They had boots—not high-heeled ones—and broad-brimmed brown leather hats. Chance had strapped on a gun belt. He was remembering who he was before he'd met and married Abby.

He was going so far west, God was going to have to come hunting him, let alone Priscilla Bradford. And Chance was going to go hunting God. He'd neglected God, as well as his son.

"We're going on a train ride, Cole."

Cole's dark-blue eyes were wide with excitement. Chance felt like he was seeing the real spirit of his son, the boy behind the careful manners.

"Let's go."

They left the boardinghouse and rode straight for the train station.

Chance had only a small satchel, for the bulk of what he owned was on that wagon train. The boy hadn't realized it, but the clothes and the horses and the haircut amounted to a disguise. Chance expected Pinkertons to get involved, and he'd done a fair amount to slip away. Probably they would be found eventually, but not for a while. Not until they were well outside of the range of Davidson Bradford's power.

The horses were going with them, so Chance and Cole oversaw them being loaded, then jumped on board. The train chugged out of the station within minutes of their arrival. A train to Lake Erie had just started running this year.

They'd take a riverboat to St. Louis and meet the wagon train there, or if, as Chance hoped, the wagons had reached St. Louis and gone on, he'd catch up to them riding horseback.

And then he'd raise his son right.

2

Chance had never seen anything so beautiful in his life. He knew without one speck of doubt that he was home.

White peaks in the distance. A vast pastureland dotted with a huge herd of cattle, ringed by rising hills covered in quaking aspen trees.

They'd been seeing the cattle and pastures for days. But today was the biggest herd of all, spread out miles in each direction with a perfectly built ranch house at the center of it all.

Mountains sloped up around the edges of the pasture. Aspen covered the nearly vertical slopes. Thousands of trees, each with yellow leaves sparkling and twisting like living sunshine.

He'd find the man who owned this house and ask where his borders lay and go just beyond. This was New Mexico, newly added to the United States and even more recently sliced off from Texas to form the New Mexico Territory.

It was a wild, beautiful land.

Looking at the expanse of rich grassland set against the grandeur of the mountains, Chance felt the stirring in his blood to give his son a birthright, to create his own dynasty, to be a conqueror.

The West was doing that to him. He'd noticed it as his hands blistered, then grew calluses. As he sat on the wagon seat in cold wind and burning sunlight. He loved rising to the challenges. The

West was making him think bigger, dream of daring things. See what he could wrest out of the land with brute strength and the wits in his head.

But Chance fought the impulse.

He looked down at his son. Cole was his future. His goal in life was to be the best father he could be. No dynasty was going to tear his attention away from what was most important. His precious boy was staring wide-eyed at the mountains before them. Chance liked that the boy was paying attention to the mountains rather than the grand house. He liked that what shined in Cole's eyes matched what had to be shining in his own.

Chance planned to live in such a way that his son would grow up to be a strong, wise, honorable, faithful man. And the only way Chance knew to teach that was to be such a man himself.

This wagon train was going all the way to California, but as of this moment, Chance was at the end of the trail. The men driving his three wagons had already agreed to stop when Chance stopped. They all planned to work for him. In turn, Chance promised to help them put down stakes of their own. They were fine men, no doubt with ambitions of their own. If they didn't want to stay, Chance would wish them well and find a way to manage alone. His newly callused hand rested on Cole's head.

The boy tore his eyes off the view and smiled up at Chance. "It's mighty beautiful, Pa."

Chance talked to his men. If they wanted to go on, they needed to stay with the wagon train, which hadn't stopped. He'd give them one wagon and plenty of supplies plus their promised wages, and wave them on their way. But the men were as enthused as he was.

⌒⌒

Chance and his men drove their wagons right into the ranch yard. Chance wound his reins around the brake and hollered for his men to wait.

He took Cole along, and they walked up the five steps to the huge stone porch that wrapped all around the adobe-and-log house. Chance had seen plenty of humble homes as they drove along on the trail, but he hadn't even known you could build a two-story home out of the dried bricks.

As he realized how much he had to learn, he decided that starting a large ranch didn't have to be his first act. Maybe instead he could start small and learn the ways of New Mexico Territory. He wondered if this man might be interested in teaching him.

He knocked on the front door, and it swung open immediately. The residents of the house had seen him coming. And why not with three wagons and twelve big Missouri mules? He had a small herd of cattle, a crate with chickens and pigs—everything he could think of.

He forgot all about his wagons and cattle when the prettiest woman he'd ever seen stepped into the doorway, her eyes snapping blue, her yellow hair piled high on her head. She was tanned, which was considered unfashionable back east among the upper classes, but who could help but be tan in the relentless sun? She wore a fancy blue gown with lace at the sleeves and neck. It made him think of the velvet pants and lacy sleeves he'd taken from his son. He'd burned them, but they were just fine on her.

Despite the delicate feminine clothing, her expression was fearless and curious, and her eyes locked on his. He reacted so strongly he forgot what he'd come for. Only moments ago he'd thought the view of the mountains was unmatched for beauty. Now, with this woman, he had a new standard.

Then Cole tugged on his pant leg. She looked down and a smile bloomed on her face.

"Hello, young man. Who are you?" She spoke to Cole with a musical voice.

Cole seemed to come alive under her attention. Chance knew what that felt like.

"I'm Cole Boden, and this is my pa, Chance Boden. We'd like to live here please."

Her smile faded as she looked up from Cole to Chance. "This land is ours."

Ours. So she must be . . . "Are you related to the owner?"

A huge bear of a man came up behind her, sounding like the most welcoming person in the world. "Ronnie, let 'em in."

The man had a full beard as bushy as fur, and his hair was overlong. He was pure muscle and stood about six feet tall, Chance's height, and wore brown broadcloth pants and shirt with red suspenders and heavily scuffed boots. No finery like his daughter.

Her eyes narrowed. "Look at them, Pa. They've brought supplies. I think this is another fool who wants to take our land."

The man's friendly manner shrank and hardened faster than adobe bricks in the noonday sun. "That right?" He looked past Chance to the wagons. "You think my land is free for the taking?"

Somehow Chance had gone from two welcoming smiles to being the enemy. "No, I do not."

Cole inched up against Chance's leg, and Chance rested his hand on his son's shoulder and spoke more calmly. "I'm Chance Boden. I'm looking to settle. My boy and I came west after my wife died, to start over."

Ronnie—which couldn't be this beautiful woman's name—looked down at Cole, and her expression softened.

"I saw this beautiful land, and when I got to your home, I told the wagon train to go on to California without me. What I'd like from you is to know the boundary of your property so I can settle nearby. I won't take property anyone else owns, but in this vast open country there must be a grassy valley somewhere that's unclaimed. My men and I and my son would settle there."

The man studied him silently for a long stretch, taking Chance's measure. A man who trusted his instincts. Chance was sure that whatever he decided, his decision would be final.

The man finally nodded. His eyes didn't lose their watchfulness as he reached out a massive hand. "I am Francois Chastain. Call me Frank. We've had trouble a time or two, so I'm primed and ready for it. Come on in."

He shook Chastain's hand, which felt like cowhide. He nodded at the wagons. "Tell your men to unhitch. They can find food for the horses around back. I've got a bunkhouse full of cowhands who will help. There'll be food for your men there and a decent bed. You can all rest overnight, and I'll give you some directions."

"I don't want to put you to any trouble," Chance said.

"We'd welcome visitors, especially a young'un." Chastain turned kind eyes on Cole. "We don't see many children out here, do we, Ronnie?"

Ronnie gave her father an exasperated look. Her gaze swung to Chance. "My name is Veronica. No one calls me Ronnie except Pa. Come in. It's late in the day and we will have a meal in about an hour. There's plenty. You can wash up and talk ranching with Pa while I add two more plates to the table."

Veronica. A pretty name for a pretty woman.

"Much obliged, Frank, Miss Veronica," replied Chance. As he said her name out loud, he realized he hadn't really noticed a woman since Abby died. In fact, he hadn't noticed a woman since he'd met Abby six years back.

He was doing some powerful noticing right now.

"Let me talk to my men."

Veronica smiled at him. "I'll take Cole in and help him wash up."

"Thank you. I'll be right back."

His *noticing* felt like unfaithfulness. It was a pure shock to find a part of his heart he'd thought died with Abby was alive and kicking. To stop the reaction, he'd have wrapped Abby's memory around him and buried himself in guilt. But he'd sworn to stop that. He needed to care for his son.

Since he couldn't let his thoughts sink into grief, he was left with not wanting to let Veronica out of his sight. She and Cole walked away. Chance turned to his wagons and went in the opposite direction of his son and that beautiful woman. It was one of the hardest things he'd ever done.

3

Veronica was so drawn to the little boy it surprised her. "Let me pour warm water for you while you wash."

Cole looked up at her and smiled. He was the most beautiful child she'd ever seen. His hands were grimy, as was his face. He had overlong hair, and she could see his clothes were coated in dust. She thought he looked underweight too, though how many little boys had she even seen?

Of course, they'd been on a wagon train. Certainly it was hard to keep clean, but everything in her wanted to help. She wanted to protect him and find him clean clothes and feed him.

She took up a cloth and washed days of trail dust off Cole's precious smiling face. She wanted to give him a bath, trim his hair.

"Cole, there is a cake in the kitchen, already sliced. Would you like me to get you a piece?"

Cole's eyes, a dark blue, widened with hunger. "Cake, miss? Oh yes, we didn't have many sweets on the wagon train."

Veronica set him up with cake and a glass of milk just as her pa came in, all washed up and rubbing his face with a towel. Veronica noticed for the first time the fine lines on her father's face. Lines that couldn't be put down to age. Pa was worried about something and had been for a long time. Yet he wouldn't discuss it with her.

Chance stepped into the kitchen. He dragged his hat from his head, his eyes going right for his son, which made Veronica's heart pang a little at his devotion. Most people who came here noticed the beauty of their home first. She never trusted folks who looked about them with awe and sometimes envy.

Then Chance's eyes came to her and, well, another pang. His son was the image of Chance, blue eyes and dark hair that had a bit of a curl. There was no denying they were both good-looking gentlemen. She looked away quickly, confused by her reaction. To fend off her unruly thoughts, she got very busy bringing Cole more milk and left Chance to Pa.

"Sit. I'll get you some coffee." Pa headed for the kitchen stove, a big cast-iron rectangle hauled here from St. Louis years ago, not long after Pa and his partner at the ranch, Don Bautista de Val, were given a half-million-acre land grant by the president of Mexico.

Then Mexico had sold this whole area to the United States in the Treaty of Guadalupe Hidalgo, and Don de Val was told that, to keep his share, he had to become an American.

He was an arrogant man who took great pride in his pure Spanish blood and his close connections to the president of Mexico. Outraged, he went home to Mexico City. His half of the land grant was nullified, and Pa changed the name of his ranch to Cimarron after the river that ran though his spread. His cattle now had a bold twisted-together CR as a brand.

Frank had no qualms about changing his citizenship. Born in Canada, his mother had died when he was young and his father had moved to the American Rockies soon afterward. Frank had grown up there and stayed to trap. Because of the laws of residency, he was a full-fledged American simply by virtue of living in the country long enough.

He'd also done some wandering, and when he met Veronica's mother twenty-five years ago, he'd settled in this area while it was still Mexico.

He was temporarily riding with Don de Val when he managed to save the life of an important Mexican official. That earned him and the Don joint ownership in a Spanish land grant on the condition

Frank became a naturalized Mexican citizen. Pa didn't give citizenship much thought, so he became Mexican and partnered up with the Don. After which the Don, a wealthy man in his own right, lived a life of wealth and ease on his half of the massive ranch, and Pa went to work and tore a fortune out of his half with the strength of his back and the sharp wits in his head. Then the land under them was made to be part of the treaty that changed it from Mexican land to American. The Don returned to Mexico City. And Pa, who'd changed countries so casually before, became American again.

At the time, it was a simple matter to be a citizen: just live in the country without committing a crime for a stretch of years and you were in. But despite the passage of more than enough years, the New Mexico territorial governor—or possibly men working in his name—didn't care for the old land grants. They allowed Pa to be harried by settlers, who didn't recognize his ownership. The governor remained loyal to Pa because Pa was generous when the governor needed money. But Veronica suspected much was done in the governor's name that he knew nothing about.

And that could be the source of his worry.

Pa filled two cups with coffee, always kept warm on the back of the stove this time of year. "Ronnie, you want a cup?"

"Yes, thank you, Pa." Veronica enjoyed the cool weather of winter. It never got too fiercely cold, and it was a wonderful break from the brutal heat of summer. Besides, she wanted to sit and listen to the men talk. And she wanted to stay by Cole.

With the kind smile Pa used only with her, he poured a third cup. When he set it in front of her, the smile was kind, but there was something else in his eyes. His gaze shifted to Chance and back again, which reminded her that Pa had been known to do some matchmaking. She didn't take it seriously, however, not when they'd only met Chance a few minutes ago. Soon the four of them were sitting around the kitchen table.

"I haven't had much time to think, Chance, but it seems to me I can help you find a mighty nice stretch of land that might be just what you're looking for. There are native folks around, Pueblos mostly.

21

They're peaceable folks for the most part. There are some Apache and Comanche, too. They can be cantankerous, but I treat 'em fair and get on with 'em well enough. I can help ease your way in dealing with them. We're a long way from anyone and we don't get much company. I like the notion of having a neighbor."

Chance smiled, and Veronica couldn't help but notice it was a fine smile. He was looking at Pa, but he glanced her way and she looked down quickly, embarrassed to get caught staring. What would he think of her?

"That is an offer I really appreciate, Frank. Is the land far from here?"

Pa leaned closer. He had a way about him when dealing with business. Veronica suspected Chance would be drawn in just as most men were.

"I own a quarter of a million acres."

"A quarter of a million acres!" Chance exclaimed. "I've never heard of a spread that big."

"Out here in the West there are plenty bigger than mine. One just to the north is four million. But I'm plenty satisfied with what I got."

"Satisfied?" Chance shook his head.

"My home is planted right in the middle of my land, so the boundary lines are a ways off. And that's what I want to talk about."

Chance held his coffee cup with both hands, warming them on the tin, looking stunned at the talk of such huge tracts of land.

"What I'm wondering about is your boy."

Veronica narrowed her eyes at Pa. What was he up to?

A furrow appeared on Chance's forehead as his eyes flickered between Pa and Cole. "What about him?"

"Who's gonna watch after him while you're trying to tear a living out of this land? I'm established now, but I'll promise you it ain't easy—especially for a man alone and with a child to care for."

"The men who came in with me are going to stay, so it's not just the two of us. But even so, nope, not easy," Chance agreed. "I grew up on my pa's farm in Indiana. I tagged after him from a young age. Ma fed us, so I know she had a big part of caring for me, but I ran after Pa from morning to night. I expect Cole will do the same."

Chance looked at his son, who was listening to every word. He seemed like a mighty smart boy for one so young. "Won't you, Cole? We're going to count on each other."

Cole nodded. "We will, Pa."

There was a long silence, and again Veronica wondered what in the world Pa had on his mind.

"Here's my idea, Boden. I am always hiring cowpokes. But they're a rootless breed, always looking to the far horizon. In the winter it's not so much trouble to get by shorthanded, but I could surely use help."

Frowning as if confused, Chance said, "You want to hire me? I'm not looking for a job, Frank."

"Nope, you look like a man who is used to being his own boss and I respect that, but hear me out."

Chance nodded.

"A ranch in New Mexico Territory and a farm in Indiana aren't the same critter at all."

There was no reaction to that.

"My idea, especially because I could use the help, is that you spend the winter here. Don't think of it as a job, though I'll be glad to pay you a decent salary." Suddenly Veronica was certain Pa was matchmaking, the old coot. "Learn about living in these parts. Get to know the land and how to handle longhorns."

"I've heard of longhorns, although I don't know much about them."

"Well, they're as hardy as scorpions and as mean as rattlesnakes."

"What's a scorpion?"

"A sort of huge bug that has a poisonous sting." Veronica was alarmed at the danger Cole would be in if Chance didn't have the sense to be wary of scorpions.

Chance's brows rose nearly to his hairline.

"If you'll spend at least a few months here, I'll teach you what you need to know about the good and bad in a rugged yet beautiful land. I'll help you scout out grazing and water holes that aren't claimed yet. I can teach you more about cactus, rattlesnakes, and which spider bites can kill you than you can believe. I'll show you where my boundary lines are and guide you to some prime grassland that's yours for

23

the taking. You can find a place that suits you, with shelter from the worst of the summer heat. You can make a choice for yourself instead of letting me do the picking. I think you'll take to the land better if I ain't standin' by saying what you should choose."

Chance kept listening.

Veronica surely did like a man who wasn't bullheaded. Maybe Chance was such a man.

4

"I'm determined to be on my own, Frank." Chance tried to hide it, but inside, even though he'd considered that he could learn from Frank, every ounce of his stubbornness reared up at what felt like charity. Did Frank feel sorry for him? That didn't sit right.

Frank Chastain was a wealthy man, and something about the offer made Chance feel like a beggar.

And he wasn't sure how closely he wanted to associate with the Chastains. This house was too much like his in-laws' place back in Boston. The lavish house was shocking in its finery, especially considering how far they were from civilization. All of it had been shipped out here, most likely at a staggering cost.

Making sudden decisions with confidence was one of Chance's best skills as a businessman and right now he made one. Though he wasn't looking for work, and intended to be his own boss soon, the only way he'd accept Frank's help was if he earned it.

"Instead of just letting me stay here and learn from you, I'll take a job. But I'll work hard for nothing beyond food and a place to sleep. Learning will be payment enough."

Then Chance had a second thought. "I'm not sure Cole will do well in the bunkhouse. I don't know your men, so I apologize if I'm speaking unfairly, but sometimes the talk can get rough."

"I've thought on that, too."

Chance felt a flare of irritation. "You've done a lot of thinking for a man who's only known me for about half an hour."

Laughing, Frank said, "I've done more thinking than you can believe."

Now what in the world did Frank mean by that?

"But I'll put some of it aside for later. I've always had a housekeeper who lived here with us. The last one married my foreman, Sarge, a few months ago. I built them a house, so her rooms are empty. Consuelo still comes in every day, and her mostly grown daughter, Rosita, with her. But there are three rooms behind the kitchen that were hers. You and your boy can use them."

"I don't expect you to take me into your house." Chance felt his hackles go up again. "I'm a hired hand, and I'll live like one."

"I'm not doing it to treat you different from the other men," Frank said, waving off Chance's protests as if they were buzzing gnats. "I'm thinking of Cole, just as you are. I don't have a place fit for him in the bunkhouse. He can tag you all he wants, but if you ever have a chore that is dangerous to him, or when the weather turns bitter cold, which it does some days, you can leave him in here with my Ronnie."

Right when Chance had been ready to tell Frank to forget the whole thing, he mentioned Cole and danger and cold. He did need the help, but how much was too much? He'd left so much to his mother-in-law that he'd almost lost his son.

Chance reached over and covered Cole's hand. "I told you I'm not going to let anything keep me from being a good father to you, son. I left you to yourself after your mama died and I won't do that again. If I say yes to this, you'll live in a better place than if we build a rough cabin, but we'd work together."

As he said it, Chance realized just how young Cole was. A four-year-old couldn't do much.

"I can still spend time with you, even though we're living in here, can't I, Pa?"

That warmed Chance's heart. He was afraid the child's head might be turned by the fancy house.

"We surely will be together. I love you, Cole, and nothing is more important to me than showing you how much. Showing you every day."

"What do you say, Cole?" Veronica asked. She drew Chance's attention again, and he realized she was looking so sweetly at the two of them, almost like she had a mist of tears in her eyes. She was as pretty a little thing as he'd ever seen.

Giving himself a mental shake, he turned his attention back to his son. After so many months of neglect, Chance had too many fences to mend with his boy. He wasn't going to even think about a woman.

Cole shrugged and smiled. "We can stay, Pa. It's nice here."

Giving his permission, as if he understood how important his happiness was to Chance.

Looking between Veronica and Frank, Chance nodded. "I'm much obliged to you folks. Thank you, we will stay. And, Veronica, I would very much appreciate your help with Cole. He's a good boy." Chance gave Veronica what he hoped was a look she'd understand was important. "Almost too good at times. He needs more time to be a boy. You won't fuss at him overly, I hope, nor keep him too quiet and still?"

Veronica looked down at Cole. "I'm not worried about a young boy being a bit unruly at times. And we'll find plenty of time to play."

⌒◦

"I'll have a meal on soon. Let me show you where you'll be staying. Then, Pa, do you want to show Chance around?" Veronica rose from the table and began picking up coffee cups.

Chance grabbed two cups and followed her to the porcelain sink.

Pa had poured the coffee. Chance was helping clear the table. She hoped Chance had a similar temperament to her father's.

She also hoped he'd let Cole stay inside with her all day every day.

5

Cole went outside with his father all day every day.

Veronica was impressed at the extent to which Chance kept Cole with him. But she was so charmed by the little boy, and he wasn't spending nearly enough time inside. Chance was out the door before Cole woke up, so she cared for him until Pa and Chance came in for breakfast. But then off he went with the men. After lunch, Cole usually slept for a time, and Veronica got him for a bit after his nap. But then would come Chance to collect him again. Chance was showing great devotion to his son.

The big idiot.

She knew things were getting bad when she found herself hoping for bitter cold.

They'd been here the better part of a month now and Cole was as sweet to her as he could be. He was also rowdier than he'd been at first. She couldn't help but be glad of that. He'd been almost painfully polite at times.

They ate with the men while discussing land, cattle, riding, and roping. Cole talked too, and Chance was careful to listen to every word the youngster spoke.

Inwardly torn up with jealousy, she did her best to smile and listen to the day's goings-on, events she'd not been included in or invited to.

She realized she wasn't really listening when Pa said, speaking too loudly, "Ronnie, will that be all right?"

By his tone she knew he'd said her name more than once. "Will what be all right?"

Pa gave her an exasperated glare. "We're going to be out in rugged country tomorrow. Chance and I have decided it's too rough of a ride for Cole."

"Cole, will you stay with Miss Veronica?" Chance, consulting with his son. It was really sweet. It made her want to strangle Chance for giving the boy a choice.

Cole looked from Chance to her and back. "I'd be happy to stay inside if you need me to, Pa."

She was thrilled at the same time she wished Cole was spirited enough to throw a temper tantrum.

"Thank you, son. We'll be out for a long, hard day. Mr. Chastain is taking me to the high-up hills tomorrow. He says there are some mountain valleys that will make likely ranchland for us. We'll have to ride hard, though, because it's hours away."

Veronica's stomach sank as she thought of them living hours away. Why, she'd never see them again. Or if they did meet, she'd be nothing but a friendly neighbor.

Why was Pa finding land for the Bodens that was so far away?

Well, she'd have a stern talk with Pa soon enough, but for tomorrow, she got Cole all to herself. "What would you say to me baking a cake, Cole? We can have a special treat to celebrate your day here."

As if he didn't live right here. But still, she felt like celebrating.

"You know how much I love cake, Miss Veronica."

"Have you ever licked the spoon used to stir the cake batter?"

"No, back home I wasn't allowed in the kitchen."

That struck Veronica as strange. The kitchen was the heart of the family. "Well, you're allowed here in my kitchen. How can I watch you if you don't stay close?"

The boy's eyes shone like little bits of blue sky. "I'd even help if you wanted me to."

"I'd like that very much. Thank you."

༄

She must have passed some test, because Chance started letting Cole stay in with her more and more. Or maybe the man didn't want his son to freeze to death.

It had turned cold. Regardless of the true reason, Veronica chose to believe the former.

Things were going well with Cole. Even Chance was acting friendly and grateful for her help.

The mystery was Pa. He had lost the matchmaking gleam in his eye, or maybe he'd learned to mask it. But those worry lines were still there, and she couldn't figure out how to erase them because he wouldn't talk.

And then Chance came in alone for the noon meal. Cole was in his room, fetching a clean shirt after he'd climbed on a chair and grabbed a gravy spoon. She was alone with Chance. Normally he and Pa came in together.

Chance looked around the kitchen. "Frank didn't get back?"

Veronica closed the space between her and Chance. His question startled her. "I didn't know he left. He's always with you."

"Not today. He rode out this morning."

"And he didn't say where?" Veronica had a bowl half-filled with mashed potatoes in her hands.

"Nope, he took off with barely a word right after breakfast. I asked if he needed help, but he said no and rode off to the south."

"Does he have part of the herd off that way?"

Chance shrugged, "He does, but he wouldn't check the herd alone."

"Pa's always preached to me that this is a rough country, full of dangers. Trouble can catch up to you in everything from a Comanche raiding party to a gopher hole that trips your horse. It's not safe for a man alone." Her worry grew as her voice rose. "He's the one who taught me that, and it's a rule he enforces with the men and lives by himself."

Chance came closer, and their eyes met; she saw Chance's concern match her own.

"I shouldn't have come in with my worries."

"Please don't say that." Shaking her head, Veronica laid a hand on his arm. "I don't want to be sheltered against hard things. I've grown up riding herd more than most women, sticking to Pa like a burr, not as much as Cole sticks to you, but plenty. He's made me stay more to the house since I've grown up. He doesn't like the way the men pay attention to me, though they are always respectful. But I couldn't stand to stay in here if I thought the ranch work, the good and bad of it, was being kept from me."

Chance settled his hands on her upper arms. It was as if his strength were seeping into her, easing her fear. As the fear left, something else stirred deep inside her.

"I understand that. My wife and I never kept secrets from each other. Her mother was always trying to cause trouble between us, and Abby was too smart to give the old terror any room to cause a rift between them. Keeping secrets is one of the best ways to drive two people apart."

Perfect Abby.

Veronica hadn't heard much about her, but she'd seen the sadness in Chance's eyes. "I'm sorry you lost your wife. You must have loved her very much."

"I did indeed. I never thought another woman would . . ." Chance drew her closer.

She desperately wanted him to finish what he'd been about to say, since she was the only woman around.

Instead, he bent down and kissed her.

The shock of it and the sweetness were things she'd never prepared for. Never imagined.

"Pa, why are you so close to Miss Veronica?"

Shoving her away, Chance rubbed his mouth and turned quickly to his son. "Uh, I was just . . . uh, we were whispering. I needed to get close so she could hear."

"Whispering what, Pa?"

"That . . . that . . . I'm maybe going to have to miss the meal. Mr. Chastain needs me outside."

Veronica had her back to Cole, and a flash of irritation must have shown in her eyes because Chance, who'd been looking everywhere but at her, seemed to notice she was in the room and he glared. Or no, not glared. It was a different kind of strong emotion. One that warmed her and drew her.

"Your Pa has to ride out to find . . . I mean, to help my father." Veronica turned to face the little intruder. She loved this boy, but for just one second she rather missed the overly quiet child he used to be. And she wished he'd have just waited a few more minutes to come back.

"Your pa thought you'd be disappointed to have him miss sharing a meal. So we were whispering about what to tell you. But you're fine here with me, aren't you?"

Cole gave her a confused look, then his eyes slid to his father. "It looked more like you were kissing."

"Well, it was whispering, son. And now I've got to go help outside." Then, as if he'd gotten past that one foolish kiss, he said, "Sarge said your pa was real clear that we weren't to worry about him nor interfere with his business, and he'd be back by the noon meal. Since we'd been working out back around the barns and corrals, I'd hoped he came in the front for some reason."

Now he looked torn between Pa's orders and all Pa had taught him. Chance seemed to be considering which set of orders from Pa to obey.

She actually caught herself wringing her hands, which was so unlike her it cleared her head. "Well, Pa's a knowing man. If he left on his own, he had his reasons."

"He, uh, he doesn't have a . . . a . . ." Chance's cheeks took on a reddish hue. He was blushing, and it was so fascinating, Veronica's attention was riveted.

So she didn't miss his meaning, he cleared his throat and asked sheepishly, "He doesn't have a . . . a lady friend, does he?"

Veronica inhaled so hard it was almost an inverted scream. "Pa? You think Pa snuck off to go courting?"

Chance held out both hands as if trying to halt her words. "I have no idea where he might be. But why does a man want to be alone? It occurred to me he might be meeting someone. And why would a meeting be a secret? I don't know your pa very well, but he seems like a man who says what he thinks right out loud. Not a lot of sneaking in him."

That was a fair description of Pa, for a fact. "So if he had a woman he was ... well, visiting ..." Veronica's mind was truly boggled. Pa had never shown a moment's interest in a woman since Ma had died.

Veronica felt like a child to have never thought of her father as a man who might want to marry again. Her own cheeks grew hot.

Chance shrugged, "I'm sure that's not it. We just need to be patient." He turned to look out the kitchen door and stood there with his back to the room for too long.

"No." His shoulders squared, and he whipped his head around, the blush gone, the awkwardness replaced by a take-charge man. "He should be here by now. I'm going hunting, taking the men with me. We aren't coming back without your pa."

Chance charged out the door and slammed it shut.

Veronica was glad Chance was going. Pa might be annoyed with a search party and people not trusting him to handle himself, but something was wrong about Pa going off like he'd done, and something was even more wrong that he wasn't back when he'd said.

She watched Chance stride away, with Sarge, John, and several other cowhands with him, thinking of how he'd touched her, remembering how he'd kissed her. There went a man she could trust. A sharp tug on her skirts drew her attention. She looked down at Cole.

His blue eyes were filled with confusion, also with affection. "So you were whispering with Pa and kissing at the same time? Why is that, Miss Veronica?"

And she felt her cheeks turning red again. "I need to check the pie I've got in the oven."

Cole's eyes gleamed with excitement.

"You go ahead and sit up to the table so we can eat." She was a very fortunate woman to have a child young enough to be distracted by pie.

6

"Over there! His horse!" John Hightree, one of the best cowhands on the Cimarron Ranch, a man Chance's age who'd become a good friend, spurred his mustang toward the gray stallion, standing with its head down. Unusual for Frank's spirited mount.

Chance was hard on John's heels, catching and passing him. Sarge only a pace behind.

The mustang started to lift its head, then lowered it again and shuffled oddly.

Slowing to keep from spooking the horse, Chance saw a rein tangled with the mustang's front leg. Had Frank dropped the reins and tripped the horse?

Chance got close enough to see beyond the horse. Frank's motionless body lay sprawled out on the ground.

Fighting back a shout of fear, Chance abandoned wondering about the gray stallion and went straight to Frank, swung down and knelt. The front of Frank's shirt was soaked with blood.

"Mateo, see to Frank's horse." Sarge's shout barely penetrated Chance's shock. "Monroe, you and Bud fashion a travois."

John skidded to his knees across from Chance just as he ripped Frank's shirt open.

They both looked at Frank's chest, then their eyes rose and locked.

Chance's voice was brutal, scraped raw. "He's been shot." Chance ripped his own shirt off, folded and pressed it against the ugly bullet wound high on Frank's chest.

John's worry switched hard and fast to rage. Chance saw him tamp it down and it helped Chance do the same.

Sarge crouched at Frank's head, took in the wound at a glance. The foreman pressed two fingers against his boss's neck. "His heart's beating. He's alive."

"He's lost a lot of blood." Chance was sickened by just how much.

Sarge's eyes snapped up. "Well, let's don't bury him quite yet."

Feeling the fury, Chance wanted to shout back. Slug someone. He and John looked at each other, then both turned to Sarge. They were all smart enough to know the enemy was long gone and there was no sense unleashing their anger on each other.

"I'll help get that travois lashed together." John leapt to his feet and was gone.

Chance didn't know much doctoring, but blood belonged inside a man, not out. He put his weight behind trying to keep what was left of Frank's blood where it belonged, holding Frank on this side of the Pearly Gates with his bare hands.

"Mateo, fetch a lariat off my saddle." Sarge barked at a steady young Mexican drover, a newcomer to the Cimarron. "We'll use it to keep pressure on the wound while we head for the ranch."

They had the rope in seconds, and Chance and Sarge used it to tie a bandage tight around Frank's chest, crisscrossing the rope over the wound. The only other way Chance could think to keep pressure on it was to walk alongside the travois all the way back to the ranch house. It was at least an hour ride and that was on a steadily moving horse. If a man had to walk, slowing the horse down, he feared Frank wouldn't live long enough to reach home.

John led a horse dragging a litter. "How's he doing?"

Chance said, "Someone needs to ride ahead to get Veronica. If she wants to see her pa again . . . she'd better come running. I know he's a strong man, but he looks bad."

Chance, Sarge, John, and Mateo, moving as smoothly as they could, got Frank onto the litter.

Once he was settled, Sarge said to Mateo, "Ride hard and don't go alone. Take Bud with you. Bring Miss Veronica here and have plenty of men ride as sentries. This might be a rustler Frank caught by surprise. But there's always those trying to take over Frank's range. If he dies, his daughter is in the way. Guard her as if she were your own sister."

"Sí. We *vamonos*." Mateo jerked his chin, understanding bright in his black eyes of the danger to Veronica, of what it meant to bring her here, of what that boded for Frank. "We return *rapido* with Senorita Veronica."

Chance didn't even watch them go. He double-checked that Frank was solidly resting on the travois, and then he and John swung up on horseback, though everything in him wanted to run for the CR. Instead they walked at a fast pace, but anything quicker would be too rough a ride and most likely deadly for Frank.

Anyway, what more could be done at home? Chance didn't know the answer to that. And a rough ride might well shake Frank loose from the fragile hold he had on life.

7

"Senorita Veronica, come! You must hurry!" Mateo, one of Pa's cowhands, rushed into the kitchen right after Cole had fallen asleep. "Your padre is hurt. You must come."

Consuelo had just come in to help with the afternoon chores. Veronica looked at her. "I have Cole sleeping."

Consuelo said, "You go, *mia* Veronica. I will care for the *niño*."

Veronica ran, terrified by the urgent way Mateo spoke and moved. A horse was already saddled for her. She swung up and tore out of the yard after him. They rode south—the direction Chance said Pa went this morning. To the east of the CR was a tiny town called Skull Gulch, brand-new and barely existing. She knew there was no doctor there. None closer than Santa Fe, over one hundred miles away.

Sick at what Chance must have found, she bent low over her mount to get every ounce of speed. Then she focused her energy on praying. God had always been a steady presence in her life, and right now she needed Him desperately.

Hooves pounded behind her. She glanced back and saw five riders hot on their trail. Behind them a wagon was coming along as fast as it could, with armed riders on horseback as escorts.

What did they need so much help for? How bad was it? Questions jammed in her throat. She didn't ask them. She couldn't even consider slowing Mateo down.

It wasn't as long a ride as she feared. They saw three riders before a half hour had passed. Sarge, Chance, and John coming home. No sign of Pa. They wouldn't have left him unless he was dead. No, not even then.

Fighting back a scream, she dug her fingers deep into her horse's mane and bent so low over her saddle the pommel pressed on her chest. Her prayers went deeper and wider. She did her best to put her trust in the Lord. Whatever happened, she would let God guide her, even through the valley of the shadow of death.

And then she saw a travois behind John's horse. Pa, injured, but surely not dead. They draped dead men over a saddle.

She could breathe again.

Chance watched them approach until they nearly met, then pulled his horse to a halt and dismounted. Sarge and John leapt down, Veronica only a second behind them. John held all the horses, especially the one pulling the travois, so they wouldn't spook.

She rushed to Pa. When she reached his side, she gasped at the blood. Horrified, she hunkered down by Pa and took his hand. Chance came to her side. They knelt there side by side, and it was a perfect time for prayer.

She'd said only a few words before Pa's hand tightened on hers. His eyes flickered open and went from her to Chance and back. Pa lifted his other hand, his whole arm and hand covered in dried blood. He reached for Chance.

When he had them both in his grasp, he said, "I'm dying, Ronnie. My precious girl . . ."

"No, Pa, don't say such a thing. We'll patch you up."

A sharp shake of his head was followed by a cough, and Veronica saw a tinge of blood on his lips. "Hush, girl, and listen."

Falling silent, Veronica prayed as Pa gathered his strength.

"I went to meet the territorial governor's man today. Fellow I've dealt with for a while. He's been riding all the way out from Santa Fe every few months, pressuring me to give over the rights to the Cimarron. He says I'm not enough of an American. I've been . . . been paying him. He has the governor's ear and will turn things against me if I don't—"

38

"Threats, extortion. If the governor knew . . ."

"Stop, Ronnie. Just let me get this out."

There was a long breath in and out, so painful Veronica feared it might be his last.

"He claims it should go to American citizens. Chance, the only way to hold it, to keep it for Veronica, is if you marry her."

"What?" Chance wobbled, and for a moment Veronica wondered if he'd fall right over on his backside.

"Pa, you can't—"

"You'll do it right now, in front of me. With these men as witnesses. That is good enough for God, and good enough for New Mexico Territory. But I want more. You." He stabbed a finger at Mateo. "There's a circuit rider in Skull Gulch helping build an orphanage. I heard he's still in the area. Go for him and go fast."

Veronica saw something flicker across Mateo's face, anger at being ordered or maybe something else. For the first time she wondered if the young man had considered courting her himself. But no, surely not.

"Pa, we can't—"

"Tell him I want prayers," he continued, still cracking out orders to Mateo, "last rites, whatever it is parsons do at a time like this. We'll head on for the CR and meet you there."

Chance turned as Mateo mounted up. "Don't ride alone."

Ignoring the words, three men headed out with Mateo.

"Chance," Frank said, nearly crushing his hand, "please save the ranch for my daughter. I was hoping things would work out for you two anyway."

She was right—Pa had been matchmaking.

"I didn't want it to be like this, but—" An ugly cough shook his body and ended his begging.

And that's just what it was. Pa was the strongest man she'd ever known. To see him reduced to begging about rent Veronica's heart.

The coughing eased and Pa went on. "Now I want your oath, your solemn promise to a dying man." He looked from Chance to Veronica. "Ronnie, you love Cole. Chance is a fine man and strong enough to hold the land. Where will you go if you lose the ranch, Ronnie? You'll be forced to marry and it'll be sudden and possibly to someone who won't treat you right."

There was only silence.

The wait was too long for Frank. "Promise. Make your vows right here before God and these men."

There were still four riders who hadn't gone with Mateo. Sarge, John, and two others. At that moment the slower-moving wagon pulled up. The men reached for Pa to lift him.

"Stop. I won't be moved until I hear your vows, right now. If you lift me and I fight you, that'll finish me."

Chance stretched his free hand to Veronica. She took it and held on tight. The three of them formed a circle, with Frank holding both of them as they held each other.

"Will you marry me, Veronica? He's right that there is something between us. This is sudden, I know, but I will admit I've wondered if there could be a future for us. You are a fine, honorable, beautiful woman. It would be my great honor if you would agree to marry me."

Veronica only kept from shaking her head no by the increasing pressure on her hand by Pa. Finally, because what choice did she have, she spoke. "Yes, I'll marry you, Chance."

Without delay, Chance raised his voice. His words rang out strong and from the heart. "In front of God and these witnesses I promise to be your husband, Veronica Chastain, until death do us part."

His words were solemn and carried the weight of a true vow to God.

She could do no less. "I swear this before God, my father, and all these men present that now and forever I will be your wife, Chance Boden. And I will honor you all of my life." She couldn't say love or obey. She just couldn't.

She knew on the frontier, when sometimes a parson didn't come around for years, many marriages started with such vows made before family. It wasn't unheard of for a parson to come by, marry a couple, and baptize a few of their children while he was at it.

Marrying Chance was an idea that appealed to her. And certainly after that kiss she'd hoped it appealed to him, too. But as he and Pa both said, not like this.

"Take me home." Pa cut into her thoughts. "I want to die in my own bed . . . after the wedding."

"But—"

"Veronica," Chance said, his voice achingly gentle, "let's get your pa home."

Chance's gaze met hers and she knew that whatever happened, their vows had been made and a promise would be kept. Whether Pa lived to see it or not, this day they would marry. They had in fact married already.

8

"What happened to Mr. Chastain?" Cole asked the question so grimly, Chance knew his son had come to care for the burly rancher. They'd done their best to staunch the blood and bandage him up, but Cole had to see how pale and wounded Frank was.

Frank had passed out on the painful trip home, and they tended his wounds as gently as they could, praying all the while. It had been more than an hour when his eyes fluttered open again. They'd been working over him on the dining room table.

He looked around. "Take me into the sitting room." Though Frank's voice was weak, his will remained strong.

Chance and John carried Frank to the room closest to the front door, a sitting room with fancy furniture. They settled him on a settee with deep-green tufted cloth covering it.

Veronica ran a hand over Cole's dark hair and drew him close to her side. Her affection touched Chance so deeply, he wanted to call it love.

He couldn't love her like he'd loved Abby. But her gentleness to Cole blended with the respect he had for her and he hoped someday it would grow into love.

"Where's that parson?" Frank said.

"Mateo's not back yet." Sarge took over the doctoring, untying the bandage, uncovering the wound.

With a frown, Sarge said, "Veronica, get your pa some water."

Veronica left to obey the order, as if desperate to help in some way. She took Cole along with her.

The moment she was gone, Sarge spoke quietly to Frank, "I can't cut the bullet out. It's too deep. My healing would kill you, Frank. If you want me to, I'll try, but—"

"We're old friends, Sarge. We both know what this wound means. I won't have you cutting on me, making my last minutes on earth torture. Bandage it and get me in a clean shirt, then I want to see a wedding."

John rushed out for the shirt. Frank and Sarge spoke in low whispers as Sarge eased the bloody shirt off his friend's shoulders. Standing back because of the way the two spoke privately, Chance saw something barely peeking out of the front pocket of his boss's shirt.

When Sarge tossed the shirt aside, Chance caught it and checked. It was a good-sized slip of paper, smeared with fresh blood. There was also blood streaked inside the shirt pocket, which had a flap on the top and was snapped shut.

"Look at this." Chance's voice surprised him. He growled and sounded more animal than man. Sarge turned.

Chance extended the note to him.

"What's that?" Frank asked.

"This note was in your shirt pocket. Unless you put it there, whoever shot you left a message."

Frank's eyes narrowed. "It's not mine."

Sarge said something harsh that Chance couldn't understand.

Turning, Sarge handed the note to Frank.

Frank read aloud, "'This is a warning. Clear out of this land you stole from Mexico.'"

Frank opened his mouth to say something just as Veronica returned. He thrust the note into Chance's hands. Sarge got back to work, getting a clean shirt on his old friend.

The men returned with the parson shortly after Frank was fully dressed and propped up in the corner of the sofa. "Someone said there's a doctor in Fort Union so I sent a rider."

To Chance it was the final death knell. The doctor wouldn't be here for hours and hours. Frank didn't have that long.

The parson, a thin, darkly tanned Mexican, rushed to Frank's side, knelt and began praying.

"I want your prayers, Parson, but first you need to hear some vows between my daughter and Chance here."

The parson looked over his shoulder at Veronica and nodded with a worried smile.

Frank watched the wedding from a seat of honor, then welcomed Chance to the family by demanding he fetch a fountain pen and paper and listen as he dictated a new will, leaving his new son-in-law, an undeniable American citizen since birth, one of the old Spanish land grants that reigned over New Mexico Territory.

"But what about Veronica? She needs to be mentioned in the will, too."

"No!" Frank slashed a trembling hand. He looked at his daughter. "You understand why I'm doing this, don't you? I love you more than my own life. All I have is yours. But the law is hard on women, and you could lose this holding if it's in your name. Chance is your husband, and in the time I've spent with him I've taken his measure. There will be no mistreatment of you personally or of your land." Frank's voice faltered. "I leave you in good hands."

Pushing forward, Chance, with Veronica on one side and Cole on the other, dropped to his knees beside Frank to catch every word as he asked the question that had burned in him for hours now. "Did you see who shot you, Frank?"

"I won't speak of it. My daughter needs to be safe, and sending you on a dangerous manhunt won't accomplish that. Marrying Veronica to you will settle things."

"How will that settle things?" Then Chance shook his head. No time for anything but simple answers. "You left this morning to meet someone. Who?"

"Chance, protect yourself and my daughter and your son. I've endangered you, and I'm sorry. But I'm hoping this will thwart the scheme."

"What scheme, Frank? Tell me what you suspect."

"I won't. Talking won't save me and it'll put you in danger. I've protected Veronica with your marriage. Now give me a minute to say good-bye to my girl."

Veronica surged past Chance to clasp her father's hands. "Pa, don't talk that way. You've been hurt before. You just need time and good care and—"

"Let me have my say, Ronnie. Yes, with a miracle I might pull through, but I will spend the next few minutes making sure that if I don't make it, you'll hear of my love before I go. I am so proud of the woman you've become."

Chance eased back to give them privacy. They murmured to each other, and Veronica kissed him on the forehead, her tears baptizing him.

Frank then said, "Now let me pray with the parson, Ronnie."

Crying, she stood and backed away until Chance held her, her back pressed to his front. She leaned so hard he was nearly holding her up.

The parson knelt again at Frank's side. Frank spoke first. "My faith is strong and my trust is in the Lord, so I have confidence where I will spend eternity. But I want to go on a prayer, with the Lord knowing I believe it is His will being done. I accept that it's my time."

Veronica was sobbing now. "No, Parson, pray for healing. Pray for a miracle."

The man glanced back at Veronica. "I'll do both, his wishes and yours. In the end it's the same—God's will be done."

His prayer was fervent and beautiful and soothing. The parson was still talking in quiet tones when God took Frank Chastain home.

9

It was early afternoon when Pa died, though Veronica felt as if she'd lived an eternity. The rest of that day was a blur of pain and loss and, for heaven's sake, marriage.

Veronica had cried until she was wrung out and numb. The sun set as her father was laid to rest, and now in the full dark she walked back from the family plot and noticed with some surprise that Chance had his arm around her waist. She was leaning nearly all her weight on him and wasn't sure she would have remained upright without his help. Cole was on her other side, holding her hand. He was so little, but he helped as best he could. Both of them maintained a solemn silence.

She barely knew them and now they were her only family. A new rush of tears flooded her eyes, when she thought she'd wept until she was a dry husk inside.

Pa rested under freshly turned soil beside her mother. His beloved Marie-Theresa. For all the elegance of her beautiful French name, Pa always called her Ma. Despite all his jumbled ancestry, Pa sounded like a western man from living in the wilds of the Rockies for a good part of his life.

And now it all belonged to her . . . and her new husband.

They were wealthy, she knew that, but it seemed like normal life to her. It had always been like this—the huge house, the lavish furnishings. Rich fabric in the chairs and drapes. Ornate carving on the curved staircases and woodwork. High ceilings and gilded mirrors. Beautiful artwork. Lushly thick carpets on the floors. Since Ma had died, Veronica and Consuelo had closed down sections of the house.

The ranch, the house, the wealth was all built by her father. A few miles away, on the half of the land grant Don de Val had owned, was another mansion that now sat empty. The proud Spanish Don's land had been split up between a few rough frontiersmen or reclaimed by the Pueblo and Apache peoples who'd roamed the land for centuries. No one knew what to do with a mansion.

Don Bautista was an arrogant old tyrant with a wandering eye, despite his equally regal wife. Pa had kept Veronica far away from him. It would be appropriate to write him of her father's death. One more thing she hadn't the strength for.

The weight of her long, sad day was pulling at her. As if she was to be pulled beneath the ground to stay with her parents. Mentally shaking the idea away, she found it creeping back in every few minutes.

Then she realized Cole was tugging on her hand.

Her thoughts were so dark, she welcomed the distraction. What if Chance and Cole weren't here? What if she had to face this alone? She held Cole's hand tight and cherished Chance's supporting arm around her waist.

"Miss Veronica?"

"You're to call her Ma from now on, Cole." Chance's instruction shocked her. She was a mother with a single spoken vow.

Cole smiled and said, "All right. Ma, do Pa and I sleep somewhere else tonight? Don't married folks pretty often share a bed?"

With a gasp, Veronica didn't respond. She hadn't allowed her thoughts to go anywhere near such a thought.

"They do, Cole." Chance answered for her. "But—"

"If you move into Miss . . . uh, I mean Ma's room to share her bed, where do I sleep? I don't like sleeping so far from you, Pa."

"Of course we'll . . ."

"Or are you going to come to Pa's bed?" Cole cut him off.

"Now's not the time—"

"Pa will want you close at hand, right, Pa? That's how a pa and ma sleep. So you can move into the rooms we're in. We'd have a good chance of finding you that way. The house is bigger than Grandmama's, and I got lost in there all the time."

"Cole!" Chance's voice was enough to silence the boy. "We are going to give Ma a little time to rest. This has been a sad day for her. She doesn't need a single new thing to worry about. So tonight she will sleep in her room and we will sleep in ours, and we will talk about such things as moving when Ma is rested."

Cole looked so subdued that Veronica was tempted to tell Chance to leave the little boy alone. Even though Veronica desperately wanted him to be quiet and she was grateful for Chance stopping the inquisition.

And then she thought of her room, right next to Pa's, so far from Chance and Cole. Hesitantly she asked, "Would it be all right if I slept in your rooms tonight? I don't want to be alone—"

Her voice broke and her knees sagged, until Chance swept her into his arms. "We'll do whatever you want, Ronnie."

Hearing her father's name for her brought the tears again. "Th-thank you."

She knew she was thanking him for carrying her, agreeing with her, and calling her Ronnie.

Chance strode toward the house, Cole at his side. He leaned close and his lips touched her temple as he whispered, "I will take care of you. You're safe. You're not alone."

Somehow it seemed as if those were his true wedding vows.

⤳

Chance carried her straight to his room. He didn't even want to see the rest of the house. Every inch of it was a painful memory for Veronica. She shook with tears, silent and huddled against him. He'd been attracted to her spirit and fire from the moment she'd opened the door to him.

Knowing how strong she was made her grief all the worse.

He carried her into the larger of the two bedrooms and laid her on his bed.

"Don't leave me alone." She gripped his arm so hard he felt her nails claw his wrist through his shirt.

He had no intention of staying. She wasn't ready to share a bed with him. It would be an intrusion at a time like this. But neither could he rip her hand free and leave her crying in the dark.

Cole came to his side, his worry for his new ma stark in his blue eyes. Chance gave his son a long hug and said quietly, "Can you get into your nightclothes, Cole, and slip into your bed?" Chance had a flicker of amusement as he remembered his son's questions about Ma and Pa and beds. "I need to stay with your ma for a while. I'll be in to say good-night as soon as I can."

With heavy-lidded eyes, Cole yawned, nodded and left. It was hours after his bedtime, so the boy would be asleep in moments. He wouldn't notice if Chance was slow in tucking him in.

He had a moment alone with his wife. At last. And she needed him. With one arm still in her grip, he pulled her close, hoping his touch would give her comfort.

"I will stay as long as you want, Ronnie. I won't leave you alone."

She wrapped her arms tight around his neck, and he either had to fight her or move closer. Unsure if it was wise, he kicked his boots off and slid into the bed beside her

"Just for a while, Chance, please. I need someone to hang on to."

It was too perfect to deny. He hadn't been near a woman in nearly two years, not since months before Abby had died. She'd been bed-ridden during most of her pregnancy.

The feeling of such a lovely woman clinging to him was pure temptation. But not all temptation led to sin, not when he was forced by her terrible grief to hold her. Not when he was possibly falling in love with a woman he'd had no intention of marrying, at least not quite so soon.

He shifted his weight until her head rested on his chest. Her grip was so tight, there could be no thought of his getting away.

And truth be told, he had no interest in getting away anyhow.

He hadn't turned on any lights. His hands had been too full as he'd carried her in. Cole was almost certainly fast asleep and would call out if he needed anything.

And holding Ronnie was pure bliss.

It was beyond his ability to resist one gentle good-night kiss. She jumped just a bit as if he'd startled her, but she didn't pull away. Instead, one of those arms around his neck tightened while the other slid forward until she rested a hand on his cheek. She offered the next kiss freely.

The brief kiss they'd shared in the kitchen, perfect except that Cole had cut it short, was alive between them.

After far too long he ended the kiss with great reluctance. Her warrior's grip lessened as she shifted to lay her head on his shoulder. Her breathing slowed and settled.

He let her warmth lull him to sleep.

10

Veronica woke up and didn't know where she was. Then the cutest little guy she'd ever seen leaned over and stared at her, so close their noses almost touched.

"Good morning, Ma." Cole smiled as if those words were the finest ever spoken.

Her heart wrenched as she remembered yesterday's sadness. And then she realized Cole was hers forever now.

I lost my father. I gained a son. And oh, my dear heaven, I've gained a husband! A husband who kissed me until I forgot my own name. Which—she had to think a minute—*is Boden. Veronica Boden.*

Drawing in a steadying breath, determined to go forward somehow and fight the tears always near to hand, and figure out how to be a good wife and mother, she reached for Cole's little-boy shoulders. She inched him back just far enough so she could sit up, swing her legs around, and stand.

"Wait in the hall while I get ready for the day, please."

He scowled. "I want to stay with you, Ma."

She was glad to see that tiny flash of childishness. He was turning more and more into a normal little boy, or at least what her notion was of how a boy should be. She had no experience.

She looked down at herself and realized she was already fully dressed, right down to her boots. A wrinkled mess, but perfectly modest.

Smiling down at him, she realized this sweet boy was her life now. He gave her purpose. He gave her something to do every day, which she hoped kept her from sinking into grief.

He and his pa were her family. Which reminded her of just how eagerly she'd responded when Chance kissed her. In fact . . . she glanced at the bed and saw two indentations, one on each pillow. Chance had slept here. She'd kissed him and clung to him, so glad for something to drive away her sadness. And then he'd held her close, and it was such wonderful comfort that she'd curled up in his arms.

Yes, she'd not only gained a son but also a husband, and so far that wasn't such a bad thing. Shocking, but not bad. Of course, it'd only been one day.

"Is your pa around?"

Cole grinned and gave a quick up-and-down shrug. "I don't know. I woke up and came to see if you were awake. He isn't here."

He'd made very certain she was awake, the little imp.

"Can you give me just a few moments to change, Cole? I'll be right out."

"All right, but hurry, Ma. I'm hungry." He dashed out of her room, slamming the door behind him.

Veronica's smile held as she made short work of washing up, smoothing her hair, and choosing a clean dress. She hurried from her room and found him two feet from her door, wriggling impatiently and grinning.

She offered him her hand, and he took it without a moment's pause. "Let's go. We'll get breakfast on and hope your pa comes in to eat. Judging by how high the sun is, he may have given up on me and gotten on with his day."

⁓

"Chance, Sarge has something to say," John said, approaching Chance in the barn, who was forking hay to the milk cows. John jerked his head at the ranch foreman.

52

Sarge was a solid man who'd earned the respect of every cowhand on the ranch. He was an old trapping buddy of Frank's and he'd come out of the mountains to see his old friend and then stayed. Sarge had seen a lot, and Chance took what he said seriously.

"Let's step away." Sarge rested a hand on Chance's shoulder. "John, I want you to hear this, too."

The men were doing morning chores. The Cimarron had pigs and chickens, sheep that kept them in wool, tame cows for milk. All in addition to the wilder cattle that earned the money and supplied plenty of beef. The animals Chance had brought west with him had all gone into their pens with the others. Even his men had joined with Frank's men and made friends and seemed to be part of the group.

Chance remembered that urge he'd felt to build a dynasty, to leave a legacy for Cole. Now he had this huge ranch dropped onto his shoulders. His few cows and chickens were nothing compared to all he'd just inherited. He was glad to protect Ronnie's land for her, but he still hadn't seen what he could do himself.

He wasn't experienced enough to run such a big ranch, and depending on Sarge and the other hired hands was proof of that. He was determined to learn all he could as fast as he could.

In the barn, there were men working all around. To not speak in their hearing meant Sarge didn't know who he could trust and that twisted Chance's gut.

"I rode with the cavalry for years; that's where my name came from. I did some Indian-fighting and saw a lot of the West before hardly a white man was out here."

Chance just listened. Not time yet to ask questions.

Sarge's eyes suddenly flared with rage. "I've seen my share of gunshot wounds and I worked with a crew of men who investigated such things. The bullet that hit Frank told me a story. You are assuming he was shot from cover and fell from his horse, but that's not the way it happened."

"The slug didn't pass through," Chance said. "Any close-up shot would have had an exit wound."

Sarge scowled impatiently. Chance wished he'd kept his mouth shut.

"There are guns small enough they don't use much powder, don't have much speed nor power behind the bullet. But up close they're deadly enough. Those guns are easy to hide in a coat pocket or up a sleeve. So a trusting man, even a knowing one like Frank, might not go for his gun before it was too late."

"So whoever shot him might have gotten close?"

"Not *might* have. He *did*." Sarge looked around to make sure they were alone. "Someone was standing facing Frank, close enough to be talking to him. He pulled a gun and fired. The way the blood flowed—not only that but the way Frank talked at the end—he knew the one who shot him."

Chance had that same impression. "Why wouldn't he tell us?"

"He wanted to keep his daughter alive. He was busy doing that, getting a marriage arranged. And he did say something to you, didn't he?"

"I asked him who did it. He wouldn't tell me. He said it might put me in danger. His only thoughts were for Veronica and her safety."

Sarge said, "I asked him, too. He said to leave it be. All he wanted was to protect Miss Veronica . . . pardon, I mean Mrs. Boden."

"Why wouldn't he want his killer brought to justice?" Chance rubbed the back of his neck and shuddered in the blustery cold wind. "Why not protect Veronica that way?"

"Frank was dying," John said, "and I don't trust all the words of a man in such terrible pain. And he was so worried about his child. Regardless, I want whoever shot Frank to hang. And I don't intend to let things stay as they are."

Sarge looked from John to Chance. "I agree."

Nodding, Chance said, "We're going hunting, men. Sarge, you're as good a tracker as there is. Let's ride out together and see if we can follow some tracks."

"I'll do it, and John can come along, but not you."

That surprised Chance, the way the old-timer gave him a direct order. But Chance didn't argue with him. Sarge was foreman, so he ordered men all the time. He was too savvy, too trail-hardened to ignore. He'd earned a little obedience, even if he was the boss.

Sarge continued, "You stay close to the house. Call it being newly married. Call it mourning, whatever you like. To my way of thinking, if someone shot Frank, and if the motive was to gain possession of the Cimarron Ranch, then you might be next. And I don't have time to watch over you today."

That tricked a smile out of Chance. It really was true that he probably needed watching. He was a newcomer out here, and for all that Frank had taught him, he was still the least knowledgeable cowboy on the place.

He wasn't completely useless, yet the men couldn't know that he was a better than decent shot, thanks to his childhood, a skill honed by hours at a shooting range back in Boston. He'd missed his country life more than even he had realized, and shooting had kept him in touch with the survival skills he'd had as a youngster in Indiana.

That same reason had sent him to a boxing club at least once a week where he sparred with some fine boxers and held his own.

Roping a calf was beyond him, though, and they hadn't branded cattle back east on his farm, but he understood livestock enough and could handle all the critters on this ranch. The business world he'd moved in had been cutthroat, yet he'd learned how to play a hard game without selling his soul. And his toughness combined with honesty had taken him far in Boston.

It had also taught him how to organize men. He knew how to lead. And he knew how to admit it if he couldn't handle something. All those were skills he intended to use to win the respect of every hand on the ranch. But by western standards, he was still a little soft.

And soft didn't survive long on the American frontier.

"All right," said Chance. "I'll stay with the family, at least for today. But I'm not hiding, Sarge. You can mention to the men that I've got heirs back east, powerful family members who'll own this land if I die. And who'll avenge my death."

He thought of the Bradfords and doubted they'd care one whit if he died. But Cole . . . yes, if something happened to their only grandchild, they'd bring every ounce of their power west to avenge him. And if Cole was alive, they'd move heaven and earth to find him and take him under their wing.

And by law, as Cole's closest relatives, the Bradfords would inherit. A modest holding wouldn't interest them much, but a quarter of a million acres and a vast herd of cattle? They knew money and they'd be greedy enough to want it all. So there was no way someone could gain this land by murder. Frank really had protected his daughter.

A spark of respect flared in Sarge's eyes and he nodded. "Git on back to the house and your new bride. We'll talk more after John and I have spent time at the place where Frank was shot."

11

Veronica got a fire roaring in the cast-iron stove, put coffee on to boil, and started heating up two skillets. Next she saw to a beef roast for dinner and set bread to rising. Meanwhile, Cole asked her questions constantly. He dragged a chair across the floor and climbed up on it and nearly leaned against the hot stove. Veronica found herself scrambling to keep Cole alive.

With dinner well under way, she turned her attention to breakfast. She noticed the half loaf of bread she had was now gone. She was glad Chance hadn't gone out on an empty stomach.

She made short work of getting biscuits in the oven, then sliced side pork and dropped it into a hot skillet with a sharp sizzle and a cloud of steam. While the pork fried she broke eggs into a bowl and whipped them with a fork. When the pork was near to done and the biscuits just turning light brown, she dropped eggs into the second skillet. The eggs hissed and popped as she turned them and cooked them through.

As the kitchen filled with the smell of fried food and the roast began to give off a savory aroma, she began scooping up breakfast. She set a platter of biscuits beside another of pork and eggs, then poured milk into Cole's tin cup. She set a glittering bowl of red jelly on the table along with a ball of butter.

She'd made a mountain of food, thinking wistfully that Chance might come in. Most likely it would go to waste, for it had become too late for a working man's breakfast.

As she chastised herself for sleeping so late and missing her husband on the first day of her married life, the back door swung open. Thinking Consuelo had come, she looked up.

It was Chance.

His breath flowed out and formed a small white cloud around his head in the cold air. He seemed to be preoccupied because he never looked at Veronica or Cole while he hung up his broad-brimmed hat and the heavy buckskin coat Pa had helped him make—right down to shooting the buck and tanning its hide.

He turned to the table, and his eyes locked on her and he froze. She had a strong suspicion he was just now remembering that he'd gotten married.

∾

Chance had been so deep in his thoughts of all it meant to be married to Veronica that he hadn't noticed his honest-to-goodness, avowed-before-God wife.

All he'd had on his mind was how to keep her safe . . . to such an extent he hadn't been looking where he was going.

A good way to get shot. Considering what had happened yesterday, and the things Sarge had said, that was all too real a possibility.

All of this boiled inside him when he stepped into the house and saw his wife sitting at the table, caring for his son.

She smiled and leapt to her feet. "You're in time to eat. I thought I was too late to serve you breakfast, but here you are." She hustled toward him and slipped past to swing the door shut. He'd left it gaped open while he thought a few shockingly married thoughts.

This beautiful woman, tending his child and making him a meal, stirred his heart and burrowed through a wall of pain left from Abby's death.

"It smells wonderful, Ronnie. I found some bread this morning but didn't want to make any noise. You and Cole got a late start on sleep."

They stood, too close, watching each other, Chance remembering their kiss and . . . well, he could see it in her eyes that she remembered as well.

With a sassy toss of her head, she said, "Come on in and eat, husband. I even started coffee and it should be done and ready for you by now."

"Sarge ordered me to spend the day with my new wife." He took her arm as if he were walking her down an aisle—there'd been no such thing at their wedding—escorting her to the table to sit straight across from Cole. "And let me bring you the coffee. You've done so much already."

"Hi, Pa. We hoped you'd come in to eat."

The kitchen was warm and smelled wonderful. Chance had been out working since dawn, and only now did he realize how hungry he was.

It was a homey room and not overly large. It didn't fit with the vast elegance of the rest of the mansion, and in the time Chance had been here he'd noticed the Chastains spent most of their time in this room. Frank had an office, and they had bedrooms of course, but the kitchen was the heart of the home.

The table sat against the wall on one side. Frank and Veronica always sat on the two ends facing each other, Chance sitting on the long side to Frank's left, with Cole between him and Veronica. Now Frank's chair was empty. Chance averted his eyes from the chair, because it hurt to think that boisterous, hardworking man was gone.

Chance poured two cups of coffee from the heavy tin pot and then set it back on the stove with the scrape of metal on metal.

Inhaling the hot, rich scent of the coffee, Chance served Veronica first then settled into his usual chair. Veronica passed the platters of food.

When their plates were full, Veronica said, "So Sarge sent you in, did he?"

Smiling, determined not to speak of Frank or yesterday's sorrow, Chance stabbed his fork into the mountain of fluffy scrambled eggs. "He didn't seem to think he'd have a bit of trouble managing without me. And he said a newly married man ought to spend a day with his wife."

"And with his son too, Pa?" Cole asked.

"With his son for sure." Chance mussed Cole's hair, and his boy, who'd given up most of the fussy ways his grandmama had taught him, scowled comically and smoothed his hair back into place. The boy did love to be neat. And maybe that wasn't his grandmother's doing, but rather just natural to the child.

"What shall we do today, Ronnie?" Chance found he liked having a special name for his wife. "Should we move to different rooms? Although I didn't mind last night's . . . arrangements." He resisted the urge to say *sleeping* arrangements, yet he was sorely tempted.

She looked down at her hands in her lap and spoke just above a whisper. "I didn't mind them either."

"Then let's stay in my rooms for the time being. It's simple and I think we should keep everything simple for a time."

"So I was right about a ma and pa sleeping together, wasn't I?" Cole piped up.

Chance was tempted to gag the little chatterbox.

"You were most certainly right, Cole." Ronnie looked up, and her cheeks were blushed a beautiful shade of pink.

"I remember you and my first ma always slept together. I crawled in bed with you one time and you were so close together it was like one of you was on top of the other. One time—"

"Cole!" Lowering his voice from a shout, Chance added, "Please, let's just finish breakfast."

Chance remembered the time and was shocked to realize Cole remembered it. There was a very good chance that their second child had been conceived that night. Cole would have been little more than two at the time. It certainly wasn't something he wanted to talk about in front of his new wife . . . or his son for that matter.

Ronnie had gone from pink to red-cheeked in the blink of an eye. These two were going to give him all he could handle for the rest of his life.

He planned to enjoy every single minute of it.

12

The morning was half gone by the time she'd cleaned up after breakfast, but they'd gotten a late start. Chance helped in the kitchen, and she found his closeness so distracting, she barely caught herself when she put the milk in the cupboard. When she quickly retrieved it and put it in the icebox, she found the saltcellar in there beside the flour.

She glanced at her husband, and he was grinning at her. She felt another foolish blush. He'd been watching her all morning and working alongside her, though he was no hand in the kitchen. Cole kept up his talking and that somehow added to the intimacy, made them a true family.

Consuelo came in with her mostly grown daughter, Rosita. She was a good friend to Veronica. Rosita hugged her, and Consuelo congratulated them on their marriage and asked Cole if he'd like to help her bake cookies. The three of them set to work.

Veronica wasn't quite sure how it happened, but she soon found herself shooed out of the kitchen and alone with Chance. Of course not for the first time since their marriage, as they'd had last night after all, but this was different. Exhaustion wasn't pulling at her now.

"Let me show you the house and decide which rooms will be yours."

"Wait, Ronnie." Chance reached out and took her hand.

She turned to face him.

"I want you to know that . . . well, last night I didn't intend to share your bed. But I think it was right that we were together. But holding each other is a long way from being . . . being . . ." He swallowed hard. "Well, it's a long way from being together as man and wife. I'll give you all the time you need. But I don't want my own room. I would like to sleep by your side. It's one of the great comforts of marriage to have someone with you so you don't have to face the night alone."

Since Veronica wanted him close with all her heart, it was simple to agree. "I do want to share a bedroom. But I'd like to know you better too, Chance. I've watched you work alongside Pa. I know you're a hardworking man, and I've only seen honesty and decency from you. Still, I'd like to know what brought you here. We see folks go by on wagon trains all the time, and they're always hard-pressed folks. Scrawny horses, few supplies, and no money to buy more. You have three loaded wagons. Hired men. Cattle and healthy mules. You're a prosperous man. And that's not the kind who strike out into the Wild West."

Chance was so quiet that Veronica wondered if she'd done wrong to ask. Surely now he'd speak of his wife and how he loved her and drive home to Veronica that she should never expect to replace the love of his life.

"I headed west because I needed to get my son away from that life before it ruined him."

"What life?"

Tugging at her hand, Chance said, "Come on upstairs. We'll decide what rooms to take, and I'll tell you about the woman who wanted my son to drink tea and wear lace."

Gasping, Veronica came along eagerly and listened. His story included his grief, but it also included him choosing to face forward, to put his mourning behind him, to make his son the center of his life. How he'd sold his company, laid down a false trail, and slipped away in secret.

"Didn't you once say you grew up on a farm in Indiana?"

"I did." More and more, Chance was taking on the speech of the West. Veronica had seen it before. Men out here could come from all over, not just in America but from all over the world. Her own father was born in Quebec, Canada. Don de Val was a Mexican citizen, but had spent many of his growing-up years in Spain. Though the Don was a bad example, because he'd always spoken Spanish and clung rigidly to his arrogant upper-class accent.

The West drew men who had the courage to face risks. Some who didn't feel fully alive unless they were pushing themselves to the limit of their strength and skill.

These men picked up the accent and slang of the West quickly, and only in the background could someone hear where they'd sprung from.

At times, Veronica could hear the East in Chance's voice, but after long days on the wagon train, he'd already shed much of that cultured sound. It was easy for a woman who loved the frontier to imagine a man wanting to come here. But how had he gotten to Boston to begin with?

So she asked him.

Smiling, Chance replied, "When I was growing up in Indiana, that was the far frontier."

"It's nearly on the Atlantic Ocean, for heaven's sake." They walked hand in hand up the stairs.

"It seems so from here, but there are mountains between the ocean and Indiana. Dense woods with rugged trails passing through it. It was a wild land. I grew up running in the hills, hunting and fishing, learning to track, learning the ways of wild creatures. I loved that part of our lives, but I had an older sister who married young and Pa took her husband into our farm. We needed to find more land to make a living for me. I could have done that, settled nearby, but I was restless. I wanted more. For some reason 'more' to me back then meant the city."

Veronica listened intently as she led the way to the rooms she thought were the right ones for them.

"Ma had family in Boston, a brother with some cousins a bit younger than me. I moved out there where Uncle Paul worked at a bank. He got me a job there and I really took to it. Somehow the numbers suited me. I could hunt for them like I'd hunted wild game, learn all their tricks, track down things that didn't add up."

"I'm a decent hand with hunting and tracking myself, Chance." She smiled at him, and he returned a grin that said he knew and he respected her skill. It was the finest feeling in the world, after all the men who'd come calling, thinking she was a pampered princess in a castle. "Go on with your story."

Chance looked like he'd rather pay attention to her. "I found a knack for making sound investments. I built that into a business and made a name for myself that led me into some high social circles. That's where I met Abby. Abigail Bradford, from one of the snootiest families you've ever seen. They had roots that went back to the *Mayflower* and they never stopped boasting about it. But Abby was down-to-earth, the kind of sensible woman who'd have probably survived on the *Mayflower*." Chance smiled affectionately, and Veronica tried not to let that pinch.

They were nearing Ma's long-abandoned room, and Veronica decided they'd talk about practical things like moving furniture and such, rather than about his dearly departed wife.

Chance stopped her from entering the room. He slid his arms around her waist and pulled her close. "I find myself in possession of another fine woman. No man has any right to be so blessed in his life. I consider myself a very lucky man to be married to you."

He bent his head slowly, giving her all the time she wanted to object.

She did no such thing.

13

The afternoon was fading away. Chance looked out the window of the room Ronnie said she wanted for them, with a smaller room right next door for Cole.

November was waning, the grass had faded to brown, and the yellow leaves were gone from the aspens. Days were short now, with the sun low in the sky behind a flat-topped butte that stood like a reigning king looking down on them all. Skull Mesa, they called it. It was nearly of mythical status because it had never been climbed, and Frank had told some funny stories about how, fresh from the rugged Rockies, he was sure he could climb anything. Even so, he became frustrated over and over as he tried to get himself to the summit of Skull Mesa. Then his old trapping buddy Sarge had come and they'd begun the whole futile effort again. The hired hands had tried. Many others had taken up the challenge too, going back as many years as folks could remember. All had failed.

Chance treasured the day with his brand-spankin'-new wife. He felt like God had given him this day to restore his soul and to form a solid bond with her.

Consuelo and Rosita had taken charge of Cole most of the day, and Chance had let Ronnie order him around, moving furniture and setting up rooms for the three of them.

They had deliberately avoided any talk of Frank or the shooting, time enough tomorrow for the trouble that loomed over them. Trouble so big it made Skull Mesa look like a gopher mound.

He thought the day was going to end as pleasantly as it had begun, until Sarge hollered up the stairs, "Chance, Miz Veronica, get down here."

Veronica smiled as she smoothed the bed they'd made up for Cole. "You're his boss, aren't you?"

Shaking his head, Chance said, "I'm taking orders just like the lowest cowhand. Let's go."

They walked down the broad staircase to find Sarge pacing in the hallway below. Any humor faded as Chance realized Sarge was here to report his day of tracking. He regretted that this had to intrude on such a fine day.

They followed him into Frank's office. There was a settee and several overstuffed chairs. Chance wasn't about to go and sit at Frank's massive oak desk.

"What did you find, Sarge?" Chance pulled Veronica with him to the settee where they sat close beside each other.

"It ain't good." He sat down in a chair straight across from them, then surged to his feet and began pacing again. "I don't have proof of it yet, but I've got enough pieces I have to suspect it."

"Just tell us what you think," Veronica said.

"The tracks were pretty stirred up by the time we built that travois and all our horses milled around where Frank fell. But we found a single set of tracks riding out of the aspens to meet Frank. The man he met must have been someone he knew because they both dismounted and stood jawing for a while. We found one of those Mexican cigars tossed into the dirt, as if they'd stood there long enough for a smoke."

"Did you recognize the boot prints or the hoofprints?" Veronica asked.

Chance knew a skilled tracker could identify a man from his tracks, a horse as well. But it wasn't that easy. Most men wore boots. Most horses were of a similar size and weight and were shod.

"I don't have to recognize them, Miz Veronica."

Chance's stomach twisted at Sarge's tone. The man was about to say something he didn't want to say, and Chance was sorely afraid that neither he nor Veronica wanted to hear it.

"Ramone's gone missing."

"What?" Veronica sat up straight at the mention of one of their best cowhands.

Chance leapt to his feet. "You suspect Ramone of shooting Frank? But he was here at the ranch yesterday morning." More thoughtfully, he added, "But not when we searched for Frank."

"Once we found he was missing, I started asking questions. You know how many cowhands are drifters?"

That much was true. They rode from ranch to ranch, worked a while, through roundup or through the winter, then wandered on.

"I just assumed Ramone was, too. But a few of the hands said he grew up around these parts. They said it was never spoken of, but a few of them knew Ramone's ma was a woman who—" Sarge cleared his throat—"who spent time with Don Bautista de Val."

"Spent time?" Veronica's brow furrowed as she stood and went to Chance's side.

Chance rubbed a hand on his chest. "Are you saying . . . ?"

"I'm saying Ramone is the Don's son. Born to a woman other than his wife. Ramone's ma was a kept woman all his life. The Don gave them a decent home with enough money to live well. He visited Ramone's mother right up until he went back to Mexico. Since he left he's had nothing to do with them, and the money stopped. Ramone came to the ranch hunting work, and"—Sarge glanced awkwardly at Ronnie—"some of the men knew because he'd spoken of it. He had plans to marry you, Miz Veronica."

With a gasp, Veronica touched her fingers to her throat.

Chance added what was most likely also part of the plan, an ugly part. "And by doing so, get the Cimarron. He no doubt thought this should have been his family's legacy. He gets by marriage what he was denied through the circumstances of his birth."

Veronica asked, "Did Pa know about Ramone? That he was related to the Don?"

Sarge rubbed his hand over a chin stubbled with a week's worth of beard, considering. "If he did, I never heard of it, and your pa talked most things over with me. But what I'm wondering is if Ramone faced him with it yesterday."

"If Ramone asked to talk with him, Pa wouldn't have thought twice about getting down off his horse."

"What's more, Ramone is a fiery one. He has a temper, and I've seen it explode a few times. But mostly he's a top hand and a hard worker. If the men are right that he had plans that included you, Miz Veronica, well, there was no way to miss that your pa was taken with Chance here. Ramone might've thought he needed to speak up, ask for your hand, or at least your pa's permission to court you before Chance was taken any more under Frank's wing."

"You think Ramone suggested he be allowed to see me and then shot Pa when he refused?"

"This is all just talk." Chance slid one arm around Veronica's waist, wishing he'd heard Sarge's story outside. "Ramone might just as well have confronted your pa about being Don de Val's son. He might have asked your pa to hand over half the remaining ranch out of some twisted notion of fairness."

Sarge's scowl twisted into fury. "I plan on hunting Ramone down, and when I find him I'll ask him just what he said before he shot Frank."

Ronnie reached out and rested her hand on Sarge's broad shoulder. "No, don't do that. Don't go hunting him. We need you. Consuelo and Rosita need you."

"I know your pa, Miz Veronica. He wanted to protect you. If your pa had lived, he'd have fought this. But knowing he was dying, he only thought of the danger his death would leave you in. And the danger to Chance if he'd go to hunting a killer. By marrying you to Chance, he protected you should Ramone try to further his plans after Frank's death. But that was a decision made by a dying man. I'm alive and I'm not going to let some kid shoot down my friend in cold blood and ride away free. I'm going after him."

"Sarge," Chance interrupted, "I don't think he had any plans to kill Frank yesterday. He was angry and his temper exploded. I suspect he's run far and fast. If he's made it to the Mexican border, you've lost all legal power to bring him to justice and you will put yourself in terrible danger. That's what Frank was worried about when he said telling us the name would put us all in danger. No lawman or posse has any rights once they cross the border. In fact, I'd imagine Ramone ran to his father in Mexico City. You'll never catch up to him before he's among folks that speak his language and may be inclined to protect him."

"And if in a fit of anger Ramone shot a good man like Frank," Sarge added, "then he's as dangerous as a rattlesnake, because he's one ugly temper away from killing again. We need to lock him up and hang him before he kills another innocent man—" Sarge paused, gave Veronica a grim look—"or woman."

Silence hung over them. Sarge was right, but Chance was right as well. Sarge was risking his neck with very little likelihood he'd catch the youngster, certainly not before he reached the border. Because if Ramone had ridden hard and fast, he was in Mexico already.

"I reckon you can go after him if you've a mind to, Sarge. You're your own man. But I wish you wouldn't. We need you here. You know with Frank gone, that is God's honest truth."

With a glint in his eye, Sarge said, "Let me scout around. If I find out Ramone made it to the border, we let him go."

Chance fought down the urge to go along. "I'm worried about running this place without you."

"I'll send out a group of my best trackers," Sarge said, "and I'll ride along. I found his trail headed south. We'll see if he's quit the country or is just hiding out for a while."

Breathing out a sigh of relief, Chance nodded. "Be careful. And remember your home is here and we'll be waiting for you. Don't stay on the trail too long."

Sarge gave one hard downward jerk of his chin. "I'll have a word with Consuelo and Rosita, then be going." He raised his dark eyes and looked at Veronica. "You know I've watched you grow up with as much pride as if you were my own child."

"I know." Veronica came forward and curled her delicate fingers around Sarge's scarred thick-fingered hands. "Please don't be gone too long. I need you here on the Cimarron and I *want* you here, because I think of you as family."

A light blush pinked up Sarge's heavily lined face, and he managed a wry smile. "I'll be back, Miz Veronica."

"You've never called me Miz before in that buzzy way. It was always Miss Veronica, even though I'd told you many times that wasn't necessary. Why are you saying it different?"

Sarge managed a much fuller smile on that question. "It's just a quick way of saying missus. I reckon it should be Missus Boden, but it's hard to change from saying Veronica."

Veronica leaned forward and kissed one of Sarge's reddened cheeks. "Be careful and hurry home."

Sarge spun away, charging toward the kitchen as if the gruff old cowpoke was afraid he might show a soft side of himself.

14

Chance looked at Veronica and thought of how bravely she'd taken such devastating news. "I am sorely tempted to ride with him."

"But you're not going to?" She sounded hopeful.

"Nope. I'm staying at your side." He walked right up and caught her face between his palms, caressing her temple and brow with his thumbs. "I am the luckiest man alive to be married to you, Ronnie. I intend to spend my life making sure you never have cause to regret being my wife."

He leaned in and kissed her as gently as a breeze. He wanted only tenderness between them. The time for passion would come later, though Chance now knew it wouldn't be long in coming. When he ended the kiss, he rested his forehead against hers and closed his eyes.

"I have spent my time here on this ranch very much aware of how beautiful you are. I've always known you were brave and strong and suited to this land in every way. But only today did I see you're as sturdy as . . . as Skull Mesa."

"You just called me a massive butte."

Chance kissed her just to make her stop talking. And probably best for him to stop, too.

When he needed to breathe again, he spoke just the barest inch from her lips. "I said all that so you'd understand why I love you, Ronnie."

A soft gasp slipped from her swollen lips. "You love me?"

He smiled and snuck in another kiss. "How could I not? When I've been blessed with such a woman as my wife, every moment spent not realizing I love you is wasted."

Her hand slowly crept up his chest, then her second followed more quickly. "I love you, too. And for me there are no reasons, though you're a fine man. For me, there is only the way my heart beats faster when you enter a room. And the simple fact that no man has ever made me so aware that I am a woman."

With a nearly silent groan, Chance said, "You are that."

When their next kiss ended, Ronnie asked, "How long would you say we have until Cole wakes up?"

The question seemed out of place, but Chance said, "After his short night's sleep last night, I reckon he'll be out for a while yet."

Something blazed in Ronnie's eyes. "You told me I could have all the time I wanted before I share myself with you as a woman does with her husband."

"You can," he said solemnly.

"I believe I've waited long enough."

He smiled, then laughed out loud as he swept her into his arms and carried her up the stairs.

Epilogue

"Justin is punching Cole again." Chance sounded weary at the howl of outrage coming from the other room.

All of Cole's overly proper behavior was gone now. He still had a liking to be neat and had taken to books at a young age. He was five years older than his little brother, Justin. So Cole had no trouble outrunning him.

"I'll go break them up," Chance said. "You stay there and rest."

Ronnie rocked in her chair and smiled. It usually started out as horseplay. Then someone, usually Justin, got too rough and it stopped being fun between them.

She looked down and adjusted the blanket so that her precious newborn daughter, Sadie, didn't get a chill. It was January in New Mexico Territory and the days were cold, especially for a three-day-old baby.

A girl. She grinned wider, thrilled to add a daughter to her precious family.

Cole howled louder.

Precious but noisy. She asked, "Does Justin ever actually land a punch?"

"If he has, Cole's not afraid to holler."

"Nope, no sign of that. Besides, if he really got hurt, I'm not sure

Cole wouldn't punch back." Chance left the room and was back in a minute with three-year-old Justin in his arms.

Cole followed, looking smug. He knew that, being eight years old, he could never really fight a little brother half his size. Instead he ducked and dodged. He had doors with knobs out of Justin's reach. Cole could open, get through, wait and taunt Justin, then slam the door in his face. And when Cole got tired of it, he just fell over on top of his little brother to pin him down until he surrendered.

And for the perfect amount of fun, Cole was quick to make a racket that brought Ma and Pa to help out.

Ronnie was a lot slower to come to the little imp's rescue since Sadie's birth. In truth she loved seeing Cole's behavior. He'd given up all his proper Boston manners and become a boy again.

Chance did his best to take the boys along all the time. Justin could already ride a horse, though usually Chance carried his son in front of him when they rode. Cole was a fine rider and could even saddle his gentle mare with just a bit of assistance.

"You don't think Sadie will grow up punching the boys, do you?" Ronnie asked.

Shaking his head, Chance looked down at the tiny scrap in Ronnie's arms. "I'm sure she'll be just as genteel and ladylike as you were when you were little."

Ronnie groaned. "I was a terror."

Chance laughed out loud as he sat in a rocking chair beside Ronnie. They enjoyed the fire and the temporary peace. Which came mainly from having Justin distracted.

Cole came up and stared at the baby. "She's so little, Ma. Was I ever that small?"

Ronnie exchanged a worried glance with Chance. Cole didn't seem to remember anything of his life before New Mexico. They never spoke of Boston or his overbearing grandparents or the fact that he had a mother besides the one he knew.

"You were the size of any newborn baby, Cole. Just like Sadie. And she'll grow just as you and Justin have."

They could have lived their whole lives with Cole not knowing his past, except they'd gotten another letter from Boston just this week. One of many. The Bradfords had spent years tracking Chance down, and they'd finally found the Cimarron Ranch and written with their intentions of sending the law to retrieve Cole.

It was a nuisance, but she didn't see how they could succeed. Ronnie's family was good friends with the governor and they had consulted with judges; they had the law on their side. Which set Ronnie to worrying about illegal methods.

She knew Chance kept a close watch on Cole when they were outside and was mindful of any new cowpokes that hired on. He'd told her he didn't put it past the Bradfords to send a Pinkerton agent in disguise to spirit their grandchild away.

They also had Sarge and John on alert. It was a well-run ranch, and the Bradfords would find they'd kicked over a hornet's nest if they tried to take Cole.

As they shared this peaceful moment, Ronnie thought back to the way they'd married, to the death of her father, to the ranch her husband found thrust into his hands. She knew he'd wished to build something of his own. She couldn't help but smile as she looked at Cole and Justin and Sadie. This was their finest accomplishment. These three children would be their legacy.

Thinking of Pa made her ask, "Did Sarge ever hear back from the Mexican government about Ramone?"

"Nope, and I reckon he never will. After all the times he's traveled down there, we have to accept that Ramone has gone into hiding, probably protected by his father. It doesn't suit me to give up, but as long as he stays in his country, we can't get justice for your pa. I'm sorry, Ronnie."

"I've never wanted to arrest him at the risk of more lives, Chance. You know that. I'd worry if I thought he was still around, a threat to us. But I won't push for bringing him in if it endangers you or Sarge or any of the men who'd ride with you."

Nodding, Chance said, "It's between Ramone and God now. He'll answer for what he's done at the Pearly Gates."

"In the meantime we'll have a good life." Their chairs were side by side. They creaked gently as they rocked. Cole clambered onto Chance's lap so he and Justin both had a knee, at least temporarily in harmony.

"And we will never let our young'uns forget that this land was held at the price of your pa's life." He looked from Cole to Justin and rubbed a big hand over each of their heads. Except for size, the two were a matched set, both a perfect copy of their father.

Then he added, "We'll teach them to respect this ranch. It will be our children's haven, their birthright and their legacy."

A LADY
OF ESTEEM

A Hawthorne House Novella

KRISTI ANN
HUNTER

To the Father of the fatherless

Psalm 68:5

And to Jacob, for reading this story fifteen times and being willing to read it a sixteenth time with equal enthusiasm.

Prologue

Amelia Stalwood winced as the tower of fabric-wrapped wooden blocks crashed to the floor. She looked to the housekeeper, tears welling in her young eyes. "I'm sorry, Mrs. Bummel."

"Don't worry, love." The woman put her quill on the desk before leaning over to kiss Amelia's head. "That's why I put the rug in here."

"Amelia!"

The man's voice echoed up the stairs into the room Amelia and the housekeeper had turned into a combination office and playroom.

When Amelia had come to live with Lord Stanford a year ago on the very distant connection that Amelia's grandmother's sister's niece had been married to the viscount's deceased brother, he'd turned her over to the housekeeper and had very little to do with her since. He passed all his requests for her to be quieter through the butler.

That he actually wanted to speak to her was somewhat thrilling.

Amelia jumped up with a grin and ran to the stairs as fast as her spindly eleven-year-old legs could go. He was at the bottom of the stairs, looking confused as he turned circles in the hall, unsure of where she would appear.

She scampered down the stairs, with Mrs. Bummel following at a more sedate pace.

"Yes, my lord?" Amelia struggled to keep the breathlessness from her voice. The viscount looked the same as when she had met him a year ago, with a too-large coat, unkempt hair, and large spectacles taking up half of his face.

"Ah, Amelia, yes. Good news! I've hired you a governess."

"A governess?" Mrs. Bummel placed a hand on Amelia's shoulder. "I must say it's about time, my lord."

"Indeed, indeed. She's taking care of packing and whatnot. Should be in London by the time you get there. How long will you need to pack? Two days?" Lord Stanford's eyes glazed over as he stared into the distance. "I wonder how long it takes to get to London. Haven't been myself since I was a boy. Where's my map?"

He started to turn toward his study until Mrs. Bummel cleared her throat. "London, my lord?"

Amelia shrank into Mrs. Bummel's skirts, while the housekeeper's arm tightened around her small shoulders.

"Yes, yes, London. Perfect place for a child—don't you think? I've got an empty house in town, you know. Lots of noise, and people, and noise. Nothing like here. It's nearly barbaric to keep the girl here." His face screwed up in thought again. For the first time his unkempt appearance frightened rather than amused. "What did barbarians do with their children? I mean, they were barbarians. Do I have a book on barbarians?"

He wandered off muttering about what kind of person would be able to write a book about barbarians.

This time, Mrs. Bummel let him go, even as she pulled Amelia closer, whispering a prayer into the little girl's hair.

Amelia wrapped Mrs. Bummel's apron strings around her fingers, mourning the plans they'd made to walk through the woods this weekend in search of wild berries. As Mrs. Bummel's rough woolen skirts scraped the tears from Amelia's cheeks, she vowed to never make plans again.

The Lord had picked a horrible time to remind Miss Amelia Stalwood that she should have been a bit more grateful that everyone overlooked her very existence. She would have given anything for a bit of that invisibility now. But no, she had this man's complete and total attention.

Tumbling off a rolling library ladder into a man's arms was a difficult thing to ignore, after all.

Amelia tilted her head back, easing open one eye to look at her rescuer. His face looked strange upside down. The lips were the wrong shape. And entirely too close.

Her other eye snapped open as she met his curious gaze. She'd never seen eyes so blue, didn't even know the shade existed.

"Oh my." Had she spoken the words or had her lips simply shaped a puff of air?

A single dark brown eyebrow lifted along with the right corner of his lips. "Oh my, indeed."

Her face pressed against a hard shoulder covered in dark green wool, limiting her view beyond the snow white cravat. High cheekbones set off the brilliant blue eyes and impeccable hair.

"Thank you for your assistance." She looked up at the dark paneled ceiling. "I believe you can put me down now."

"Actually, I can't."

Amelia's gaze darted back to his face, then followed to where his eyes were pointing. Her feet and skirts were tangled in the rungs of the library ladder, exposing her boots and ankles—proof that impulsiveness led to folly.

She couldn't even do someone a good turn without it ending in catastrophe. Visiting her friend Emma had seemed like such a good idea this morning. So did volunteering to help the ill maid with her chores, despite the fact that Amelia didn't know the first thing about being a servant.

"Not that I mind," the man continued.

She grasped the edge of the ladder and, with the man's assistance, heaved herself back into a standing position. After regaining her footing and straightening her skirt, she braved another look at her unexpected companion.

He was tall. She could have run her fingers through his thick waves of chestnut brown hair without having to stretch. Not that she would. But she could think about it.

The dark coat topped a pair of tan breeches and well-used but expensive riding boots. A patch of white on his shoulder drew her attention. Was that her cleaning rag? Horror filled her as she saw the small streaks of grey on his shoulder made from the dust she'd been clearing from the massive amount of bookshelves.

"May I assist you down?"

"No, I rather think I can manage. Thank you." Given the flock of magpies making a home in her midsection, the words came out surprisingly steady.

She descended the ladder, plucking the cleaning cloth from his shoulder as she went. A puff of dust drifted into the air.

Her backward momentum continued until she'd crossed the room and put her back to the bookcase she'd recently been cleaning. That put two tufted leather chairs and a tea table between her and the man.

And the man between her and the door. Not the smartest maneuvering she could have done.

He exuded casual confidence, with one shoulder leaned against the bookshelf and one booted foot propped on the bottom rung of the now vacant ladder.

How had he gotten in? A swarm of servants covered the house, preparing for the owner to return in three days, ending his two-year hiatus from London. A man would have to be very skilled to avoid them all.

Or know the house very well.

Panic unfurled in her toes and worked its way to her throat as the man's identity became obvious.

She was in a room alone with the notorious Raebourne Rake. Reputations had been ruined for less. Amelia needed her reputation, or rather her utter lack of one. Her lack of scandal was the only asset she could truly claim if she found herself searching for work after her next birthday.

She wove the dust rag through her fingers, twisting until the rough fabric cut into her skin. "Lord Raebourne, I presume."

He inclined his head in a mock bow. "You seem to have the advantage."

Good manners opened her mouth to answer his unspoken question. Good sense snapped her teeth shut. He did not need to know who she was.

Pushing away from the bookcase, he ran a finger along one still dusty edge. "Thank you for cleaning my bookcase. I apologize for interrupting your endeavors."

"If you require this room, I can finish the job at a more convenient time." The lie burned her throat, but what else could she do? Besides it was only a partial lie. Someone would return to finish the room. Someone actually employed here.

"Can you? How interesting." He paced forward to lean on one of the tufted leather chairs. "When do you intend to do that?"

Never. "At your convenience, my lord. It is your house after all."

He nodded. "And you spend a great deal of time in it?"

"I'm usually in the kitchens, my lord." Amelia restrained a wince at yet another partial lie. Despite her many visits to the house, this was the first time she'd ever ventured farther in than the kitchen.

She doubted he'd be interested that the reason she'd done so this time was because her friend Emma was sick. The man's housekeeper was a dreadful viper who threatened to fire Emma for neglecting her chores, unconcerned about the maid's inability to move five feet from the chamber pot.

"I'm curious," he said, once more inspecting the bookcases. "I know I've been away a while, but I don't recall the servants of this house dressing in well-crafted muslin gowns before."

Amelia's free hand clutched at the front of her gown, crushing the fine muslin between her fingers. It was simply cut and the drabbest of browns, but he was correct about the craftsmanship.

"You are known as a rather generous employer." Amelia pinched herself. He was known as a cad. A cad who'd left town two years prior to avoid a duel with a young lady's angry brother.

His eyebrows lifted even as his mouth turned down. For a moment the look of playful curiosity succumbed to a dark cloud of resignation. "I think we both know my reputation points in another direction."

Amelia blinked, and the sophisticated man of rumor returned, wielding his social power as casually as a riding crop. His face relaxed until it was poised on the edge of a smug grin. "Why don't we start with you telling me who you are, since I don't believe for a moment that you work for me."

Why, oh why, did the first nobleman she'd encountered in a decade have to be the devastatingly good-looking and debonair Marquis of Raebourne? Life would have been ever so much easier if she could have started with a nice baronet.

A homely viscount would have worked as well. Preferably one who was easily distracted, like her absent-minded guardian. He walked around his Sussex estate with unkempt hair, a too-large coat, and three pairs of spectacles tucked in various places on his person because he kept forgetting where he put them. It all testified to the somewhat endearing absent-mindedness and total harmlessness of her guardian.

The marquis did not strike her as absent-minded and he certainly wasn't harmless.

He rounded the furniture and advanced toward her. "I believe, under the circumstances, we can introduce ourselves. As you have surmised I am Anthony Pendleton, Marquis of Raebourne."

He bowed and looked at her expectantly. "And you are . . . ?"

"Not supposed to be here." The words spilled from Amelia's mouth before she could catch them.

The dark eyebrows climbed toward his hairline. His lips twitched as if they wanted to curve but he wouldn't let them. "Do tell."

She had to tell him something, and it had to be true. As a liar, she was abysmal. Most days she was happy to claim such a failure. "I don't work for you. Not really. I was . . . visiting. And Mrs. Banks required that this room be cleaned today."

Dear Lord, please don't let Mrs. Banks find out I've done any of Emma's cleaning. If the housekeeper found out . . . "Please don't tell her I was here."

His eyes locked with hers. His steady gaze became too much, and she looked down, stunned to discover she'd moved forward during her plea.

"I won't."

Amelia's shoulders slumped in relief. As long as Mrs. Banks never knew Amelia had been here, Emma's job should be safe.

"I can't," the marquis continued. "You haven't told me who you are."

She intended to keep it that way. "God, help me," she whispered.

Hurried footsteps sounded down the hall, breaking Amelia's trance. Both she and the marquis turned toward the door. *No, not like that!* She couldn't gain her escape at someone else's expense.

Amelia ran along the edge of the room, her shoulder grazing the bookcase.

She collided with the tall, breathless maid running into the room.

Jane grabbed Amelia by the shoulders to keep both of them from falling. "Cook told me about Emma! She'll be in the suds if Mrs. Banks finds out you've gone past the kitchens to do her cleaning."

All efforts to shove the woman out the door failed. The maid was lost in her emotional rant. "You shouldn't be working. You're Quality, Miss Amelia!"

Amelia darted a look at the marquis, who wasn't missing a moment of the exchange. Jane turned as well. Her mouth dropped open.

Shivers skittered up Amelia's back and her stomach, twisted like Cook's kneaded bread dough. What if the marquis blamed Jane for Amelia's trespass?

She had to get Jane out of there. She needed a distraction or the marquis could stop them before they reached the back stairs.

More out of alarm than inspiration, she flung the cloth she'd been using on the bookcases toward his head.

The marquis snatched the fabric as it connected with his nose. A puff of dust settled in his hair as one corner of the cloth slapped against his forehead. The stunned look on his face was the last thing Amelia saw before she shoved Jane down the corridor.

They half slid, half ran down the back stairs. The hollow echo of their feet on the bare wooden treads mirrored the pounding in Amelia's chest. A swift glance over her shoulder revealed they were not being followed. A relief to be certain, but not enough of one to calm her frantic flight.

They stumbled into the kitchen, clutching each other to keep from falling. Momentum from their mad dash down the stairs sent them careening across the floor with little balance and even less grace. Cook shrieked and dropped a bowl of flour.

"Oh, I'm sorry!" Amelia searched for a rag to help clean up the mess.

"Miss Amelia!" Jane pulled on her companion's arm. "*He* could be on his way down here!"

"But I—"

Words failed as the sound of footfalls reverberated in the servant stairwell. They sounded too light to belong to the marquis, but Amelia wasn't going to wait around to find out.

2

Anthony rested his head against the back of the seat in his carriage. Arriving three days early had thrown his house into turmoil, but if he'd stayed at his country estate any longer, he'd have talked himself out of coming at all. The friends who had convinced him it was time to reestablish his place in London society had returned to Town almost two weeks ago, leaving him brooding back in Hertfordshire.

To spare the sanity of his cook, he was dining with those same friends this evening.

Maybe they could help him forget the enigma he'd found cleaning his study. He'd become entranced the moment he saw her perched on the ladder, humming as she ran the cloth over the books and shelves. Her giggle of happiness as she kicked off the bookshelf and sent the ladder careening down the wall had fascinated him to the point that he forgot to move out of the way before the ladder connected with his boot.

Then she'd landed in his arms.

Two years ago the situation would have delighted him. He'd have flirted instead of remaining a good distance away from her after she was back on her feet. Those old instincts had been difficult to fight during the encounter.

Difficult enough to keep him from pursuing her.

Difficult enough he should avoid her. He was attempting to prove to himself and God that he was indeed the new creation the Bible said he was. Obsessing about a woman he'd met only hours before seemed too much like the old creation for his peace of mind.

Not that she fit his old ideal. With dark hair pulled back into a serviceable bun—devoid of a single face-framing ringlet—an unadorned mud-colored dress, and well-worn boots, she'd been a. head-to-toe column of nondescript brown. Pretty but not classically beautiful, and without a hint of anything fashionable about her appearance.

He'd never seen someone so happy to be where they were, though. Her joy in the midst of the degrading act of cleaning was like nothing he'd ever seen.

Being attracted to goodness and joy was a sign he was changing for the better, wasn't it? It didn't hurt that goodness and joy was wrapped in the body of a woodland fairy.

The carriage stopped in front of the London home of his good friend, Griffith, Duke of Riverton. More proof that he wasn't the same man.

Up until two years ago, Griffith had been nothing but an aristocratic neighbor. He'd never set foot in the man's home for a gathering of anything less than one hundred people, even though their country estates sat within five miles of each other. Now Griffith and his siblings were the closest thing Anthony had to family.

The butler showed him to the drawing room, and Anthony grinned as he spotted Miranda, the elder of Griffith's younger sisters. "You provide a splendid welcome to Town."

Miranda returned Anthony's grin as she crossed the drawing room, her green eyes brimming with humor. "I shall accept the compliment, despite the lack of competition. Tell me again after the masses have a chance to greet you. I give it two days at most until they all come 'round for one reason or another."

"I haven't officially told anyone I'm back in London."

Anthony would have sworn it was impossible to snort in a ladylike manner, but Miranda managed to accomplish it. "That won't matter."

He couldn't stop a groan of discomfiture, though it lacked Miranda's refinement. He reached past the decanter of brandy to grab the lemonade. "I only want a chance to settle in without being pestered. It sounds unbearably egotistical, but I do believe my arrival in town is going to make me the prey instead of the hunter."

The very thought was enough to make Anthony long for his country estate once more. As he poured the lemonade he noted Trent, Griffith's younger brother, sitting in a chair by the fire. "Are Griffith and Georgina joining us this evening?"

"Griffith departed Town earlier this morning. He wants to get through some pressing ducal business at a few of his estates before the heart of the season." Miranda cut her eyes toward her brother. "Trent is irritated. Griffith promised to help escort me this year, and Trent claims big brother is shirking his duties. I adore being a burden."

Anthony counted himself grateful that he wasn't on the receiving end of Miranda's glare.

Trent coughed as he stood and tugged at his cravat. "Yes, well, Georgina should be along at any moment. Next to her I look positively cheerful. She is irked at us for not allowing her to participate in society yet."

"She was soothed considerably when I informed her she could join us for dinner this evening." Miranda turned her pinning gaze from her brother to her guest. "I believe she has a *tendre* for you, Anthony."

"All the smart women do." Anthony favored Miranda with his most charming grin. "I have been biding my time until you come to your senses and fall at my feet as well." He raised his glass in her direction.

Miranda grimaced. "That would be like marrying my brother."

Trent tried to hide his wide grin. "I doubt there'll be room for her once you make your first social appearance, Anthony."

Miranda cast a sideways glance at her brother. "Honestly, Trent, he hasn't set foot in the city for two years. You have to take into account that many of his acquaintances might have forgotten him."

Anthony coughed, trying to remind the siblings that he was in the room.

Trent gripped Miranda's shoulder and looked at the floor, slowly shaking his head. "My dear, dear sister, this man is a legend." He raised his head and pointed his glass in Anthony's direction, a crooked smile on his lips. "He told me himself."

Anthony's neck got hot. If he was going to blush for the first time in years, shouldn't it be about something much more risqué than that offhand comment?

"Yes, yes." Miranda waved her hand through the air. "The enormously popular bachelor possessing both title and fortune, notorious for racing, women, and various other pleasurable pursuits. While rare, men of that ilk are not impossible to find."

"What do you know of his 'pleasurable pursuits'?" Trent's gaze jerked to Miranda, his face bearing the stern cast of big brother instead of charming gentleman. Their green eyes, so similar to each other in shade and shape, locked across the room. His narrowed as an impish smile formed on his sister's face.

Anthony shifted, trying to avoid a deeper blush. He didn't like Miranda knowing anything about his former pleasurable pursuits either.

"Only whispers, I assure you. Women love to gossip when they visit, but no one tells unmarried ladies any details. They only share enough to scare all the decent young ladies away."

As the dreaded heat crawled farther up Anthony's neck and onto his ears, Trent's deep laughter filled the room. He laughed so hard he had to bend over and take huge gulping breaths of air in order to catch his breath back.

"Miranda, Tony is a marquis, and a rich one at that. He could have a string of debauched virgins—"

"Trent!"

"—and a passel of illegitimate children trailing behind him and still have his pick of any unattached woman in town."

"I suppose." Miranda hid her smile behind her glass. "Imagine if they knew he had the ability to climb apple trees while completely foxed."

Trent toasted him once more. "Not to mention his skill at remaining in said tree after passing out."

Anthony could have done without the reminder of his final drunken stupor, despite its fascinating and embarrassing conclusion in an apple orchard. It was, however, the event that brought Griffith into his life, changing it forever, so he couldn't completely detest the experience. At least the memory was sobering enough to cool the flush from his skin.

Miranda looked Anthony in the eye. "As long as you steer clear of any scandal, we should be able to find you that rare jewel who will overlook your past and see the changed man you have become."

What was he supposed to say to that? "Um, thank you?"

"Don't forget to watch for a jewel of your own, dear sister. I don't relish carting you around again next season."

Trent was saved becoming the victim of fratricide by the entrance of a vibrant young woman with masses of blond curls and laughing green eyes. Georgina danced into the drawing room, an engaging smile decorating her face. "At last, I have arrived. So good of you to wait for me."

Anthony stood as the spritely female dipped low in a curtsy of greeting.

She then twirled to Anthony's side. "If only you would consent to wait for me, my lord. My overbearing family will let me out of the schoolroom next season, and we can dance away in wedded bliss."

Anthony laughed and kissed the outstretched fingers, thankful for a less serious conversation. "Alas, fair maiden, I fear I am not worthy of your dancing slippers. I shall have to comfort myself with someone within the reach of these lowly arms."

"Oh pish!" Georgina, swatted Anthony on the shoulder. "You shall be the catch of the season. I wish I could watch all of London fall at your feet when they discover you are seeking a bride." Her sigh threatened to extinguish the candles across the room.

Picturing the beauties of London at his feet brought the morning's mishap to mind. "Miranda, do you know of a rather short brunette miss named Amelia?"

The footman entered to announce dinner.

"I am afraid you will have to be more specific, Anthony," Miranda murmured dryly as she rose to take Anthony's arm.

"I found a young woman dressed considerably better than your average maid dusting my study when I arrived today."

Trent laughed. "Was it a marriage-minded miss trying to get your attention?"

"If it was she did a terrible job of it." Georgina placed her hand on Trent's arm. "He can't call on her if he doesn't know her full name."

"I am sorry, but I cannot think of any women who would be dusting your study, Anthony," Miranda said as they passed the wide-eyed footman.

Anthony sighed. "Be a diamond and keep an ear out for me, would you? I would like to know who she is."

3

She had to be vacant in the attic to even consider the request. Amelia choked down her bite of toast as she tried to come to terms with Mrs. Harris's request. "You want me to *what*?"

The loving housekeeper was the closest thing to a mother Amelia had experienced. Amelia would have done anything for the woman who'd done her best to show Amelia around London when the viscount had sent her here almost ten years ago.

Anything, that is, except return to the marquis' house.

Mrs. Harris plunked a bottle on the scarred worktable. "Take this tonic to Emma. You said she was still feeling poorly yesterday."

The bottle tilted as one side settled into a thick groove on the table.

Amelia had never thought much about the many dings and dents of the old table. She'd sat here for breakfast every morning and had eaten dinner at the table as well until Miss Ryan, her governess and companion, had declared it unfit for her station. Then they'd all moved to the dining room for the evening meal.

All it did was create more work in Amelia's eyes, but it made the servants feel as if they were doing something right so she never complained.

"Do you really think she needs it?" Amelia asked.

"Do you think that dragon of a housekeeper will keep her around if she misses any more work?"

Amelia ran her fingers over the rough surface until they wrapped around the smooth glass bottle. "Perhaps Lydia could take it," she asked hopefully, referring to the parlor maid with a mop of blond corkscrews popping out around the edges of her mob cap. "Or perhaps Fenton?"

Even before Mrs. Harris could spear her with a quizzical stare, Amelia knew her suggestions were nonsensical. As the lady of the house, such as it was, she was the one who should visit their friends and see to their care when needed. Sending the maid or the butler, who each had a full day's work to do, would be impersonal and strange.

If only she could claim other lady-of-the-house duties such as dinner parties and afternoon social calls. But when one only knew the servants of London's elite and not the lords and ladies themselves, a social presence was hard to come by.

"Is there something you aren't telling me?" Mrs. Harris placed a fist on one skinny hip and looked at Amelia with the same glare that had gotten her to confess to eating all the gingerbread cookies her first Christmas in London.

The housekeeper's eyes narrowed. "You look guilty. Like the time you snuck young Celia Scott into the dressmaker's shop every night for two weeks as if she was the shoemaker's elf."

"She got the job, didn't she?"

"At the expense of every candle in this house. I thought I was going mad when I couldn't find any." Mrs. Harris crossed her arms but didn't relax her accusatory glare. "What have you gotten yourself into now?"

If Amelia's choices were to deliver the tonic or tell the tale of the marquis, there was no need for debate. She clutched the bottle to her chest. "Not a thing. It's probably the busyness of the season getting to me. All the extra noise and traffic." Amelia popped up from her stool. "I'll take it now. As you said, she can't afford to miss another day." But even as she buttoned her spencer jacket and slapped a bonnet on her head, Amelia tried to come up with a reason to avoid going.

As she walked down the street, her mind swirled with all the reasons returning to the scene of her humiliation was a bad idea.

Once she'd cut through a back alley, the top of the marquis' house could be seen over the roof of his mews. The unfamiliar stench of horses and leather tickled her nose, reminding her how different his life was than hers. It was surprisingly encouraging.

He would likely still be abed. If he had risen early, he'd be off at his club or one of those other places men of leisure spent their time. He wouldn't be home, and he certainly wouldn't be in the kitchens. She'd be in and out without any additional embarrassing encounters.

By the time she was creeping through the enormous hedges toward the kitchen entrance of the marquis' Grosvenor Street home, her mental assurances had almost convinced her heart to resume its normal beat. A masculine chuckle caused it to stop altogether.

Amelia's feet grew roots. It couldn't be *him*.

She squatted low to see beneath the hedge. He lay on a blanket, a tray with a half-full pitcher of lemonade a few feet away and a large pile of cards on the ground next to him. He picked up a card. His low groan reached her ears before he tossed the card over his head and into the grass beyond. What could he be doing?

He sighed. "Lady Charles is hosting a soiree, hmm?" The white card hit the grass behind him. "I wonder if she stopped serving raw meat to her guests yet." He shuddered and moved on to the next card.

"A ball given by the Countess of Brigston. A crowd of that size would allow me to greet people quickly." A card went into the stack nearest his hip.

"Perhaps it's better to start small, though. I liked Harry Wittcomb well enough at school. A dinner party at his home could be enjoyable." The card went toward the pile at his knee.

She should move. This was the man's private garden. He had every right to expect that his verbal musings were falling on no ears but his own.

But what kind of man had a picnic in his own garden and threw invitations willy-nilly about the yard?

For goodness' sake, Amelia. It doesn't matter if the man is a paragon of virtue; he deserves his privacy.

But this behavior was too intriguing for her to leave.

Anthony picked up the next in the seemingly endless stack of invitations. Were all of these events occurring in the next few days?

He sighed and opened another invitation.

"A garden party. Dreadful bore those are, unless you know the other guests well. Who is Lady Galvine? I assume she is married to Lord Galvine but I've never heard of him either."

Snickering at his own wit, Anthony tossed the parchment over his head.

He picked up the next one.

"What are you doing?" The irate voice of his valet, Harper, sounded from his right.

A quick glance around the clearing confirmed that Anthony was not the target of Harper's verbal attack. Which begged the question of who was. Anthony rose and started running around the line of greenery.

Was Harper hurt? Was someone attacking him? Harper was a wiry little fellow, an odd choice for a valet, but the man could tie an impeccable cravat.

"Harper!" Anthony called out as he rounded the edge of the hedges. His foot slipped in the dirt, but he quickly steadied himself.

The last thing he expected to find was a woman snared in his valet's glare. And not just any woman.

The familiar brown dress, the alarmed chocolate-colored eyes, the severe bun. His mystery woman had returned.

She squealed as recognition dawned in her eyes. Both of her hands flew up to her face, leaving only her big brown eyes showing. Her gaze connected with Anthony's, and her eyes widened even more until a full rim of white surrounded the deep brown.

Harper's hand wrapped around the woman's upper arm. Her eyes cut to the valet. She whirled with such force that Harper was knocked sideways and required several steps to regain his balance.

Then she ran.

"Wait!" Anthony ran after her.

The woman darted a look over her shoulder. His call seemed to spur her to run harder. Anthony, however—in possession of much longer legs and not encumbered by skirts—was faster. He skidded to a halt, grabbing her shoulder and spinning her around.

Her gaze connected with his. Breath backed up in his lungs at the sadness mingled with fear he could read on her face. For the space of several heartbeats he stared into her big brown eyes, watching an emotion he couldn't quite name build within them.

"Go to Lady Galvine's," she whispered in a rush. "She treats her servants well and has spent an entire year planning the party. Her only daughter is in love with the Earl of Lyndley's eldest son and he with her, but they don't think that the earl will let his son marry her. Lord Galvine is only a baron. If you announced your arrival in London at her party it would increase her consequence enough that Miss Kaitlyn might be allowed to marry the earl's son."

She pulled away and ran behind the mews.

He gave chase, but by the time he reached the alley, she was nowhere to be found. His mystery woman had escaped again.

⌒

"Why are we here?" Amelia frowned at the row of glinting shop windows marching down Bond Street. After her encounter with the marquis and his valet she'd wanted nothing more than to hide in her room and wallow in useless grumbles and futile daydreams.

Daydreams in which her encounter with the marquis had taken place in a respectable place, she'd known exactly what to say, and her dress had been something other than serviceable brown.

"You've been moping about the house for over a week, grumbling about hedges and cleaning cloths. You needed to get out. Besides, you need a new dress." Miss Ryan, her governess turned companion, nodded to punctuate her statement, causing her black ringlets to bob against the sides of her bonnet.

Amelia blinked out of her reverie and looked down at her skirts. "There is nothing wrong with this dress."

As long as one didn't compare it to anything else walking down the street.

"Aside from the two layers of trim we've put on the bottom to hide the ragged edges, the pull in the back from where you mended a hole under the arm, and the fact that the waistline is three years out of date—no, there's not a thing wrong with it," agreed Miss Ryan.

Amelia didn't want to accustom herself to upper-class finery only to have it ripped away from her when she reached one and twenty in a few short months. Who knew if the viscount would continue to support her? Or if he even remembered she existed?

"My dress is suitable for what I do. None of my friends care that I've had to repair a tattered hem or two." Over the years she'd made lots of friends and she'd even invited them over to the house for tea occasionally. But they weren't the type of friends to help a girl socially.

Miss Ryan shook her head. "You can't marry if you limit your socializing to the servants. You're a gentleman's daughter."

"I like the servants," Amelia mumbled. They'd been the only ones willing to talk to her when she'd been dumped in London at the age of eleven.

"Servants don't marry, dear." Miss Ryan ran a comforting hand along Amelia's arm.

"Neither do unknown wards of forgotten viscounts." Amelia crossed her arms and dared the companion to contradict her statement.

"This is London. You never know what the good Lord will make happen. Perhaps with the right dress." Miss Ryan smiled but didn't meet Amelia's gaze. "It changed Cinderella's life, didn't it?"

Before Amelia could ask where Miss Ryan was stashing a fairy godmother, she found herself grasped by the elbow and hauled into the shop.

Two elegant women sat in chairs near the window, sipping tea. Another cluster of three ladies looked at a book of fashion plates while two more perused a selection of fabric.

Amelia sputtered. "But this is Madame Bellieme's. It probably costs money to simply breathe her air."

"We've been stashing money away for ten years." Miss Ryan shrugged. "We aren't here to see her, anyway."

"We're not?" Amelia clapped a hand to her bonnet to keep it from flying off as Miss Ryan pulled her behind the golden silk curtain.

The sun coming through the back windows of the store was considerably brighter than the shadowed front room. Amelia blinked rapidly to adjust her vision.

"Miss Amelia!"

Amelia shook her head to focus on the speaker, a middle-aged woman in a light blue dress with her light brown hair pulled into a low bun. It took a moment for Amelia to recognize the impoverished gentry woman she'd met in the free pews at St. George's nearly five years prior. "Oh! Good morning, Sally. I haven't seen you in an age."

"Not since you helped me get that job in Hampstead Heath. I can't thank you enough for putting in a good word with the housekeeper there. I was privileged to act as companion to Lady Margaret until she passed on. I'm a lady's maid, now." Sally peeked at a folding screen partitioning part of the back room off from the rest of the work area.

Amelia looked at the screen as well. Sally's mistress must be behind there being fitted for a dress. "Are you not needed back there? I would have thought the lady's maid would be part of the fittings."

"I usually wait out here. Sometimes I visit with Celia. Her brother, Finch, is a footman for the family I work for now."

Miss Ryan turned from the folding screen that she'd been staring at since they passed the curtain. "Celia was very excited to know we were coming today. She said that sometimes she still slips in here at night to work by candlelight so that she can remember how badly she wanted the position."

A tall, blond young woman bustled out from behind the screen, smoothing her skirt over her hip. "Have those delivered to the house when they're finished, Madame Bellieme. I won't need the second ball gown until next week."

"Of course, my lady." The modiste was older than Amelia remembered, although it had been at least three years since she'd seen the woman.

"Sally, let's be going."

Amelia couldn't begin to guess what the elegant lady was thinking as her brilliant green eyes took in Amelia and the two servants, none of whom belonged in the inner sanctum of London's finest dress-maker—but at least the woman knew why Sally was there.

"Yes." Sally stepped away from their little gathering with a small wave. A green reticule, likely belonging to Sally's mistress, dangled from her wrist. "Have a good day, Miss Amelia."

Amelia nodded, not wanting to say anything to get Sally in trouble. Her mistress kept glancing back and forth between her servant and Amelia.

As the two pushed past the curtain Celia came out from behind the screen. "Miss Amelia!" She bounced across the back room and wrapped Amelia in her skinny arms.

Madame Bellieme gave Amelia a smile and a pat on the shoulder as she made her way back to the front of the store.

Amelia extricated herself from Celia, whose smile remained as strong as the hug.

"I'm happy to see you!" The younger girl reached out to give Amelia one more squeeze.

The enthusiasm inspired Amelia's own smile. "How have you been, Celia?"

"Better than I ever dreamed. Come, come, I've got your dress ready." Celia pulled her toward the screen, Miss Ryan pushing from the back.

Amelia's slight weight was no match for the two of them, and she found herself propelled across the floor even as the rest of her froze in shock. They already had a dress made for her? How? When?

"Madame Bellieme's fingers aren't working as well as they used to, and she's made me her secret apprentice. She says my eye for fashion and hand with a needle are almost as good as hers." Celia bounced in excitement, her dark bun bobbing about atop her head.

She hauled out a dress of beautiful green-sprigged muslin. "And there's a matching redingote as well. Come, come. Let's get you fitted."

The women pulled at Amelia's dress, eager to get her into the new gown. Amelia began to feel a bit of excitement herself as the soft fabric draped over her body.

Celia had used one of Amelia's old dresses for size, so it didn't require much altering to fit her perfectly. A few quick stitches along the seam of the coat and Amelia was ready to go in the most gorgeous afternoon ensemble she'd ever laid eyes on.

After folding Amelia's old dress into a bandbox, Celia gave her another hug and told Miss Ryan to let her know when they wanted more dresses.

"This one is too beautiful." Amelia swayed back and forth, enjoying the swish of her new skirt. "I may never find another dress acceptable again."

They all laughed as they left the partitioned area.

"Oh dear." Miss Ryan's voice was stilted, almost toneless.

"Oh my," Celia added.

Amelia looked around, but didn't see anything to cause their wooden surprise. "What?"

Celia stooped to scoop up a green reticule from the floor.

4

"That can't be good," Miss Ryan said. "How could Sally have left it behind?"

"Can't you have it delivered?" Amelia looked around the little group. Why was this causing such concern? The solution was simple. The tall lady couldn't have been the first to leave her belongings behind.

Celia shook her head. "The footman is out already."

"I hope Sally doesn't get fired." Mrs. Ryan bit her lip.

Why the sudden concern for everyone's position? First Mrs. Harris feared for Emma, and now Miss Ryan mentioned Sally? Did they think everyone in eminent danger of unemployment?

"Lady Miranda is kind, but as a child she could be very emotional and unpredictable." Celia looked up at Amelia from the corner of her lashes.

Something strange was afoot, but Amelia couldn't begin to think what. "Lady Miranda?"

Celia nodded. "Lady Miranda Hawthorne. Sister of the Duke of Riverton."

Amelia hadn't realized what a prestigious position Sally had managed to get.

Resigned to another aristocratic encounter, Amelia took the bag. "Hawthorne House isn't far out of our way."

It was miles away socially but a mere two streets over physically. Amelia never visited Hawthorne House, despite knowing the butler and a few servants. It was too intimidating.

With the gorgeous green bag clutched in her hand, Amelia led Miss Ryan back out onto Bond Street.

They left the shopping district behind, chatting about the pretty wares in the various windows. Then, without warning, Miss Ryan fell into Amelia, nearly sending her to the pavement.

"Oh! Oh my, Miss Ryan. Are you all right?"

The older woman made her way to the side of the pavement to lean on the building. Her limp was drastic.

Amelia bit her lip. "Should we call a hack?"

Miss Ryan waved toward Grosvenor Square, within sight but in the opposite direction of their home. "I can make it back home. You go ahead without me."

"You . . . but . . . I can't go alone!"

"I'm sure Finch or Gibson will see that you get home safely." Mrs. Ryan squared her shoulders and limped down the side street that would take her toward Mount Street. "Remember Sally is depending on you."

Amelia looked back and forth from the companion to the distant square. Had Miss Ryan lost her mind? The reticule felt heavy in her hand. She couldn't take it home with her. It was either continue on to Hawthorne House or return the bag to Bond Street.

Since walking alone down Bond Street was an even worse idea than walking in Grosvenor Square, she continued on.

Hawthorne House loomed as Amelia crossed Grosvenor's Square. The grand columns were daunting even if one didn't know who lived there. Few homes in London were larger, but then few men were more powerful than its owner.

Amelia smoothed her skirts. The ensemble was still the most beautiful thing she'd ever worn or even seen in person, but it felt unequal to the task of socializing with the sister of a duke.

"Lord, be with me," she whispered before taking a deep breath and climbing the stairs. Her knock was so timid she didn't think anyone would hear it, but it was immediately followed by the scrape of the latch.

"Miss Amelia?" The butler's surprise was evident as he opened the door.

Amelia bit her lip. Should she have gone to the servant entrance? "Good day, Gibson. I'm making a delivery." She extended her arm, the green bag swinging from her fingertips like a clock pendulum, counting down the minutes to her next humiliation.

"Bless you! Come in. My lady discovered the loss of it moments ago." Gibson ushered her into a beautiful drawing room decorated in white and gold. "Please have a seat."

"There is no need for that, Gibson. I can leave the bag in the hall." The pleading edge to her voice made Amelia wince. Cowardly or not, facing and conversing with Lady Miranda seemed like a bad idea. Amelia's encounters with the marquis had proven how inept she was at interacting with aristocracy.

"She will insist on thanking you in person. Wait here, Miss Amelia, if you please." Gibson hurried from the room.

Throwing the reticule on a chair and leaving seemed like an inspired idea, but Gibson knew where she lived. The last thing she needed was Lady Miranda on her doorstep.

The blond woman from the modiste entered the drawing room, a warm smile on her face and open curiosity in her eyes. "Gibson tells me that you have my reticule?"

"Er, yes, my lady." Amelia stabbed her arm forward, the reticule once again dangling before her. Lady Miranda accepted it.

"We found it as we were leaving. Everything is in there. Celia knew it was yours so we didn't need to open it."

Small creases formed at the corners of glittering green eyes and the edges of slightly curved lips. Was she amused by Amelia's assurances? Perhaps she found Amelia's lack of composure entertaining. Amelia's fingers began to play with the drawstring of her own reticule.

"Thank you." The lady set the bag on a nearby table. "I am Lady Miranda Hawthorne."

"I know. That is, Celia told me who you were." Amelia clamped her teeth shut. She would not prattle on and reveal her discomfort. She was going to limit herself to three-word sentences. That allowed her to say little more than "Yes, my lady" and "No, my lady."

Lady Miranda dipped her head and raised her eyebrows.

"Oh!" Amelia cried. "I am Miss Amelia Stalwood." That was five words, but perhaps her name could really be counted as one. "Pleasure to make your acquaintance." Five words again. Very well, she would limit herself to five-word sentences so long as they were intelligent five-word sentences.

Lady Miranda smiled as if every visitor lost her wits. Maybe they did. It was a duke's house, after all. "That is a lovely dress. Were you picking it up?"

Gibson appeared in the doorway before Amelia could answer. "Would you care for tea, my lady?"

"Oh no, Gibson, I don't—" Amelia froze. That was her voice answering the butler. Heat rushed to her cheeks and her ears. Her nose felt like ice. She cut her eyes to Lady Miranda and found the other woman just as still, with her mouth slightly agape, as if she, too, had been about to answer the butler.

"Miss Stalwood, Amelia Stalwood, was it?" Lady Miranda recovered her composure first. "Do please stay. Gibson, tea would be lovely."

The butler bowed and spun on his heel to leave room.

Lady Miranda waved an arm in the direction of a white brocade chair. Amelia perched on the edge, ready to flee if the opportunity arose.

Celia's brother, Finch, strode in with a laden tea service before Lady Miranda could finish adjusting her skirts on the adjacent sofa. Had he been standing in the hall, filled tray in hand, when Gibson came in to inquire if they wanted tea?

Amelia blinked in surprise. Lady Miranda hesitated before indicating Finch should leave the tray on a low table.

"Thank you, Finch." Amelia closed her eyes. That had been her voice, again, acknowledging someone else's servant, by name no less. Lady Miranda was sure to boot her out through the kitchens at this familiarity.

Silence filled the room. Not even a clock ticked to fill the quiet. Amelia hadn't felt this exposed since she was ten years old standing on the viscount's doorstep with nothing but a trunk, a valise, and a letter from her grandmother claiming the most distant relational ties imaginable.

What was the woman sitting before her looking for? Was she finding it?

Finally, Lady Miranda concluded her inspection. She nodded her head and began fixing tea. "You know my servants?"

"Er, yes, my lady." Amelia tried to mirror the graceful restraint of the woman across the table.

Lady Miranda paused in silent inquiry after pouring a cup of tea. Her hand hovered over the pitcher of cream.

"Sugar, no milk, please." A thrill of confidence twirled down Amelia's spine. That had sounded almost cultured and sophisticated. Granted it was merely a request for tea, but—

"Are you on good terms with many servants?"

They were back to the awkward inquisition.

"I suppose." This was not going at all the way Amelia had anticipated. She wasn't ashamed of her acquaintance with lower London, but she never imagined a highborn lady asking her about it.

"I myself have always tried to be on good terms with those I hire, but I have never been able to refer to those in other homes by name." Lady Miranda held out a cup of tea.

Willing her fingers not to tremble, Amelia accepted the cup. Her definition of "good terms" was likely different than Lady Miranda's.

"You know my maid as well?" Another cup filled with tea. A splash of milk and the slightest bit of sugar joined it.

Amelia hastily swallowed her sip of tea. "Yes, my lady."

Lady Miranda added a selection of biscuits to a small plate and offered it to Amelia. "It isn't everyone who would make an effort to return someone's belongings."

"It was no trouble." What else should she say? Amelia nibbled at a biscuit to buy herself some time.

Another young woman entered the room, her astounding beauty

108

making Amelia blink. Blond curls piled atop her head, with ringlets framing features that would make a porcelain-doll maker swoon. "Gibson mentioned tea." Her green eyes assessed Amelia. "Good afternoon."

Lady Miranda fixed another cup of tea. "This is my new friend, Miss Amelia Stalwood. Miss Stalwood, my sister, Lady Georgina."

Amelia slid her cup onto the table. Was she supposed to rise and curtsy? This was a duke's sister, after all. There had to be some form of proper address in this situation. In the end she performed an awkward head nod, which drew a smirk from the younger woman.

Amelia directed her eyes back to the floor, wishing she could sink through the floorboards into the servant domain below. She'd be ever so much more comfortable.

The sisters talked and sipped tea, occasionally asking Amelia a question. After the first few times, Amelia stopped stumbling over her responses and managed something resembling a normal conversation.

"You've been so gracious, bringing my bag here that I hate to ask you this." Lady Miranda poured a bit more tea into her cup. "But would you do another favor for me?"

Amelia swallowed. Could she say anything other than yes?

"Would you come to dinner tonight?"

Amelia bobbled her tea cup. Lady Miranda tried to hide a smile with a sip of tea.

When Amelia didn't answer, Lady Miranda spoke again. "It will be very informal. Family and one or two close friends."

Amelia felt skewered by Lady Miranda's green eyes, like one of the animals she had read about scientists studying.

"You would be a great help. Georgina isn't able to join us tonight, so our numbers will be off if you do not come."

Lady Georgina shot her sister a scathing glare. "Actually, I—"

Lady Miranda gracefully kicked Lady Georgina in the shin. Amelia's eyes widened. How long would it take to learn how to do such an uncouth thing with ladylike grace? Who would take the time to develop such a strange talent?

"I understand. I was sixteen once." Lady Miranda patted her sister's hand.

"I'm seventeen."

"Miss Stalwood, please say you will."

Amelia plucked at her skirts. It was impossible. How could she come?

"I need you." Lady Miranda clasped her hands in her lap, her eyes filled with pleading.

Amelia heard herself agreeing before she could think it through. Excitement tingled along her fingers, making her bury them in her skirts to hide their shaking. She couldn't back out now. All she could do was pray she wouldn't regret it before the night was over.

5

"*En garde.*" Sunlight glinted off the thin metal as Anthony slashed his sword in Trent's direction. Sweat rolled down his back, making his white lawn shirt stick to his skin. Finding such a well-matched fencing partner had been an unexpected benefit of befriending the Hawthorne family. Spending time with the younger man was surprisingly enjoyable.

"How goes the bridal hunt?" Trent grunted.

Even if he was an insolent pup.

Anthony blocked Trent's sword, not about to let his opponent distract him with mere words—even though the hunt had thus far been an utter failure. "Dismal."

Trent laughed as he danced forward, jabbing his sword toward Anthony's belly. "No one you find appealing? What about the Laramy girl? I haven't met her yet, but all accounts are that she is incomparably beautiful."

"She is." Anthony knocked Trent's sword upward to force him backward a step. "Beauty is not the problem, but I'm beginning to think intellect is."

Anthony's foot slipped sideways, and he felt the blunted tip of Trent's sword strike against his ribs. Acknowledging the hit, Anthony pulled off his mask. "If all the aristocracy is as lacking in wit as this year's crop of marital hopefuls, our country is doomed."

"Lady Miranda and Lady Georgina," the butler intoned from the terrace doorway.

"Present company excluded, of course," Trent murmured, grinning.

Miranda's nose wrinkled as she stepped onto the terrace. "The two of you are . . . disgusting." She gestured vaguely in the direction of their sweat-matted hair.

Anthony ran a hand through his disheveled locks, feeling awkward in only his shirtsleeves. Had he brought his coat out onto the terrace with him?

Georgina's expression was more admiring than disgusted. "They have been exerting themselves, Miranda. It is a most gentlemanly pursuit. Did you know Trent was going to be here?"

"You see?" Trent said. "Intelligent."

"Of course I did." Miranda speared her sister with a look that called the young woman's intelligence into question. "I would hardly have come here if Anthony were home alone."

Anthony turned to put his fencing equipment away. It was best if the ladies didn't notice him snicker at their spat. After composing his features, he turned back to them and gave a slight bow. "Ladies, please excuse me if I don't greet you properly. I am, as you noticed, a bit disheveled."

Trent gave a dismissive wave. "Bother that, it's just Miranda and Georgina." He turned to his sisters. "What are you doing here?"

Miranda turned her back on Trent, while Georgina stared daggers in his direction.

Anthony became unnerved by Miranda's blank expression. Normally the most confident of women, she seemed a little unsure of herself.

"Whatever you were planning tonight, I am afraid you will have to send your regrets. I need you at dinner."

Dinner? She wanted his presence at dinner? He'd expected something considerably more painful and difficult. In truth, a respite from the social whirl would be more than welcome. After enduring more tedious introductions, boring conversations, and lackluster dance partners than he would have thought possible in a short two weeks, he was inclined to disappear for another two years, with or without the wife he sought. A quiet dinner with intelligent friends sounded like Miranda was doing him a favor instead of the other way around.

"You're inviting him to dinner?" Georgina's despair added to Anthony's confusion. Since when did Georgina not want him at dinner?

"Unless Griffith returned this morning, Anthony's presence is required." Miranda turned from her sister back to Anthony. "It is of utmost importance."

This was obviously about more than a mere meal, but he could handle whatever it was. Miranda was as near to a sister as he had. If it was important to her, he could suffer through it. "I am, of course, at your service, my lady."

Georgina gave a little sigh. "I wish I could be there."

Trent left off his experimental sword swinging to join the conversation. "May I be excused as well?"

Miranda glared.

Anthony laughed, grateful God had brought this close-knit family into his life and suddenly looking forward to his evening.

⌒⌒

Amelia stood in front of the same house, wearing the same dress, for the second time that day. Would she repeat the same blunders? Dinner was considerably more involved than tea.

A breeze rustled the leaves in the park behind her, luring her to turn and run. She could be back at her own home within fifteen minutes.

It wasn't really a viable option. If she wanted to eat tonight she was going to have to march through that front door and dine with Lady Miranda. Mrs. Harris would refuse to feed her.

Gibson's face appeared from behind a curtain, sealing her fate. If she ran now, every servant in London would know by morning.

She walked resolutely to the door and knocked.

Gibson answered the door, a wide smile stretched across his lean face. "Good evening, Miss. May I take your coat?"

His happiness bolstered Amelia's spirits, and she grinned back.

She handed him her redingote and bonnet, but couldn't make her feet follow him toward the drawing room.

She was terrified.

"Hullo, there," called a voice from the stairs.

Amelia jumped and covered her skipping heart with her hand. A man was crossing the hall. Was this the duke? She knew the duke was young and handsome, but wasn't this man a bit too young?

Blond hair formed a neat cap against his head, skimming his ears and collar and almost brushing his eyebrows. His green eyes seemed friendly, though curious as he looked at Amelia standing three feet inside his front hall. There was little doubt that he was related to Lady Miranda.

"May I be incredibly bold and present myself? Lord Trent Hawthorne, at your service." He picked up her limp fingers and kissed the air directly above her knuckles.

Amelia watched her hand as if it belonged to someone else. She should say something. Her brain was forming the appropriate words to introduce herself as well, but more than her hand felt disconnected. Her mouth had forgotten the motions. Her lungs felt devoid of air.

This inability to express herself around these people was becoming tiresome. If she couldn't bring her tongue and brain into communication within the next ten seconds, she was leaving.

Ten . . . Nine . . .

"Not to worry." Lord Trent placed her hand on his arm. "I often have the effect of speechlessness on the lovelier half of the population. Mothers, of course, live in quiet fear of me attending a social gathering and rendering their daughters mute. The men, on the other hand, beg me to come so that they can enjoy some sensible conversation."

Eight . . . Seven . . .

A giggle sputtered through Amelia's lips. Was that enough noise to count?

Six . . . Five . . .

Finch stood at the door to the drawing room, his eyes wide. As they approached, he cut his eyes to the interior of the room and back to Amelia. Was he trying to communicate with her?

Four . . . Three . . .

"Alas, our other dinner guest has already arrived so I shall have to share your charms this evening. My sister will be down shortly. A small wardrobe issue. You know how that goes, I'm sure."

Two . . .

Amelia's cheeks turned bright pink. The man next to her was certainly aware that her wardrobe was inappropriate for the occasion. His blatant ignoring of that fact was both embarrassing and endearing.

One . . .

Her time was up. Amelia took a deep breath as she stepped across the threshold of the drawing room, but nothing came out as her eyes landed on an all-too-familiar sight.

Her feet comprehended what she saw first and came to a complete stop, causing Lord Trent to stumble. Then her blood understood and drained from her face, leaving her chilled and likely pale as death. The blood must have told her heart, because it began increasing in speed until a dull roar filled Amelia's ears. Finally her voice joined the party. "Oh my," she whispered. "You."

It was not the stellar conversational gambit she'd intended.

"My sentiments exactly," the marquis said.

Lord Trent looked back and forth between the two dinner guests. "You have already met?"

"Not formally. I do believe she likes to trespass on my property, though." Lord Raebourne smiled.

"Ah," Lord Trent gave the woman on his arm an assessing look. "Your devious duster."

"So it would seem." Lord Raebourne relieved Lord Trent of Amelia's arm. "Please have a seat, my dear. You're looking a trifle pale. I believe I introduced myself at our first meeting, but I quite understand if you have forgotten. Anthony Pendleton, Marquis of Raebourne."

All the blood that had previously left Amelia's face returned with reinforcements. She could feel the heat in her neck and cheeks and prayed that it was not as bright red as it felt. "Mishamtalwood."

Lord Trent and Lord Raebourne both leaned forward. "I beg your pardon?" Lord Trent asked.

Amelia cleared her throat and straightened her spine. She focused on a delicate green vase on a table behind and between the two gentlemen. "Miss Amelia Stalwood."

"I am *very* pleased to meet you, Miss Stalwood." A smile accompanied the statement, making Lord Raebourne's face engaging as well as handsome.

"And I you, my lord." Amelia thought her blush was a deep as possible, but when Lord Raebourne kissed her hand in a repeat of Lord Trent's earlier gesture, she positively flamed.

"I had a most splendid time at Lady Galvine's party. Her daughter is a jewel. I am sure that she and Lord Owen will do famously together." The corners of his mouth twitched.

Amelia's eyes grew larger with every word he spoke. Could eyes fall out of one's head?

"I . . . " Amelia struggled to find her tongue.

Lady Miranda burst into the drawing room, her breath coming short and fast. Had she *run* down the stairs? "Miss Stalwood, you have arrived!"

Both men in the room quirked a brow at her. Lord Trent looked decidedly amused while Lord Raebourne seemed almost accusatory.

The arrival of Lady Miranda helped Amelia feel like herself again. Still dismayed by the unexpected connection, but herself. Taking a deep breath, she stood, determined to make their last impression better than their first.

"Lady Miranda, I must apologize." She swallowed. "I am afraid I have to bid you farewell. You see, I was . . . That is to say, I have met your other guest, after a fashion, and I fear my behavior at the time would not reflect well on anyone claiming an acquaintance with me."

Amelia turned from Lady Miranda's wide-eyed amazement to the marquis. "My lord, please do not hold this against Lady Miranda. I have done her a small good turn, and she sought to repay it. For what it's worth, I do apologize for intruding upon your privacy. It shall not happen again."

Amelia looked at the occupants of the room. They all appeared to have eaten something disagreeable. She was slipping past Lord Trent when all three aristocrats burst out in laughter.

"I know, Miss Stalwood." Lady Miranda gasped for air. "Or I should say I suspected. Please, stay for dinner. No one is mad at you for dusting a library for a sick maid. Confused perhaps, but hardly angry."

Amelia's eyes flickered from one person to the next. They were smiling. Not polite we-don't-want-to-be-rude type of smiles, but broad smiles, the kind born of genuine amusement.

Lord Raebourne's grin was accompanied by conspiratorial gleam in his eyes. Was he recalling their second encounter?

It seemed her humiliation had to be complete. Amelia sighed. "It is not the dusting of which I am ashamed, my lady." Her voice was barely audible, even to her own ears. "I returned the next day, and—there is no polite way to say it—I spied upon his lordship in a private moment and was caught by his valet. It is all dreadfully embarrassing and—"

Amelia had to stop again as Lord Trent and Lady Miranda looked at Lord Raebourne and collapsed into a new round of laughter.

The marquis kept his bemused gaze on Amelia. "It is not quite the way it sounds. I was in my garden sorting through invitations."

Wasn't that what she said? Maybe not in so much detail, but . . .

Amelia closed her eyes in mortification as she realized that her phrasing implied she had spied upon him in much more intimate quarters. She needed to leave.

Head down, she made for the door, keeping her eyes locked on the veining of the marble floor. Polished shoes stepped into her view, forcing her to stop or collide into Lord Raebourne's chest.

Again.

She stopped.

"Please," he said softly. "Do not leave."

A single finger caught under her chin, forcing her gaze up to his. "Stay and dine with us this evening. It will give us a chance to start afresh."

Amelia searched his beautiful blue eyes and found nothing but kindness and sincerity. "Very well." The unspoken forgiveness lightened her, allowing the corners of her lips to edge upward. "I shall stay."

He offered her his arm. With some hesitance, she gave him her hand, hoping there wasn't a right and wrong way to do so. Heat emanated through his coat, sending a thrill spiraling up her arm and into her lungs.

As they passed through the main hall to the dining room, Amelia spied Finch, Gibson, two housemaids, and Miranda's lady's maid huddled behind a large plant in the corner of the front hall, enormous smiles on their faces. One of the housemaids saluted her.

The support of her friends calmed her. Surely she could get through this dinner with what remained of her dignity intact.

6

Anthony watched Amelia throughout dinner, noting the tremble in her fingers, and her wide, bright eyes. Even though he knew her full name now, he couldn't think of her as anything other than Amelia. It was all his imagination had to go on for days.

The knuckles on her hand were white as she gripped her serviette. Likely she was measuring every word and action to ensure there were no more embarrassing moments like the one in the drawing room.

He wanted to help her relax, free the engaging woman he'd caught glimpses of. How had Miranda found this woman?

As the fish course was cleared, he heard a low murmur from Amelia's direction. Had she thanked the servant for clearing her dish? His father had been a stickler for gentlemanly manners, but even the most polite in his acquaintance didn't make a habit of thanking the servants.

Which was rather inconsiderate when he thought about it.

His ears strained as the next course was set in front of him. Would she thank him again? Surprise made Anthony fumble the fork he reached for. Not only had she thanked the footman, but she'd used his name. His mysterious trespasser was on friendly terms with more than just *his* household staff.

The man answered with a quiet "You are most welcome, Miss Amelia."

A desire to learn everything about this woman rose within him.

Did she like the food? What was her favorite color? Did flowers make her sneeze?

"Tony!"

Anthony jerked from his reverie to find Trent and Miranda looking at him with expressions of amusement. He cleared his throat. "Yes, Trent?"

"I asked if you'd been to Tattersalls since your return. They had some prime horses there last week."

Horses. Tattersalls. Had he been? "No, not yet."

Miranda smiled. "Too busy settling back into the glittering ridiculousness that is London, are you?"

The only response Anthony could generate was a grunt. His weeks back among the social whirl of the elite had convinced him more than ever that he had to marry this year. The temptation to drift back to his old life was so much stronger in Town.

Was that what drew him to Amelia? She embodied the simplicity he missed from the country, where he had learned who he was beyond cards and drink and women. She might not be the one he should spend the rest of his life with, but he couldn't think of any woman he'd rather get to know.

A smile tugged at the corners of his mouth as Amelia twirled a spoon through her turtle soup. It was obvious she didn't care for it, but she kept trying to choke down bite after bite. The footmen cleared the bowls before she'd managed to eat half of it.

"Anthony?"

Miranda didn't bother to hide her amusement as she tried to catch his attention.

He dabbed the corner of his mouth with his serviette and raised his eyebrows in inquiry.

"Miss Stalwood mentioned attending St. George's at Hanover Square. I asked if you intended to take up a pew there."

She had spoken? And he'd missed it?

Anthony cleared his throat. "Griffith has invited me to join your family pew at Grosvenor Chapel for now. I see no reason to rent a pew myself without family to share it with."

120

Miranda's eyes cut to Amelia and then swiftly on to Trent, her throat convulsing in her obvious attempt to choke down a laugh. His own gaze flew back to Amelia—its favorite place this evening. Was Miranda implying that Amelia should share his pew or . . . Oh. Anthony bit back a chuckle himself.

The poor woman was trying to slip bites of spicy bread pudding into her serviette. The footman behind already had a clean one at the ready, waiting until the appropriate time to exchange the cloths. Anthony pinched himself to prevent the encroaching laughter.

He forced himself to pay more attention to the conversation around him. Staring at Amelia all evening wasn't going to help her relax or allow him to know more about her.

"Trent, what are your plans now that you've finished school?" Perhaps discussing the young man's future would lead to discussing Amelia's. Anthony couldn't bring himself to direct personal questions to Amelia when she looked so uncomfortable.

Trent gave a vague, noncommittal answer, then proved he did not share Anthony's aversion to interviewing Miranda's new friend. "Did you grow up in London?"

"No. I lived in Suffolk until I was eleven." Amelia fell quiet for a moment, her fingers wrapped in the folds of the clean serviette.

Miranda's eyes narrowed. "Why haven't we met? Didn't you say your guardian is a viscount? Surely he didn't give you a season before my first one. You'd have been a child."

A brilliant pink washed over Amelia's cheeks, deepening to red as she looked around the table. "I-I'm not positive the viscount remembers he sent me to London. It was almost ten years ago."

Anthony choked on the very idea. How could a grown man of title and responsibility essentially turn out a young child?

His fingernails bit into his palms, and he glanced down, surprised to find his hands curled into fists underneath the table. It had been two years since he felt the desire to hit anyone. The unpleasant sensation was not welcome now. He barely knew this woman and he wanted to physically avenge her childhood wrongs?

Silence fell over the room. Miranda shifted her spoon to the other side of her empty bowl. Trent cleared his throat and decided his finger-nails were utterly fascinating.

Amelia's eyes darted from one dinner companion to another. The poor girl must be panicking, thinking that once again she had said something to put her entirely beyond the pale. He couldn't go back and save her from abandonment as a child, but he could rescue her from her current awkward discomfort.

"Trent, did you hear about the new tailor that set up shop behind White's? Superb workman. Made Struthers look almost fit."

The small smile of relief on Amelia's face was all the reward he needed.

~⁀~

Amelia kept a mantra of proper behavior running through her mind. *Think before you speak. Sit straight and tall like a lady. Don't talk to the servants. Don't talk about the servants. Stop staring at the marquis.* Nervous laughter threatened to bubble up from her chest.

As she collected her redingote and bonnet from Gibson, she realized she was smiling. She had enjoyed herself despite the agonizing atten-tion paid to every word and movement. Even if this taste of refinement made it difficult to return to simplicity, she was glad she'd come.

Anthony collected his own belongings from Gibson. After such an intimate dinner she found it difficult to continue to think of him as Lord Raebourne. "May I see you home, Miss Stalwood?"

"Oh!" A ride with Anthony would be considerably nicer than braving the walk home. She looked to Gibson, delighted when he gave a slight, almost imperceptible nod. "That would be lovely, thank you."

"Excellent." Anthony led her to his waiting carriage, a small smile gracing his handsome features. The kind of smile people wear without even knowing it.

The highborn ladies he socialized with probably thought noth-ing of being handed into a carriage by a charming, handsome man. For the orphaned daughter of a landed gentleman, it was all a bit overwhelming.

Amelia's nervousness grew as Anthony sat in the carriage seat across from her. She fiddled with the strap of her reticule as they rolled forward.

"Thank you." The words burst from her mouth in a rush. She hadn't intended to say them, but it was all she could think of, and the words of gratitude spilled from her lips before she could stop them.

Several moments passed before Anthony spoke. "You are most welcome, I'm sure, but I generally like to know what a lady is thanking me for."

Amelia swallowed her groan. She sounded like a complete ninny. The reticule strings twisted around her fingers as she gripped them together. "I am sure I was the last person you expected to dine with tonight. You could have made it a humiliating experience, but you were most gracious. Thank you."

Anthony's gaze fell to her fingers. Could he see her nervous habit in the low lantern light? A downward glance revealed a sliver of moonlight cutting right across her hands, highlighting the red-and-white splotches on her skin caused by the tightly wrapped strings.

She'd forgotten to replace her gloves after dinner. Her last hope of obtaining a modicum of sophistication drifted away on her sigh.

With a quiet clearing of his throat, he crossed the open expanse between the seats and settled next to her, sliding the gloves from his hands. Amelia's heartbeat sped up. What could he be thinking?

"Here now." Anthony gently took her hands in his. "You're going to hurt yourself."

His skin was warm and rough against her own. With utmost care, he untangled the strings, tsking quietly as he revealed the deep red marks on her fingers. He massaged the feeling back into her hands. "Bizarre meetings can make the best of friends. I have no wish to embarrass you. I confess to curiosity about your relationship with my staff, though."

The grin he gave her brought to mind a little boy trying to convince the cook to slip him an extra biscuit. At the same time, though, his hands held hers in a shockingly intimate gesture that she had never experienced in her life. Her brain couldn't decide where to settle.

His eyebrows drifted up in a questioning look. He still wanted to know about her connection to his staff.

"One of your maids is the niece of the cook next door. We played together as children. Through her I met others of your staff, and we have been friends since, though it is rare that many of us are able to meet together." Mortification shot through her. "Not that I think you don't give your staff adequate time off."

Anthony coughed and rubbed his hand over the bottom of his face. Amelia slid her freed hand into the folds of her skirt. He must disapprove of her association with his staff. Did he fear she would disrupt his household? "I would never ask you to adjust your household's schedule for my convenience."

His cough modified into a sputter.

"It would be dreadfully rude." She slumped back into the seat, her voice little more than a mumble.

The carriage rang with the sudden release of his laughter. "Miss Stalwood, you are without a doubt one of the oddest women in London."

Was that a good thing?

His laugh subsided to a wide smile. What was he thinking? Amelia started to reach for the strings on her reticule again. Anthony captured her hands in his once more.

"We must do something about this nervous penchant you have for creating tourniquets for your fingers." His thumb rubbed across her knuckles while Amelia ducked her head. His hands were large and warm, wrapping around her fingers in a way that made her feel cared for. She would gladly sit in this carriage all night if he would keep holding her hands in his.

He bent low, bringing his face into her downturned vision. "I have never met my servants' friends. Probably because they themselves are most often servants. I've never known anyone, gentry or peerage, who knows the names of someone else's footmen."

"I am merely a gentleman's daughter," Amelia whispered.

"You live in a home in London. You must be attached to someone of consequence." They stared at each other for several moments.

Why was he acting like a man fascinated with what he saw? She glanced down at their joined hands.

There were tales that among the *ton* a closed carriage was often used to steal a kiss or two during a courtship. This wasn't a courtship by any definition of the word, but this breathless anticipation and excitement must be what those other women felt. The sway of the carriage and the warmth of his hands lulled her into a fantasy where he would whisper to her and beg her for a kiss, like in *Much Ado About Nothing*, the only Shakespeare play Miss Ryan had been able to get Amelia to read.

"There was a time, not too long ago, when I would have taken this moment and kissed you."

Amelia crashed back into reality at his harsh whisper. She was always careful to keep her musings contained in her head, but had it slipped out this time?

"Trust me," Anthony continued, "you are safe now. I am a changed man." With a final squeeze, he released her hands and returned to his side of the carriage.

A burning sensation covered her eyes. She couldn't cry. Not here. Especially when there was no reason for tears. This man had promised her nothing, hadn't even implied anything. He'd been nothing but kind to her all evening. Yes, the idea that he would consider her as a potential wife had crossed her mind at dinner, but not with any thought of that becoming a reality.

Perhaps the notion that he might have found her a pleasant dalliance before his decision to pursue matrimony had spawned the threatening tears. One more indication that she didn't really belong anywhere.

The coach came to a stop. The soft scuff of the footman jumping to the ground to open the door sounded like a shot through the silent confines of the carriage.

Anthony sat back with a small frown. "I never asked where you lived."

Amelia lunged for the door as soon as it swung open. She stepped to the ground before turning back to face him. "I am also friends with your coachman. And your cook. She makes wonderful ginger biscuits."

She dredged up a smile. "Good night, my lord." With a glance at the coachman, she waved and turned to the stairs. "Good night, James."

"Good night, Miss Amelia."

The steps to her front door had never felt so steep. She wanted to turn and get one last look at the marquis, to store up one more memory for her fantasies, but the tears slipping down her cheeks chased her into the house.

7

Spending the evening comparing the calculated flirting of London's eligible ladies to Amelia's honest innocence was unappealing to say the least, so Anthony welcomed Miranda's suggestion of an outing to the opera.

He welcomed it even more when he learned she intended to invite Amelia.

Miranda shook her head and laughed as Trent and then Anthony followed her out of the carriage to collect Amelia. "You've left Aunt Elizabeth alone in the carriage."

Trent pointed at Anthony. "He's the one who left her alone."

Anthony crossed his arms over his chest. "She's your aunt."

The discussion was interrupted by the opening of the door. Miranda halted one step into the front hall, blinking in surprise before continuing across the floor. "Miss Stalwood, don't you know you are supposed to make a gentleman wait so that you can make a grand entrance as you enter the room?"

"You are not a gentleman." Amelia's brows drew together in confusion.

"How very true, but they are." Lady Miranda stepped aside and indicated Anthony and Trent.

The blush he was coming to adore spread across her cheeks. She was beautiful. He recognized the dress as one Miranda had worn to several country assemblies last year, but the style suited Amelia as if she'd picked it out herself.

Her hair was adorably off center. Proof her maid was unused to such elaborate coiffures. Anthony considered suggesting Amelia find someone to teach her maid about hair. It was becoming apparent that many more outings such as this one were going to be in her future.

Anthony intended to see to it.

Miranda jabbed him in the ribs with her elbow. He shook himself out of his contemplation and glared at her. She tilted her head toward her brother, who was fawning over Amelia. The pup had already told the girl how beautiful she looked. Repeating it would make Anthony look like a simpleton.

He cleared his throat before stepping forward. "Might I escort you to the carriage?"

"Of course." Amelia accepted her cloak and reticule from the butler before waving in the direction of the drawing room. Three servants clustered in the drawing room doorway, waving back and grinning.

The carriage was a tight fit, with the three ladies on one side of the carriage and the men on the other, but all agreed it was better than taking a second carriage. It didn't take long to reach the opera house, and most of that time was taken up with introducing Amelia to Trent and Miranda's aunt, Lady Elizabeth Breckton.

Anthony marveled at the wonder on Amelia's face. The opera had yet to begin—they were, in fact, still taking their seats—and already she appeared rapturous.

Miranda linked arms with Amelia as they entered the private box. "Miss Stalwood, you must sit up front. You shouldn't miss a moment of your first opera."

As Amelia settled into a seat at the railing, Trent wedged himself past Anthony, aiming himself for the seat next to her. He was brought up short by a heavy hand on his shoulder. Anthony was surprised to realize it was his own. He didn't remember moving it.

Trent turned to face him with a huge grin.

"Yes, Anthony?" His face was the picture of innocence. Anthony knew better.

Trent was teasing him, the obnoxious pup. Anthony tried to regain his dignity. "I believe, since it is my box, that I will take the prerogative of the other front seat."

"If we wanted to be proper, Miranda should get the other front seat." Lady Elizabeth tapped Anthony on the shoulder with her fan before settling into the backmost seat, an indulgent smile on her face. "I've seen the show already, so I'm perfectly happy to sit back here where I can make sure all of you behave yourselves."

Anthony sighed, looking from the empty chair to Miranda's grinning face. Being a gentleman could be irritating at times. He bowed and gestured toward the front of the box. "If you please, my lady, your chair awaits."

"Thank you, my lord." Miranda took the seat next to Amelia, grinning like a fool.

Once Miranda was seated, Amelia began talking about all the elegantly dressed people in the boxes around them and the extravagant sets on the stage.

Anthony moved to his seat in the row behind the young women. Hooking his foot around the back leg he angled the chair before sitting down, anticipating it being more pleasurable to watch Amelia watch the opera than to enjoy the show itself.

The show began, and all of the box's occupants fell into silence as the story played out on stage.

Just enough candles had been left flickering for Anthony to watch the emotions cross Amelia's face. It was the best show in town.

At intermission Miranda announced herself positively parched and dragged Trent and Lady Breckton off in search of refreshment. Anthony slid into Miranda's vacated chair.

"It's so beautiful," Amelia whispered. "What language is it?"

Anthony's eyebrows shot upward. "French."

It was hard to remember sometimes that Amelia's upbringing was unconventional. Every woman he knew had at least a passable knowledge of French.

"I don't know French, but it doesn't seem to matter. The story is very sad."

He considered her profile, pondering the best course of action. Assuring her that the story took a turn for the better might ruin the experience for her. She turned and he found himself drowning in her glistening brown eyes. Was she about to cry? "She is not going to die is she?"

When was the last time a woman of his acquaintance had shown this much emotion over anything, much less simple entertainment?

"There is a happy ending." He couldn't resist the urge to smooth an escaped curl of hair back behind her ear.

Her eyes widened. He could feel his heart beat, his chest expand with each passing breath. What was she thinking? He searched her eyes, looking for any spark of interest. Something in her expression that told him maybe, just maybe, she wondered about him as he wondered about her.

"Miss Stalwood, I—"

"We have returned. I forgot to see if you were as parched as I, Amelia, so I procured you a glass of lemonade." Miranda's voice and manner were overly bright as she reentered the box.

Anthony sighed and looked out over the opera house. What had he been about to say? Words had been forming in his mouth but not in his head. He should probably thank Miranda for interrupting him, but he mourned the moment as he relinquished the front seat back to her.

∽◯

Amelia had never seen anything like the crush of people outside the opera house after the show. Even more amazing was how everyone strolled about talking to each other as if it were a party, calling to each other and carrying on as if rows of carriages weren't waiting to be filled.

Even as Amelia climbed into the carriage, she heard people calling for Anthony and another woman grabbed Lady Miranda by the arm.

Lord Trent clambered in behind her, settling back to wait as if it were the most natural thing in the world. Amelia tried to copy his nonchalance.

"There is a bit of a chill in the air this evening. Is your cloak warm enough?" Lord Trent asked.

"Oh yes." Amelia was so light-headed from the evening she wouldn't have noticed if her toes had turned blue. "I hope this doesn't cause a setback on your head cold. Are you fully recovered?"

"Yes, quite, I—" Lord Trent frowned. "How did you know I'd been ill? That was weeks ago, when I first arrived in London."

"Oh, well, I think Fi . . . someone might have mentioned it to my maid Lydia. I didn't think a thing of it until now." Amelia gripped the edges of her cloak and tried to smile. The effort felt wooden at best. How did one tell someone they'd been the subject of gossip without making it sound like a horrible breach of privacy?

Lord Trent looked thoughtful. "This *someone* was a servant, I assume?"

Amelia swallowed. "Yes, my lord."

He laughed. "Does that happen often? Servants sharing about our health and the like?"

"Servants gossip worse than any member of the *ton* ever could." Amelia winced at how awful that sounded, but it was the truth.

Lord Trent looked skeptical.

"It's true!" Amelia defended. "*Ton* gossip is strictly speculation, from what I understand. What someone might have seen or overheard filled in with conjecture and suspicion. Do they ever know for a fact?"

"Rarely," Lord Trent conceded.

"Servants *know*, my lord. They see and hear everything, and they like to talk about it."

His gaze grew thoughtful again as the rest of their party finally climbed into the carriage and the conveyance made its way back across London.

"That was splendid, Lady Miranda. Thank you for inviting me," Amelia said.

"I cannot remember the last time I had as much fun. It is most refreshing to see things through a new pair of eyes." Lady Miranda reached over and clasped one of Amelia's hands. "You must call me Miranda. I believe we're going to be great friends."

"Then I am Amelia." Under the cover of her cloak Amelia pinched herself.

"I intend to drag you to the Hofferham ball with us next week, Amelia. Are you available Thursday?"

Amelia bit her lip. The true question was whether or not she would be able to procure the appropriate clothing between now and then. The dress Miranda had sent her was lovely, but it was not a ball gown.

"I have no other engagements." Amelia wound her fingers together and held them tight to keep from shouting her happiness out the window. No doubt Miss Ryan would have her on the doorstep of the modiste at the crack of dawn.

"Does this mean that I have to go to the Hofferham ball Thursday?" Lord Trent grumbled.

"Of course." Miranda huffed and crossed her arms over her chest. "Who else would escort me?"

"Anthony will be there. Can he be your escort?"

Miranda frowned. "Anthony is not a relation, you ninny. Besides, how do you know Anthony is attending?"

Lord Trent grinned. "If he wasn't before, he is now."

Anthony opened his mouth but closed it again a moment later with a bit of sheepish shrug.

"Nevertheless, Trent, you are accompanying me and Amelia." Miranda gave a decisive nod. "Resign yourself now."

Amelia looked at London passing by outside the window and smiled.

8

Memories of the opera outing filled Anthony's head the next day, finally sending him from his house in a desperate attempt to find distraction. He let his head loll back against the coach cushions, allowing it to rock back and forth with the swaying conveyance. If God felt charitable today, there would be someone interesting at his club. Waiting five more days to see Amelia was driving him to Bedlam.

Perhaps he should have James change the direction of the coach and head over to Mount Street instead. There was no reason why he couldn't pay her a call, other than a lack of proper chaperonage and a great deal of potential embarrassment on her part. Considering her clothing situation, he was afraid that her housing might be less than amenable as well, despite its fashionable location.

The last thing he wanted to do was cause her shame, but he'd be lying if he said her situation wasn't part of her appeal. What he could give her would far outweigh the scandal of his past.

The rocking stopped, and moments later the footman opened the door. Anthony poked his head out and found a scene vastly different than the white-blocked edifice he expected. Instead of seeing Beau Brummel in White's prestigious bay window, he saw women. Lots of women.

What were all of these women doing on St. James Street? They weren't supposed to even walk down St. James Street, much less patronize the establishments lining the gentlemen's road.

A closer look at the shops revealed the glittering windows and wares of stores catering to decidedly female customers. "James! Where the blazes are we?"

"Bond Street, sir."

Anthony looked up to find the insolent coach driver staring straight ahead. A look to the footman proved that he, too, found the passing traffic of immense interest. "I know we're on Bond Street," Anthony growled. "The question is why?"

James looked down at Anthony, eyes wide. "You said you wanted a hat, sir."

"I wanted a . . . ? I don't want a hat." He turned to scowl at the frippery in the nearby windows. "Even if I did want a hat, I wouldn't come here. I'd go over to— Miss Stalwood!"

Amelia was exiting the milliner, a pink hatbox swinging from her fingertips. A tall woman with a tight black bun showing beneath her plain bonnet stood behind his captivating brunette angel. What amazing luck.

He looked over his shoulder at James, only to find the man once more enthralled with the traffic. Luck had nothing to do with this little encounter. His coachman appeared due for a small bonus.

"My lord, I didn't expect to see you here." Amelia stepped forward, shock lining her face, her fingers twisted in the twine holding the lid on her hatbox.

"I must admit I didn't expect to be here." He bowed and sent a look in the other woman's direction.

Amelia's arm jerked as if she had intended to gesture to the woman beside her, but couldn't. Probably because her hands were so twisted in string. The woman's fingers were going to fall off if she kept doing that. "Lord Raebourne, this is Miss Ryan, my companion."

The woman smiled at Anthony and then emitted the worst fake gasp he had ever had the misfortune to witness. "Oh dear," she muttered. "I believe I left . . . something in the shop."

He liked the companion, fake gasps and all. His attention reverted

KRISTI ANN HUNTER

to Amelia and her tangled parcel twine. A single step brought him close enough to reach down and untangle her fingers. The worn gloves bore creases from the string's loops. "The pleasure is mine, Miss Stalwood. A new bonnet?"

"Oh . . . well, yes. I recently purchased a few new dresses and none of my bonnets match my new pelisse . . . But you don't really want to hear about that, do you?"

No, not particularly. "Of course. I find it beyond interesting. Do you have any more shopping to do?"

"Not really. Although one can always look around even when they aren't shopping for anything in particular." She looked into his eyes. Her shoulders began to pull in a bit and he feared uncertainty was setting in. This woman was just now getting comfortable enough to look him in the eye without blushing. He couldn't let her retreat back into herself.

"Have you been to Gunter's?" The popular tea shop was just the thing. The afternoon was warm and no one would think it odd for them to partake of one of the establishment's famous ices without a chaperone.

"I adore Gunter's! I'm particularly fond of the chocolate ice. Not very original of me, I know, but it seems to be what I always end up with." Her smile broadened a bit more.

"I insist you let me get you one, then. I'll have my men fold down the top of my—" Amelia's restrained giggle stopped him midsentence. A glance over his shoulder revealed that his servants had already taken care of converting the carriage into an open-air conveyance. Yes, a bonus was definitely in order.

"Shall we remove to Gunter's, then?"

"Oh yes." She looked down at her hatbox and then back at the shop behind her. Miss Ryan exited, nothing new in her hands, which surprised him not at all.

"I'll take that home for you," she said, pulling the hatbox string from Amelia's fingers with a deft twist. "Going to Gunter's?"

Anthony tried to be stern as he caught his coachman's eye, but he was afraid his frown looked more like a smirk. He was being

135

manipulated, but he couldn't bring himself to care. Maybe he'd en-list this creative band of servants to aid him further. If this was what they could manage on their own, things could only improve with his cooperation.

"Yes." Amelia looked stunned as she watched Miss Ryan give a small wave and trot over to a tall man with a skewed wig, hatbox securely in her arms. A puzzled look crossed her face. "Fenton?"

Anthony offered a hand to help her up into the carriage. "My lady?"

Amelia drew her gaze from the retreating maid and gave him a wry smile. "I'm not a lady."

No. But she could be. He grinned. "I know."

He clapped his coachman on the back as he climbed into the seat across from Amelia. "To Gunter's, James. Unless you have another surprise for me."

"I hear he has added a new flavor, my lord. It is a berry Miss Amelia is rather fond of." The coachman guided the carriage into the flow of traffic.

Anthony couldn't get the wide smile off his face. Definitely giving that man a raise.

❧

Anthony stared at the Bible lying open on his desk. Since returning to the city, he'd had a difficult time maintaining his morning Bible reading. The different hours and increased distractions reminded him of the way his life used to be, making him feel unworthy of the sacred words.

Restless energy pulsed through him, making it impossible to remain in his seat. He stood in a rush, reaching for the darts he used when he needed to think.

He thumbed the tip of a dart. What did London mean to him? He flipped the dart in his hand and flung it at the board.

"Drinking." *Thunk.*

"Revelry." *Thunk.*

"Women." *Dink. Clank. Clatter.* Anthony watched as the third dart spun a wide circle across the floor. That was the crux of the problem.

Drinking had been easier to avoid than he anticipated, though he was finding many of his former friends were much less entertaining than he previously thought them.

The revelry of London was still alive and well. A good card game or conversation at his club, the crush of social gatherings, all things he had enjoyed before and found pleasure in again.

The women were the problem. Or rather a single woman. His infatuation with someone as sweet and pure as Amelia was at odds with the memory of his previous peccadilloes. No amount of praying and Bible reading would change his past. Even if God didn't hold him accountable for it anymore, Anthony couldn't see how she wouldn't.

Amelia was a ray of sunshine whenever he saw her. She scattered his thoughts even as she brightened his day.

While they'd enjoyed ices at Gunter's she'd confessed that she hadn't read much, but she enjoyed fictional tales of other lands and historical travels. They let her imagine she was somewhere else, far from England. Anthony smiled as he recalled her blushing and ducking her head until her nose nearly touched her shoulder.

The gold lettering on the spine of a copy of *Gulliver's Travels* caught his eye. He'd liked the book as a child, imagined little people living under his bed for a year after his governess read it to him. He stooped and slid the book off the shelf. It was as good an excuse as anything else.

His free hand reached out and scooped up the wayward dart. Straightening, he weighed the book in his hand. With barely a glance, he launched the dart at the board. The ends quivered as it struck the target.

He rolled his shoulders, a satisfied smile creeping across his face. It wasn't easy to force his new life in where his old life had flourished, and he looked forward to finding a wife and retreating back to the country where things were simpler. If loaning a book brought him a little closer to that goal, then he'd willingly pack up the whole library.

～⌒○

Amelia and Miss Ryan tripped over their feet. Again. Amelia stifled a giggle as Miss Ryan frowned. They'd cleared the drawing room of most of the furniture and were attempting to dance. Miss Ryan's efforts to remember the dance steps her friend had taught her were admirable, but Amelia knew she would never feel confident enough to step onto the floor of a London ballroom.

Still, she loved Miss Ryan for trying.

"Now I believe that you and the gentleman place your hands on each other's shoulders." Amelia and Miss Ryan awkwardly tried to hold each other's shoulder with a low degree of success.

"This cannot be right," Miss Ryan muttered.

Amelia laughed. "I don't think it will matter if I know how to waltz or not. I doubt I'll even dance. The experience of a London ball will be enough."

"Pish posh!" cried Miss Ryan. "You listen to me, young lady. I've seen you in that new gown, and I know that some young buck is going to ask you to dance. Why, those two young lords who have been escorting you around town will ask for certain. Let's try again."

Since it made Miss Ryan happy, Amelia returned to the middle of the floor.

"May I be of assistance?" a deep male voice inquired from the doorway.

Amelia whirled to find Anthony handing over his hat to a grinning Fenton, a book tucked under his arm. Her neck began to flush, and she prayed that it would not spread over her cheeks. She forever found herself blushing in front of this man.

"We are learning to waltz." Amelia's voice was so soft she wasn't sure he heard her.

"It is quite difficult when neither of us is aware of the proper forms." Miss Ryan relinquished her spot on the impromptu dance floor.

"How fortunate that I came along, then." Anthony's eyes never left Amelia's. The anticipation of being held in his arms made her skin prickle. Even when she dared to dream that he'd ask her to dance, it hadn't been for a waltz.

He held the book out. "Have you read *Gulliver's Travels*?"

She shook her head and reached out a hand to accept the volume. "I'm sure it will be delightful."

Miss Ryan swept by, snatching the book as she crossed to the settee by the fireplace. Fenton stood in the doorway with a twinkle in his eye.

Anthony took Amelia's hands in his own. "Your hand does go on my shoulder." His voice was low, causing Amelia to lean in to hear him. "Mine rests at your back. I hold your right hand in mine."

Amelia stared at their joined hands. How long since she'd been in the arms of a male? Fenton had never been much for hugging, but he had stopped entirely when she turned fifteen. She had forgotten the sensation of being protected and cared for that a man's arms could project.

"Now we twirl about the room." Anthony began to hum a tune.

He guided Amelia in the steps of the waltz, occasionally correcting the placement of her feet. "No, when I step in this direction, you will step to the other side and our arms will meet here, above our heads."

Amelia tried to follow and ended up stepping on her own foot. As she strove to catch herself, her toe caught and shifted her slipper off of her heel. The following step sent the slipper skittering across the floor to bump against the wall.

She froze, staring at the offending shoe, unsure what the correct etiquette was for returning a slipper to one's foot when in the presence of a man. "I believe, my lord, that I am destined to embarrass myself at every one of our meetings."

Sighing, she maneuvered herself into the corner of the wall, holding her skirts to retain her modesty while she wiggled her foot back into her slipper. When she turned to face him, Anthony was grinning.

And alone. When had Miss Ryan and Fenton left the room?

"Perhaps we should try a quadrille. As you stated, you are unlikely to dance the waltz at your first ball."

For the next hour, Anthony instructed Amelia on the basic steps of London's more popular dances. While she would hardly shine as the most graceful woman in the ballroom, if she were asked to dance Thursday, she felt that she would indeed be able to execute the basic steps without crashing into too many people.

"Thank you, for a delightful afternoon." Anthony accepted his hat and coat from Fenton, whose immediate appearance proved her servants hadn't left her quite as alone as she'd thought.

"It is I who should thank you," Amelia said. "If you had not come by, anyone seeing me dance Thursday would have immediately labeled me a provincial."

"Anyone seeing you dance Thursday will be too busy being jealous of the gentleman you partner to worry about you missing a step or two." He lifted her hand in his and brushed a light kiss over her fingers.

Amelia blushed once more, amazed she hadn't caught fire in the past hour and a half, with the many compliments the marquis gave her. He must think her complexion was permanently flushed. With one last look into her eyes, Anthony donned his hat and hopped lightly down the stairs to the sidewalk.

9

Despite the bleakness of the next morning, Amelia's spirits remained high. How could they not after the most amazing week of her life?

She rushed through her breakfast, anxious to put together a tray for Miss Ryan. Sometime in the night, the older woman had become quite ill. She would probably be in bed for days, but even that didn't faze Amelia.

It was doubtful that Miss Ryan would be able to partake of anything more than tea, but Amelia loaded the tray with toast and a warmed mug of broth as well.

A loud knock echoed through the house as she crossed the hall to the main staircase. Fenton rushed by her to answer it. Though she was curious to see who would be calling this early in the morning in dismal weather, the tray was getting heavy and she still had to climb the stairs with it. She didn't wait.

"May I help you, sir?" Fenton asked.

Amelia shook her head at the mix of condescension and graciousness in his voice. He was getting much better at answering the door of late. After seeing Anthony out the day before he'd claimed to be fitting in with the rest of the upper-crust butlers.

The rasp of hacking coughs greeted her as she shouldered her way into Miss Ryan's room.

"Tea. Bless you!" Miss Ryan flopped back against her pillows, fever making her look pale and flushed at the same time.

"I brought some broth and toast as well. Perhaps you can stop coughing long enough to partake." Amelia set the tray on the small writing desk and set about preparing Miss Ryan's tea. She was handing Miss Ryan the cup when Fenton appeared in the doorway.

"Miss Amelia? There is a solicitor downstairs to see you."

A solicitor? Here? What on earth for? She glanced to the window, now streaked with rain. "Oh my, he must be soaked. I'll grab a blanket as I go down. Miss Ryan, I shall return as soon as possible. Fenton, please ask Mrs. Harris to come help Miss Ryan finish her soup."

"Right away, ma'am."

Amelia grabbed a blanket from the chest at the foot of the bed before scurrying down the stairs. A solicitor. Had he been sent by the viscount? Was he there to give her instructions on vacating the property by her birthday?

She bustled into the drawing room with part of her mind still abovestairs with Miss Ryan. The companion's discomfort was a more immediate, though significantly less permanent, problem than the viscount's cessation of support.

Awaiting her in the drawing room was a very short, very round man wearing round spectacles. Round water droplets ran slowly down his round top hat to splash in small round dots on the worn rug at his feet.

She extended the blanket. He didn't take it.

"My name is Mr. Alexander Bates of the offices of Chandler, Bates, and Holmes. I need to speak with the personage in charge on a very important legal matter." The man pulled himself up to his greatest height—which put him at the same height as Amelia's nose—and made every attempt to appear as important as possible.

"I am in charge." Amelia clutched the blanket to her chest. Dear Lord, help them. He was going to kick them all out immediately.

"Ah, the governess."

"I beg your pardon?" She had thought of becoming a governess but as of yet hadn't even applied for any such position. Had one of her friends taken it upon themselves to find her a position?

142

"The governess," he repeated.

"The governess?"

The man harrumphed loudly. "For the child."

"The child?" What was he talking about?

Mr. Bates looked very grim. Amelia thought about offering him the blanket again, but it didn't appear as if he realized he was wet. Perhaps he had the wrong house.

"While it is no nevermind to me if a person hires those who are lacking in wits, you can be sure I will relay this exchange to the heir." He snapped a packet of papers from his greatcoat pocket and held them in front of his eyes.

Heir? Oh no. A sinking feeling hit Amelia in the stomach. If there were an heir, then that had to mean—

"On behalf of Chandler, Bates, and Holmes, I would like to extend heartfelt condolences for your recent loss." The little man's voice held no emotion as he read from the papers.

Amelia felt her jaw slacken. He was going to call her a lackwit and then carry on delivering his message without any explanation or apology?

The truth of her changed circumstances began to sink in. Amelia dropped into the closest chair. A soft *whoosh* hit her ears as the blanket fell to the floor. What was going to happen to them all now?

"As I am sure you are aware, there was no direct heir. An extensive tracing of the family tree has located the next male relation and he has been notified of his inheritance. He has agreed to take up the wardship of one Miss Amelia Stalwood, age eleven . . ." Here Mr. Bates paused and glanced up. "Though I suppose she might be twelve now." He looked back down at his papers. "Regardless, the care of Miss Amelia Stalwood has been taken up by the new holder of the title.

"The heir has arranged for the child to live with his mother and stepfather at their estate in Essex until further arrangements are made. He wishes to place her with his family as soon as possible to help her deal with her grief. You and the child are to depart at nine o'clock tomorrow morning."

Amelia felt cold and pale. She never knew someone could actually feel pale. She couldn't leave tomorrow. The ball was tomorrow. She didn't want to leave London at all! There must be a way to delay their departure. "There is an engagement tomorrow—"

"Your comfort matters not." The little man frowned, the first emotion he shown since he arrived. "He wishes the child stabilized immediately. It is your job to see that she is prepared."

Were Amelia actually a child, she would likely appreciate the sentiment.

But she wasn't a child. "I am not eleven."

The man frowned. "I should hope not."

"Amelia Stalwood is not eleven. Nor is she twelve. I'm afraid your information is outdated."

He looked at his papers, as if he couldn't fathom being wrong. "She is still here, isn't she? The papers indicate she is to remain under the guardianship of Lord Stanford until she reaches the age of one and twenty."

She could lie. Add a few months to her age and be free. But honesty was a trait that God praised, wasn't it? Mrs. Bummel had always thought so. Would He honor her honesty? "Yes, I still live here, and—"

Mr. Bates continued as soon as he heard an affirmative answer. "The quarterly allowance will be adjusted accordingly for the departure of the ward and the governess. Further arrangements for the house will be made at a later date."

Mr. Bates tipped his hat in Amelia's direction, placed his stack of papers back into his coat, and exited the room, stepping on the blanket that had fallen from her cold fingers. He had never even taken a seat.

Amelia ran after him. "But, I—"

"Nine o'clock tomorrow. Good day."

And then he was gone, leaving the drawing room before Amelia could draw in a breath.

"Sir, I insist you stop." She chased the solicitor into the hall. "There's been a misunderstanding and it must be corrected."

He paused with his hand on the door latch, condescension and exasperation in every line on his round face. "We have established that Amelia Stalwood is not yet of age. Therefore she is bound by her guardian's wishes. I have done my job by delivering the message despite this dreadful weather. If you have further problems, I suggest you take them up with the new guardian. Good day."

He opened the door enough to slip from the house and slammed it behind him, as if he were afraid she'd chase him out into the street.

Rain continued to pelt the window, seeming to echo the words of the departed solicitor. *"Amelia Stalwood, age eleven . . ."*

She knew that the viscount never loved her, did not even think much of her. But to have meant so little to him that once she was out of his sight neither he nor his solicitors remembered that she would continue to age?

Tears were inevitable. Once the shock wore off, the hurt and fear would remain. She would curl into a little ball and feel the pain. But she welcomed her current numbness more than she would have ever imagined.

Placing one foot in front of the other, she trudged up the stairs and into Miss Ryan's room, where she found the entirety of her little servant family. Lydia, the parlor maid, was changing Miss Ryan's sweat-soaked sheets. Mrs. Harris was trying to convince Miss Ryan to take one of her homemade remedies. Fenton was replacing the chamber pot. Miss Ryan must have cast up the soup Amelia had coaxed her into eating.

All activity stopped as Amelia stood in the doorway. How awful did she look? She felt small and thin, a piece of parchment poised to blow away in the wind. All three able-bodied servants began to rush toward her until Amelia held up her hand.

She looked into the face of everyone in the room before speaking again. "Lord Stanford has passed away. A carriage will arrive to carry me to my new guardian in the morning. Miss Ryan can follow once she is well." If she needed to come at all. Perhaps Amelia could secure a position and Miss Ryan could seek work in London, where their connections could work in her favor. "Now, if you will excuse me, I need to pack."

Amelia did not meet anyone's eyes as she turned and walked down the corridor to her own room.

It would not take her long to pack all that she considered her own. She had little left from her parents and had no reason to acquire many personal objects to remember life in London.

The new pink ball gown hung on the outside of the closet, reminding her of how close she'd come to a different life. There was nothing to do now but pack it up and let it remind her of the joyful moments.

More than anything, Amelia wished for the courage to stay, but there was little doubt she would be supporting herself soon. As soon as her true age was revealed to the new viscount, she'd be looking for work.

It would be better to find work in Essex. London held too many reminders of what almost was. Once away from those remembrances, she could be happy. She would make herself be happy.

A deep, steadying breath filled her lungs. As it whooshed out again, she wiped her hands firmly down the front of her skirt. Clothing wasn't going to pack itself. There was much to do before the carriage arrived in the morning, and she still had to help take care of Miss Ryan.

Lydia appeared and began folding and packing Amelia's few dresses in a trunk. "Why do you have to go?" Lydia whispered.

"I have no way of supporting myself if I don't go. I confess I thought that I had months before facing the day I would be on my own. We were so ignored here, away from Lord Stanford's books and studies, I thought I would be able to ease into making my own way in the world. I'm afraid I'm at the mercy of the new viscount."

Lydia's grin was as shaky as it was cheeky. "Maybe he'll be young and single. The marquis seemed to like you well enough. A viscount's not as good, but he'd be able to support you right and proper."

Amelia threw a pillow at her friend. The beginnings of a smile reached the edges of her lips. With a shake of her head she turned back to the trunk.

Silence remained as they finished packing, but the air felt a little lighter.

10

The scene was too reminiscent of the one that took place when she left the viscount's for London ten years ago. Amelia sat on a trunk in the front hall, clutching a valise, waiting for the promised carriage. A basket of Mrs. Harris's best cooking efforts sat on the floor at her feet. She, Miss Ryan, and Lydia had said their good-byes an hour ago. Only Fenton remained, pacing from window to window.

A strong knock on the front door made Amelia jump. The second had her clutching the valise to her chest. The third sounded like a death knell.

Fenton wrenched open the door to reveal a liveried footman standing tall and straight like the guards in front of the palace. "The carriage for Miss Stalwood and Miss Ryan has arrived."

Amelia placed one foot in front of the other with deliberate precision. There was no room for hesitation today. God had promised her nothing but this moment, and she would make the best of it. "Good day. I am Miss Stalwood, but please call me Miss Amelia. And you are?"

The footman shifted his weight. "M'name is Gordon, miss. Jeremy Gordon. I thought there was to be a child?"

"I am pleased to make your acquaintance, Gordon. I'm afraid there's no child today. Only me. Miss Ryan is unfit to travel, unfortunately. If you would be so good as to assist me with my trunk, I will not delay our departure any longer. I have a basket of scones and biscuits and other good things prepared by my housekeeper that I will be more than willing to share on our journey. Shall we be off?" Her tension uncurled as she discovered her voice could remain steady. She even managed a smile.

Gordon gave her basket a strange look but said nothing about it as he hefted her trunk. "Will this be it, miss?"

"Yes, that is everything." Everything she had to mark twenty years of life fit in a single trunk. "Thank you, Gordon."

The driver helped Gordon secure the trunk. He started to yawn and ducked behind the carriage out of sight.

Amelia followed him. "Are you well?"

The man flushed. "I beg your pardon, miss. We didn't arrive from Essex until late last night."

And now the man had to make the drive back. Amelia couldn't help but wish they'd taken a day to rest. Then she could have attended the ball tonight. She felt a bit guilty over that. The driver and his employer thought they were rushing to the aid of a distraught young girl. She held up the basket. "Would you like a raspberry scone?"

The driver and footman exchanged glances again but then graciously accepted her offer of pastries.

Gordon handed her into the carriage and toasted her with his last bite of scone. "These are quite good, milady."

"My— That is Mrs. Harris is an extraordinary cook." Amelia fought back the tears at the thought that Mrs. Harris was no longer her cook. She had no claim to the woman anymore. "Please, call me Miss Amelia. Everyone does."

"Very well, Miss Amelia." His smile looked a bit more genuine as he shut the door and climbed atop the carriage. "You get comfortable. It shouldn't take us long. The roads seemed fairly empty this morning."

The steady clop of the horses' hooves gave Amelia something to cling to. All she had to do was maintain her composure until the next hoof fell. If she could manage that, by the time they reached Essex she would be in complete control of her faculties.

She watched the buildings roll by, expecting to take the same road out of London that she'd arrived on so many years ago.

The sudden turn took her by surprise. This road took them deeper into the heart of Mayfair. Were they lost? Perhaps they'd gotten turned around, unfamiliar with the tight streets of London.

After a bit of struggle, she managed to open the window and lean her head out. A fat raindrop fell on her forehead before she could ask if they needed assistance. Another soon joined it and within moments the sky was full of pelting rain.

Amelia jerked her head back inside. They must be staying in London somewhere overnight instead of risking the country roads in the rain.

A trickle of hope wormed into her mind, even as she tried to squash it. If they were staying in London for the night, could she make it to the ball?

A few more turns took them clear to the other side of Mayfair. Amelia had never visited this area, so she wasn't likely to find anyone willing to help her get to the ball. The warm glow of hope faded away.

They stopped in front of a simple but stately terrace house, at least six windows across.

Gordon flung open the door and lowered the step, water dripping from his nose.

"We're stopping here?" Amelia hated making him stand in the rain, but she couldn't just walk into someone's house without knowing who they were or what they expected.

"Of course, Miss Amelia. Lady Blackstone is expecting you." Gordon reached out a hand to help her alight. "She thought a trip to Essex might be a bit much for a grieving child, so she came to London to meet you."

A scraping noise preceded the driver carrying her trunk down to the servant entrance.

Gordon rubbed a hand along the back of his neck. "'Course, you're not really a child."

"I'm afraid that's going to take a bit of explanation." Amelia took a deep breath and stomped out of the carriage. Her determination caused her to slip on the stair, nearly sending her bottom first into a puddle.

Gordon righted her before resuming his formal stance.

"Thank you." She stared at the steps to the front door, all determination replaced by fear.

"You're getting wet, miss."

"Yes. Right. I should go in, then." She flew up the stairs as if another moment's hesitation would make everything disappear. The front door swung open as she approached, and her momentum sent her careening into the front hall. Her slippers slid across the slick marble, and Amelia managed her second narrow escape in as many minutes. It wouldn't do to meet her hostess by sliding across the hall on her backside.

The butler closed the door slowly. He didn't have a smile on his face, but his eyes crinkled a bit at the corner. "Would you care for a towel?"

Amelia gratefully accepted the length of linen he extended toward her.

"There is a fire laid in the drawing room. I'll have Lady Blackstone summoned. You're a bit earlier than she anticipated."

The butler took her wet pelisse, but the dress underneath was still damp. Amelia retreated to the room the butler indicated, but she refused to place her sodden clothing on any of the beautiful upholstered furniture. Instead she stood by the fire, enjoying the warmth on her skin as cold trepidation seeped through her blood. Who was Lady Blackstone? What had she been told? She had a vague recollection of a Lady Cressida Blackstone getting married last year. Had that been her name before or after she'd gotten married?

Another carriage clattered to a stop outside the house. Had Lady Blackstone been away?

Curiosity propelled Amelia to the window, but she couldn't tell anything about the people who alighted from the carriage. Two women wearing deep-hooded cloaks and a man with his greatcoat pulled up close to his top hat rushed up the stairs.

Amelia heard footfalls in the hall as she crossed the drawing room. She recognized the butler's quiet gait from earlier, but the heavy tread of boots and the swish of slippers were new.

Wanting to know the situation before bumbling into it, Amelia peeked around the partially closed drawing room door. She couldn't see the people entering from the street, but she saw the elegant woman coming down the stairs from the upper floors and the mountain of a man approaching from the back of the house.

The woman had touches of grey threaded through her dark blond hair. She reached a hand toward the large blond man in riding clothes. "I'm glad you managed to be here this morning. I must have misunderstood—they told me a woman had arrived."

The man gestured toward the front door, where presumably the newly arrived party had shed their coats and cloaks.

"Mother!" a young, slightly familiar female voice called.

Amelia tried to see the front of the hall without opening the drawing room door any wider, but it was impossible.

The girl continued. "I'm begging you to convince Miranda to stop this mission."

Amelia jerked away from the door. *Miranda?* It couldn't be the same Miranda. That was impossible.

"She's not a mission. Besides, she sent me a note this morning canceling our plans for the evening and then had her butler tell me she wasn't home when I went by. I think she's scared and means to drop our friendship entirely. Mother, you have to help me make her see reason."

It *was* the same Miranda. Amelia had wanted to tell her good-bye since she had little intention of returning from Essex, but she put off writing the letter until all she had time to do was scribble a note that she wouldn't be able to go to the ball. But how could she . . . ? Why would she . . . ? Had they called the woman *Mother*?

"Of whom are we speaking?" The older woman's smile was indulgent. Definitely that of a mother.

"Some poor girl Miranda has decided to yank into society as a sacrificial lamb," Georgina muttered.

Amelia paused in the act of reaching for the door latch. Were they talking about her?

"That is not true," Miranda grumbled.

"Trent has decided to court her," Georgina continued.

"That's not true." Trent walked into view. "Good morning, Griffith. What brings you to town? By the by, I think she was lying in that note she sent this morning. It was rather vague."

Miranda huffed. "Why would she lie to me?"

Amelia crossed her arms and frowned. She hadn't lied. Unforeseen circumstances was a perfectly acceptable explanation for why she wouldn't be attending the ball.

"Beg pardon," a voice she assumed was Griffith's said, "but of what are we talking? Aren't you all here to meet my new ward?"

"I met a lovely young *disadvantaged* gentlewoman and have befriended her." Miranda paused. "Trent does appear to have decided to court her though. What do you mean you have a new ward? Who died? No one close or I'd have heard about it."

Amelia's head was spinning. She looked for a second door out of the drawing room. She couldn't possibly face them now, not after hearing that conversation. How could she face Trent when her heart was already Anthony's?

"Nonsense, Miranda. I have merely befriended her as well. I value my head, you know. Anthony would kill me if I courted her when he's already claimed her for himself."

There wasn't another door. She was going to have to face them. With the towel pulled tight around her shoulders, she eased the drawing room door the rest of the way open, but no one noticed her.

The man she assumed was Griffith was looking from one family member to another.

His mother looked delighted. "Anthony is courting her?"

"Of course not," Georgina said. "He has a marquisate to think about."

"I do so love it when you're wrong," Trent said, smugness oozing from his smile. "He's been to call on her already. Even took her to Gunter's for ices."

"That was her?" Georgina pouted.

Miranda clapped with glee. "Everyone's talking about that. No one could see the lady for the tree. Rebecca Laramy claimed he'd taken her, but I knew it couldn't be true."

"This is all fascinating," Griffith said, "but a young girl is going to be arriving here soon—"

"How young?" Georgina's eyes narrowed.

"You never said who died," Miranda said.

The import of Griffith's statement penetrated Amelia's spinning brain. *He* was her new guardian. But how was that possible? How could God do that? The one friendship she'd formed where the other person had nothing to gain but her company was about to be tainted with obligation. "Oh my."

Five heads twisted in her direction.

"Amelia!" Miranda danced across the hall and wrapped her arms around Amelia.

"Who are you?" Miranda's mother walked forward with a frown. "Are you the governess? What did you do with the child?"

Georgina coughed. "She's a servant?"

Miranda frowned. "But I thought you were the ward of the Viscount of Stanford."

Amelia swallowed. "I am, but—"

"No," Griffith said, "the viscount's ward is an eleven-year-old girl, I'm expecting her here any minute."

"But the maid told me the girl had already arrived." His mother, who was presumably the Lady Blackstone who lived here, looked very confused. "So you must be Miss Ryan."

"Miss Ryan is sick. She couldn't accompany me. I'm—"

Trent grinned. "I like Amelia better than an eleven-year-old girl. Can we keep her instead?"

"Mind your tongue." Lady Blackstone poked Trent in the chest. "We take care of the less fortunate in this family, and a young girl who's been uprooted twice is most unfortunate."

"Her name's not Ryan—it's Stalwood." Miranda crossed her arms over her chest.

"But the ward's name is Stalwood," Griffith said. "Amelia Stalwood."

Everyone stared at Amelia in silence. The sudden quiet was heavy. She gave a tiny wave. "Hello."

"You," Lady Blackstone finally said, "are not eleven years old."

11

It took only five minutes for them to explain that Lady Blackstone was Miranda's mother, who had remarried the year before.

It took almost an hour for Amelia to relate her story to the curious family. She didn't know who was more surprised—them at finding out who the ward truly was or her at discovering she was now connected to a duke. It was a step up in society she couldn't have even dreamt of.

"How did you manage to inherit a viscountcy?" Trent asked.

Griffith shrugged. "The first Duke of Riverton was the second son of the fourth Viscount of Stanford."

"That must have made family gatherings fun." Trent grinned.

"They weren't a very prolific bunch. The viscounts that followed each had one son who married and produced one son of his own." Griffith shook his head. "A couple of them also had daughters, but they had to trace back nine generations to find another male heir."

"The Hofferham ball!" Miranda cried.

"What?" Lady Blackstone set her cup of tea aside gracefully, despite her obvious confusion.

"You can't still be thinking of going," Georgina said.

"Of course I am!" Miranda wrapped an arm around Amelia, who sat next to her on the settee. "It is the perfect time to announce Amelia's new status."

"But we haven't unpacked her trunk yet," Lady Blackstone said.

"Perfect. Don't. I insist that she come live at Hawthorne House anyway. The rain has stopped, so we can lug her trunk over there now." Miranda smiled at everyone in the circle, excitement bursting from her.

"I don't have a maid," Amelia said. Not that Miss Ryan had proven to be of much help when it came to dressing Amelia in finery. The hairstyle she'd worn to the opera had taken hours and even then it'd been a bit lopsided.

"Sally can help you. Or Iris. Iris is the upstairs maid. She's fabulous. If I didn't have Sally I'd hire Iris in a moment."

No one could come up with a sufficient objection, so Amelia bundled herself and her trunk into a carriage once more, though with a considerably lighter heart than that morning.

In the whirlwind that only a competent household can accomplish, a room was prepared, her trunk was unpacked, and clothes for the evening pressed. Amelia had barely caught her breath before she found herself in the hall of Hawthorne House, Gibson smiling like a proud papa.

"Now, my dear, do not worry about a thing. You will be marvelous tonight." Lady Blackstone, who had insisted on being called Caroline, because there was no place for formality among family, smoothed a piece of Amelia's hair back. "Doesn't Amelia look lovely this evening, William?"

Lord Blackstone, who had married Caroline the year before, smiled at Amelia and then his wife. His daughter was the one whose marriage Amelia had heard about. "That she does, my love, but I think your encouragement is causing more flustering than bolstering."

Amelia snapped her fan out, moving the air toward her face in an attempt to ward off the impending blush.

Trent, Miranda, Amelia, and Griffith rode in one carriage with Lord Blackstone and Caroline in a carriage directly behind them.

Miranda talked incessantly about how much fun it was going to be having Amelia around the house. Amelia didn't say a word. Breathing was about all she was able to manage. After all the ups and downs, the gaining and losing of hope, she was on her way to the ball.

The horses slowed to a stop, jolting her against Miranda. The footman, Gordon, swung the door open and stood stiffly, waiting to assist. He broke form for a moment, glancing sideways into the carriage to wink at Amelia. The wink gave Amelia more confidence than anything Miranda or Caroline or even Griffith could have said.

Amelia stared up at the house, unable to believe she was here. She remembered over the years seeing the glow of houses lit up with so many candles they were visible from the next street. Now she would see what was going on inside with her own eyes. Her heart filled with bubbly happiness. God was good. Even if He'd taken a bizarre route to get her to this place.

Trent gave Miranda his arm and grinned like a mischievous little boy. "I can't wait to see Anthony's face."

The brother and sister trotted off, leaving Amelia to revel in her dream world as she and Griffith waited for Lord and Lady Blackstone. People streamed by her in a beautiful rainbow of silks and satins. A sudden urge to see if the interior was as awe-inspiring as the exterior released her feet from their invisible prison. She glanced around to find her companions and discovered them a few steps away with small smiles and damp eyes.

"How long have I been standing here?" She hated how her voice trembled, but there was nothing she could do to stop it.

"However long you needed." Griffith offered her his arm and led her into the building.

The noise of the ballroom reached her first, an indistinct swell of voices and music. Amelia's heart sped up, and her palms began to sweat. Thankful for the gloves, she gripped Griffith's arm tighter.

The ballroom was like a painting come to life. Beautiful people, beautiful music, and beautiful decorations swirled together in a mass of splendid color.

A small flight of six stairs led down into the ballroom, giving Amelia enough height to see two blond heads cutting a swath through the crowd. Miranda and Trent were making good on their intention to rush to Anthony's side. Her gaze followed their intended path until she found him dancing. Her overactive imagination made her think she could see the vibrant blue of his eyes.

Seeing him again when she'd thought she never would made her feel funny inside. Her rapidly beating heart rose from her stomach to her throat. She couldn't breathe anymore but at least she was no longer queasy.

When he'd come by the house, she'd begun to hope his apparent interest was genuine. Surely that would only continue now that her circumstances had changed.

Wouldn't it?

⁓

Anthony wasn't sure why he had arrived so ridiculously early to Lady Hofferham's ball. Griffith's vague note ensuring his attendance had intrigued him, but he doubted the mystery would provide enough distraction from his disappointment over Miranda's early-morning note telling him Amelia wouldn't be coming.

He murmured the appropriate pleasantries to his dance partner as he handed her to her mother. She was nice enough, but so were many of the other dozens of women he's danced with of late.

Perhaps he should return to the country and try again next year. His obsession with the absent Amelia kept him from considering any other candidates. It was insupportable. He had been in her company a scant number of times. Surely it had not been enough to warrant this incessant comparison of every other woman to her.

Miranda and Trent accosted him as he walked away from the young woman whose name he had already forgotten. The beauty of Miranda's wide smile took him by surprise. Wasn't she supposed to be nearly as disappointed as he was?

Lady Helena Bell was working her way across the ballroom toward him. There was another problem he could do without. She'd been following him since his first public appearance in London. Miranda told him she was bribing people to tell her where he went each evening so that she could show up as well. Her intentions were embarrassingly obvious, but he wanted no part of them. Why wouldn't the lady simply go away?

"Hullo!" Miranda called cheerfully, snagging his arm and pulling him back around to face her. Trent stood behind her rocking back and forth on his feet, grinning like an idiot.

"Good evening," Anthony said cautiously. "Where is Griff? He said he was going to be here."

"Oh, he is here." Miranda giggled.

Anthony braced himself. Miranda never giggled.

Trent cleared his throat. "We convinced him to delay his entrance until we found you."

Anthony began to worry.

Trent's grin got even wider.

"He has a solution for your doldrums caused by the impossible infatuation you have with Amelia," Miranda chirped.

"His Grace, the Duke of Riverton, Lord and Lady Blackstone, and Miss Amelia Stalwood!" the bailiff cried from the doorway.

Anthony's head snapped to the front of the ballroom. Had he heard correctly? Was Amelia actually here?

A vision in pale rose stood beside Griffith. It was her. Even from this distance, he could see the banked excitement on her face. He could almost feel her pulse race under his fingers, see the blush behind her ears, threatening to spread charmingly to her cheeks if she became the center of attention.

He pushed past Lady Helena as he crossed to the entrance, ignoring her huff of indignation. Miranda and Trent could deal with his pursuer's hurt feelings.

His mouth dried as he took in every detail. Her dress was elegant, a ball gown any woman in the room would be proud to wear, yet still quintessentially Amelia in its simplicity. Her brown hair had been piled on her head with a single large ringlet draped over her right shoulder. His fingers itched to bury themselves in that ringlet. It was wide enough to wrap around his wrist. How had she gotten it to do that?

She wasn't looking at him, was enthralled with everything around her, swiveling her head from side to side in an effort to take everything in as she walked down the stairs. When she finally saw him, her eyes lit from within and pink tinged her cheeks. He had never seen anything lovelier in his life.

"Miss Stalwood." He bowed over her hand and kissed the knuckles. He'd never despised a glove more in his life. "It is a delight to see you again."

Two people come up behind him. The rustle of her gown as she bounced in excitement gave Miranda away.

Anthony spared her and Trent a scathing glance before directing his attention back to Amelia. "I thought you weren't coming."

"Neither did I. So much has happened since yesterday, I can't even begin to understand it all," Amelia said.

Anthony offered Amelia his arm. Her smile was small and sweet as she laid her hand in the crook of his elbow. Over her head, Anthony caught a glance of Lady Helena glowering in their direction. He shrugged. He had never given her a reason to believe he was interested. It shouldn't take long for her to move on to some other unsuspecting nobleman.

❧

The evening whirled by in a swirl of colors and sensations. Anthony escorted her straight from the stairs to the dance floor. Terrified that she would forget the steps, she barely managed two words to him. He didn't seem to mind, giving her an understanding smile as he escorted her back to Caroline.

While she'd been dancing, the news that she was the duke's new ward had circulated through the ballroom, and a queue of gentlemen awaited her arrival. Introductions and requests to dance arrived with such regularity Amelia began to feel light-headed. Her frequent pleas of breathlessness were not always because she didn't know the dance being done. Her dancing lesson with Anthony hadn't been extensive enough for this level of popularity.

After two hours, Caroline allowed Anthony to dance with her again.

"How are you enjoying your first ball?" Anthony led her onto the floor.

Amelia's hand tingled as she felt the warmth of his arm through her glove. Dancing with Anthony was more exciting than any of her

159

other partners. "I know a lot of the attention is curiosity over the duke's new ward, but it has still been a wonderful experience."

The dance pulled them away from each other for a time, but when they came together again, he asked, "Did I hear Sir Hollis reciting poetry earlier?"

Amelia tried not to giggle at the memory. The man's hastily constructed ode to her pink gown had been sweet, but horrible. "Yes. He was quite enthusiastic about it."

They parted again, and she could only smile at him as the dance moved along. Eventually they stood in the middle once more.

"I never understood before what drove all the young fops to spout flowery bits of terrible poetry." Anthony took her hand to walk her around the end of the line of dancers. "I think I do now."

Amelia couldn't hold back a small smile.

The dance drew to a close. Griffith was waiting by Caroline and Miranda when they returned. "My drawing room is sure to resemble a hothouse by tomorrow afternoon."

"Gibson will have to station himself permanently by your door," Anthony added.

Miranda looped an arm through Amelia's. "I've no doubt the man is looking forward to it. Didn't you notice the maids clearing the flower arrangements from the hall tables as we were leaving? I think the servants are anticipating your success as much as I am."

Caroline cocked her head to the side. "Gibson *did* seem more exuberant this evening. Why is that?"

"Because everyone loves our dear Amelia."

Miranda could not have said anything that would please Amelia more. As long as her old friends knew she hadn't forgotten them, she could enjoy everything this new life had to offer.

A tall woman with icy blond hair walked by, eyes narrowed as she looked at Amelia and Anthony.

Perhaps everyone wasn't as happy with her new good fortune as Miranda seemed to think.

12

Trent, Amelia, and Miranda strolled slowly down the path beside Rotten Row. The place bustled with society's upper crust, but Amelia was content to focus on her strolling partners. Over the past three weeks the sheen of the promenade had worn off a bit as she realized others were looking around in judgment instead of fascination.

"It feels odd having Trent out of the house," Miranda said.

Amelia thought of all the school stories Trent had shared. "Hasn't he been out of the house for years?"

"But his home was still with us. Now he has lodgings of his own."

"Imagine how strange it is for me. He's living in my old home." Amelia grinned at Miranda, hoping to disguise how strange it truly made her feel. She'd been visiting several times a week with Mrs. Harris, Lydia, and Fenton. Those visits would have to stop since Trent had officially taken possession of the house yesterday.

"You realize I'm here, don't you?" Trent asked.

Miranda continued the conversation without acknowledging his interruption. "I suppose it would be difficult for you. I mean, he's eating at your old dining table." A wide grin split Miranda's face. "Do you think he kept all the curtains? I believe I remember seeing lace in a window or two."

"Mrs. Harris planned to remove the more feminine frippery from around the house."

Trent coughed. "I am walking between the two of you, even."

Miranda frowned. "That is no fun at all. I shall continue thinking of him drowning in ruffles. It makes me laugh."

Amelia rolled her eyes. The image was certainly a funny one, but it was also disturbing. Trent was eating off dishes she used every day in her former life. He was sitting on the sofas that she'd had re-covered. At least Mrs. Harris had set him up in one of the other bedrooms so she didn't have to picture that awkward scenario.

"How was your first evening in your new home, Trent?" Amelia hoped hearing Trent's stories would make the house more his than hers.

"Oh, so we've decided I can be part of the conversation now?" Trent straightened his cuffs. "You neglected to mention that you lived in the strangest house in London."

Amelia frowned in confusion.

Miranda laughed. "I've been in the house, brother. There's nothing strange about it."

Trent grunted. "They ate dinner with me."

Amelia giggled.

"Who ate dinner with you?" Miranda's brows drew down over her eyes.

Amelia's giggles grew into a laugh. She could visualize what must have happened.

"Who do you *think* ate dinner with me?" Trent stopped and crossed his arms over his chest.

"You couldn't have invited guests over. Half of your things are still at Hawthorne House."

Amelia gave in. The idea of Mrs. Harris and Fenton sitting down to dinner and treating Trent the way they had treated her was too comedic to resist. The brown ringlets Iris had so carefully fashioned that morning bobbed happily against her head. It certainly wasn't fashionable to laugh this loud or this long, but Amelia didn't care.

That realization distracted her brain enough to allow the laughter to begin to ebb. She didn't care! From the first moment Amelia had met Miranda, she had been constantly worried about her dress, her manners, and her speech. The desire to impress engulfed her, even after securing a place in the family.

Her gaze flew around the circle, touching on the now familiar faces. Miranda smiled though confusion filled her eyes. Trent's disgruntled frown was exaggerated in an obvious attempt to make her laugh harder. She loved these people, and they loved her back.

A blessed freedom she hadn't realized she'd missed the past few months filled her heart. It was a new confidence that would probably falter at the next ballroom door, but for that moment she was nothing but herself. It felt glorious.

"Wasn't it better than eating alone, Trent?" Amelia's giggles settled into a wide grin.

"I wouldn't know. I didn't have the chance to find out."

"Find out what? If it's as delightful as Amelia's smile indicates, I want to be included in the revelation."

Amelia turned, a smile still stretched across her face, to see Anthony dismounting from his horse. Tossing the reins to his groom he approached the group. Amelia felt some of her peaceful confidence sliding away. She clung to it with ruthless determination.

"What are we talking about?" Anthony looked back and forth from Amelia to Trent.

"Trent bought the lease to my house," Amelia said.

"What?" Anthony all but yelled the question and sent an accusatory look at Trent.

"Well, she wasn't living in it any longer. And to be fair, it wasn't actually her house. It was Griffith's."

Miranda crossed her arms and huffed. "Would somcone please tell me what happened last night that is so funny? Trent, did you or did you not enjoy a quiet dinner at home?"

"Oh, I was at home. No guests over at all."

"Then what could have possibly happened?"

Trent gestured at Amelia. "Why don't you tell them what you neglected to warn me about?"

Amelia blushed as she smiled. "I would have to wager a guess that Mrs. Harris and Fenton ate dinner with you."

"No!" Miranda shook her head in shock.

Trent nodded. "Lydia too. Afterward, Fenton and I even sat down to a glass of port."

Amelia's giggles started all over again.

"Isn't that the butler?" Anthony asked.

"Yes. Yes, he is." Trent's voice was flat as he closed his eyes and hung his head.

Miranda and Anthony joined in Amelia's renewed laughter.

"Would you like me to speak to them?" Amelia offered.

"No, I don't need you to speak to my servants. How awful would that be if every time I wanted to get something done I had to go across town to collect my brother's ward."

A horrible thought crossed Amelia's mind. "You're not going to dismiss them, are you?"

Trent smiled at her. "No. I think, given time, I'll enjoy having the most unconventional house in the neighborhood. Truth be told, I was wondering how I would handle living alone. It was going to be quite a transition, having no one to question my comings and goings, no one to talk to in the evenings. I'm sure it will be tricky finding the right people to fill in the rest of the staff, but I think it might work for me."

"I'm glad. I'd be happy to help you find suitable employees. I know several people who might fit in well."

"I'll manage." Trent shook his head, but his smile was bright. "Well, Anthony, care to help me see these ladies home? Then I believe I shall go spend a few hours at the club and make Mrs. Harris wonder what happened to me."

Anthony offered Amelia his arm. "I would love to, Trent."

The walk back to Hawthorne House was uneventful, filled with meaningless chatter about the weather and the upcoming parties. As Amelia climbed the stairs, she realized she had gotten through an entire conversation with two attractive, titled gentlemen, and she hadn't once twisted her ribbons around her fingers.

She smiled and danced the rest of the way to her room. Life was good, indeed.

❦

Anthony slapped his gloves against his palm as he climbed the stairs to Hawthorne House. The betting book at the club had convinced him that his behavior now was nearly as bad as it had been two years before. If he allowed it to continue, someone was going to be hurt.

There was an entry for a bet that he'd be married to Amelia by summer.

Underneath that was a bet that Lady Helena would manage to drag him to the altar.

Two pages over, a line stated that Lord Howard had bet twenty-five pounds that Griffith would call Anthony out for his dealings with Amelia.

It didn't seem to matter that Anthony had never declared himself, at least not in so many words. All of London saw his infatuation.

But they also knew his reputation.

He couldn't let Amelia get caught up in the tentacles of his past, not when she had so many opportunities now. Being Griffith's ward meant the men were lining up to dance with her. The drawing room saw a never-ending stream of gentlemen on days when the ladies were at home.

How could he ask her to choose him over one of those more respectable men?

The door opened before he could lift the brass knocker.

"I'm afraid no one is receiving visitors today, my lord," Gibson said.

Anthony thought through all the plausible reasons why he should be allowed entry when it was obvious that no one else in London was making it past the portal.

Before Anthony could speak, Gibson continued, "It would be a shame to waste your walk here, my lord. Perhaps you'd like to borrow a book from His Grace's library before you return home?"

A book? The butler was offering him a book? Anthony narrowed his gaze as he saw the glint in the eyes of the otherwise stoic servant. "A book, you say?"

"Yes, my lord. I would feel obliged to grant you, as a friend of the family, access to the library." Gibson raised a brow.

"A book is the very reason I'm here, Gibson. How very astute of you."

Anthony thought Gibson might have rolled his eyes as he gestured Anthony into the hall, but the crafty butler turned his head so Anthony couldn't be sure.

After shedding his coat and hat, Anthony jogged up the stairs to the library, hoping he'd interpreted the hidden message correctly. Knowing Amelia's close relationship with the servants, he wasn't sure what he would find. Amelia, anxious to see him, or Griffith, demanding he declare himself.

His heart beat faster as he approached the library, anticipating seeing Amelia curled up with a book or lazily browsing the shelves. The fact that he'd come here with the purpose of breaking their unofficial courtship fled his mind and a grin broke across his face. Maybe she would be on a ladder cleaning. There would be a much different outcome were she to tumble into his arms now.

He slammed a mental door on the path his mind tried to take.

The object of his musings was not lounging, but furtively searching the library. "Looking for something in particular?"

She whirled around, eyes wide. "Anthony!" She slapped a hand over her mouth. "Er, I mean, Lord Raebourne."

"I think I like Anthony." He knew he liked *Anthony*. Hearing his name on her lips sent a shiver from his heart to his toes. Maybe it was selfish, but he couldn't find the will to walk away from this woman.

"I hear you referred to in that way—I mean, here in the house. I did not mean to presume—"

"Stop." Anthony crossed the room and took her by the shoulders, relishing the precious, fragile feeling of her small bones under his hands.

A blush stained her cheeks as her gaze darted to the floor. Feeling pained at the loss of her deep brown eyes, he hooked a finger under her chin to regain her attention. His voice was hoarse and quiet when he spoke. "I like hearing you call me Anthony. I like it very much."

Her smile was small and shy but reached all the way to her eyes. "Truly?"

Pleasure at her smile drowned his guilt. Maybe he could be enough for her. He was willing to spend his whole life trying.

"Truly." Anthony slid his hands down her arms until he clasped her hands in his own. "May I call you Amelia?"

She nodded.

He wanted to kiss her. To take her in his arms and mark her as his own. But he'd just promised to give her the best he had to offer. With great reluctance he released her hands and forced himself to take a few steps to the bookcase, putting a globe between them. "What were you looking for?"

"Oh! Nothing, well, not nothing. It would be silly to look for nothing. I thought that with the number of books here there might be a family Bible, but I suppose it is at the country house."

Of all the answers Anthony had expected, the family Bible wasn't among them. "Are you wanting to check up on the births and deaths of various Hawthornes?"

"I was more interested in the Bible part than the family part." Amelia twisted her fingers into her ribbons.

He'd told himself he wouldn't touch her again, didn't trust himself to do so, but he couldn't bear to see her tie her fingers up in knots. "As adorably charming as I find this little habit of yours, I would rather you not be nervous around me."

"I can't help it, my lord."

"Anthony." He gave her freed hands a squeeze and trailed his fingers along her wrists, feeling like the cad everyone assumed he still was.

"Anthony," she whispered.

"As it happens, I can solve your dilemma. What you seek is in Griffith's study. Come along." With a clear objective in mind, Anthony gave himself permission to take her hand. It helped him overcome her obvious reluctance at invading Griffith's private space.

The door was ajar, and Anthony poked his head in to determine if they would be disturbing Griffith. The room was empty, so he pulled her in behind him. He directed her to a pair of wingback chairs angled in front of the fireplace with a small table in between. "He keeps it here. His habit is to read first thing in the morning."

Amelia picked up the black leather-bound book. She sank into one of the wingback chairs and placed the book in her lap. She opened the heavy tome and lovingly riffled the pages.

"I've never held one," she whispered. Her smile of reverent anticipation punched Anthony in the stomach, sending him into the other chair. Sheer joy covered her face.

"It's wonderful to hear the parts the bishop reads in church, but I have often wondered what the rest of it says." She ran her hand along the gold-embossed spine. "The housekeeper at Lord Stanford's house used to tell me Bible stories." Amelia smiled at the memory. "She always told me to remember that someone even more powerful than King George loved me."

Anthony dredged up skills left dormant since his days of high-stakes card games and forced himself to relax and reveal nothing. Amelia had never talked about her childhood, so he didn't want to risk distracting her from revealing this glimpse into her young life.

⁂

Amelia took a deep breath and adjusted her position in the chair. Anthony was waiting patiently for her to tell him more. Maybe he needed to know more of her background before declaring serious intentions.

"My parents didn't want me." Amelia winced at the abruptness of her statement, questioning her intent to share her past. It might be more than he'd come for, might even convince him to cease his attentions.

She forged on regardless. Better to know now if her past would scare him away. "They wanted a son. Father despised my uncle and he needed a son to inherit the entailed estate."

Pride had kept them from ostracizing their daughter. She was educated, dressed according to her station, and paraded about in front of their friends as an attractive young girl who might someday make a wonderful match and become a credit to the area. But she was never loved, never coddled or hugged or even taken for a walk.

"They weren't bad parents," Amelia said with a shrug. "They just didn't love me. All their attention went to trying to conceive a boy."

In the end, that desire had killed them. "The doctors said the benefits of sea bathing might help my mother conceive, so they planned a trip immediately, even though I'd come down with a dreadful fever. They stopped at a posting inn on the way to Brighton. There was an argument in the tavern below and a fire broke out.

"Uncle Edward arrived within days." He'd offer to let her stay, but he had no intention of raising her as his own. Amelia'd had no desire to follow in Cinderella's footsteps as companion and maid to his daughters. "Grandmother took me in, but it was too much of a strain on her limited finances."

Amelia glued her gaze to her toes. How hard it was to admit that no one wanted you, particularly when sitting next to the man you hoped would want you more than anything else in the world. "The viscount took me in but left me in the care of his housekeeper."

Memories of Mrs. Bummel had always made Amelia smile, and now was no exception. The woman had taken one look at the lost little girl and deposited her at the kitchen worktable with a plate piled high with biscuits and a large mug of hot chocolate.

"Mrs. Bummel did the best she could, but she had work to do and I was only ten," Amelia said. "I followed her around a lot. She was nice. Even when the maids burnt food or broke something.

"The other servants talked a lot about the viscount and what a disservice he was to the title. She never did. I thought it was just because she was a higher servant, but she said Jesus wanted her to treat the viscount with respect, so she would." The only time she'd complained about the viscount was when he decided to send Amelia to London.

"When I left for London, she said I didn't have to go alone. That Jesus would go with me everywhere if I committed my life to Him." Amelia shrugged. "It's been good, knowing I wasn't completely alone, but I know there's more." She ran a hand over the worn cover once more. "I never had a chance to look for myself."

The book covered her entire lap, but the awkwardness of handling it didn't bother her. As she flipped the pages, the words began to swim in front of her eyes and she realized tears had formed. "Where do I even begin?"

"Griffith told me to start in John," Anthony whispered before rising and kissing the top of Amelia's head.

And then he was gone. Amelia felt him leave. She had poured her heart out to him, telling him things she'd never told anyone. And he was leaving. She couldn't blame him. Who would want someone of her background?

"He's right—John is an excellent place to start."

Amelia turned in the direction of Griffith's voice.

He crossed the room and knelt in front of her. "Keep this one. I can get another."

Amelia looked down at the book. She had known for years that Jesus was with her and that He had promised to take care of her, but this was a gift she had never expected. She may have lost Anthony, but gaining a family who cared for her would mean so much more. "Thank you."

"You're welcome." Griffith grinned. "And if Mrs. Bummel still works at Harmony Hall, she is going to get a large bonus."

13

Over the next two weeks, Anthony gave up any pretense of avoiding Amelia in public. He kept as much distance as he could, wanting to give her the chance to enjoy society she'd never had, but he was never far away.

His reward was that her smiles came more frequently, her blushes lessened. Confidence grew until she had no problem meeting his eyes. The ribbons she'd added to her dresses to accommodate her nervous habit had swung freely as she danced.

Until tonight. Anthony frowned as he watched her wind her fingers tightly in the ribbons. Her normal wide-eyed fascination had become subdued and withdrawn.

Something was definitely wrong. People had been talking all evening, their stares becoming more open with every passing minute. Old gossip couldn't be that interesting. He racked his brain for anything he could have done recently to inspire such avid talk.

Whatever the news, if his name was part of it, his past was surely part of it as well. Amelia would hear of it.

And then she'd have nothing to do with him.

Anthony hid himself in an alcove behind the refreshment table, unfit company for anyone but unwilling to leave. Despite the covering of potted plants, Griffith found him.

"We have a problem."

If Griffith thought there was a problem, it was already very bad. And personal. Nothing set up Griffith's bristles except problems directed at his family. Anthony took the offered glass of lemonade and leaned a shoulder against the wall, trying to appear casual.

"It would seem some people are questioning whether or not Amelia is truly my ward."

Anthony took another sip, focusing his eyes on the whirling couples as the blood rushed through his head. Possibilities swam through his head, but he took a deep breath to clear them. There was no use in jumping to conclusions. "Nonsense. Who else would she be?"

"Lord Howard implied she could be my father's by-blow."

Anthony froze with the glass an inch from his lips. That scenario had never run through his mind. "No one of any intelligence would believe your father had an affair, much less an illegitimate child from it. Your parents were quite famously devoted to each other. Even I have heard the stories."

"Nevertheless . . . " Griffith said. He looked as if he didn't know quite what to say next. He didn't have a chance to figure it out before Lord Geoffrey Chester stumbled into the alcove, nearly ripping a tied-back curtain away from the wall.

If the fumes emanating from his laughing mouth were anything to go by, Lord Geoffrey was already deep in his cups. Anthony turned his head in search of cleaner air.

"I commend you, my man." Lord Geoffrey waved a finger in Anthony's direction. "I thought you'd gone soft in the country, but this is masterful. A mistress in the London ballrooms!"

Anthony saw Griffith's eyes dart in his direction. He didn't dare meet them. If he saw censure or belief in his friend's gaze . . . No, it was better to remain directed at the pompous windbag threatening Anthony's attempt to rebuild his reputation.

He'd been so careful. How could anyone think he harbored a mistress?

Anthony considered punching Lord Geoffrey, but it would likely leave him passed out on the floor and that wouldn't get Anthony more information. Instead he raised his glass and took a small sip of lemonade. "Of what are you speaking?"

Lord Geoffrey turned toward Griffith and laughed. "Must say I never figured you for playing into one of his rakish schemes, though."

Anthony could almost taste the whiskey on the other man's breath as he leaned closer.

"Tell me, man, did your skirt really cry at the opera? Got you a softhearted one?" Lord Geoffrey reached out and took a swig of Anthony's lemonade.

He coughed loudly and frowned before slamming the glass back into Anthony's hands. "Are you buffle-headed, Raebourne? Don't you know the good brandy is in the card room?"

Anthony set his cup on a nearby ledge, trying to find the right words. He'd been to the opera but once since returning to London. Yes, Amelia had cried, but that had been weeks ago, before anyone in this room knew of her existence.

Lord Geoffrey clapped a hand on Anthony's shoulder before stumbling away, talking over his shoulder. "Not sure what you mean to accomplish but it's right entertaining for the rest of us."

Anthony turned his back to the crowded room. "Who could have started such a rumor? It certainly did not originate from a man who cannot tell the difference between brandy and lemonade."

"We need to get out of this alcove." Griffith straightened the sleeves of his coat and ran a finger beneath his cravat. "Hiding behind these plants won't gain us any information."

∼◯

Amelia went through the dance by rote, her mind occupied, as it often was, with Anthony. He seemed out of spirits this evening. Her partner mentioned something about the weather. Why was it always the weather? Did other ladies find the temperature and amount of cloud cover fascinating? She certainly didn't.

The whole evening had been strange. Most people had accepted her warmly or been indifferent to her presence the past few weeks, but tonight most of their greetings were cold. The unmarried ladies had given her the cut direct.

Even her hostess, Lady Mulberry, had looked unsure when Amelia arrived. Had she not been on Griffith's arm, Amelia might have found herself escorted from the house.

After the final curtsy of the dance, she pled the beginnings of a headache and took herself off to the retiring room, hoping to find Miranda along the way.

It took her an hour to cross the ballroom, with the number of people who refused to step out of her way or scowled at her until she decided to change directions.

How fickle the world she'd thought she wanted was. In a single evening Amelia became all but ostracized. She considered spending the rest of the ball in the kitchens. At least the servants still liked her.

Amelia held her head high even as she trembled. Behaving as if everyone weren't dragging her name through the mud was harder than she'd imagined it would be.

Whispers followed her everywhere. Even from people she hadn't met. Some were shocked that she dared to show her face. Others questioned their hostess's taste in letting her in the door.

Just as she found Miranda, a bold slur to Amelia's honor was hissed from within a passing group. Miranda's fingers curled into a fist. "The next so-called lady who dares to open her mouth against you will feel my wrath."

Amelia appreciated the desire to defend her, but what could Miranda do? "Do you intend to engage her in fisticuffs?"

Miranda shrugged. "I could pull her hair out. That would send a message."

When the next derogatory whisper came their way, Amelia pulled Miranda from the ballroom before her vow could be tested.

"Where are we going? That vile woman deserved a good dressing down. You are the ward of a duke. You don't malign someone under the protection of a duke." Miranda stumbled after Amelia as they walked down the hall.

"I need somewhere to breathe." Amelia pulled Miranda into the ladies' retiring room, where two young women were working to clean a pale pink slipper.

174

"Champagne! All over my shoes. They are completely ruined."

The other girl looked up from the soiled shoe. "How did this happen? It's soaked through."

"I was taking a glass from the tray and suddenly it tipped. The footman caught all of the glasses, but the contents of half a tray of champagne spilled down my front." The girl pouted as she held her skirts away from her body.

"It's quite fortunate you can't see it on your skirt. You would have had to go home."

The two girls looked up at Amelia and Miranda standing in the doorway. The girl in pink, who had earlier told Amelia that she had seen through her disguise of innocent niceness from the beginning, grabbed her sodden shoe and stomped out of the room. The other girl hastened after her.

With the retiring room empty, Amelia and Miranda took some time to pray and breathe. The Lord answered by keeping the room empty a full twenty minutes and calming their spirits.

"We could leave," Miranda said.

Amelia shook her head. "No. I didn't need them before, and I don't need them now, but I refuse to hide. I finally feel I know who I am and won't let them take that from me."

Miranda nodded, and they returned to the ballroom arm in arm.

The dance floor was far less crowded than normal. With such a luscious piece of gossip to chew on, everyone gathered in groups around the edge of the dancing area.

Amelia didn't know what to do now, so she stood near the doorway, clinging to the notion that she hadn't let them chase her away.

One bitter spinster who'd called Amelia a bit o' muslin passed by them wailing about huge globs of melted candle wax in her hair. No one in her party could figure out how it happened.

Amelia looked around. Had anyone thought to ask the little maid smiling in the corner as she affixed fresh candles in the sconces? She probably knew.

"We could still leave," Miranda whispered.

Amelia swallowed hard. "Perhaps that would be best."

❧

"Did you really teach her to dance?" Griffith leaned a shoulder against the wall as he and Anthony reconvened in the alcove.

Anthony grunted. "It was a brilliant idea at the time. I spent nearly two uninterrupted hours in her company."

"Two inappropriate hours you mean." Griffith grinned. "I should call for pistols."

"You'd make Lord Howard a good bit of money."

Anthony looked around the ballroom. An entire evening of questions and they'd come no closer to fixing the problem. Around the ballroom, groups of London's elite bent their heads close to each other, no doubt discussing him or Amelia.

He took a few steps to the refreshment table and snagged an éclair before stepping back to the wall. It gave him a reason to stand around. Griffith selected a glass of lemonade.

Trent approached them with both eyebrows raised. His hands were clasped behind his back as he strolled, seemingly without purpose but managing to cover the distance in mere moments. "What are we contemplating as we scowl across the ballroom?"

Anthony knew him well enough to feel the tension behind the joviality. "I am trying to figure out who despises me enough to have me watched."

Griffith started visibly. "What makes you say that?"

"People are mentioning things they shouldn't know about. One pup had the audacity to ask me if I often had my mistresses clean my house. How could anyone know that?"

"I've had no luck determining where the rumors started." Griffith raised his glass to his lips only to realize it was empty.

Anthony hid a grin as Griffith tried to pass off the blunder by placing the glass on a passing servant's tray. "Nobody will say, but an inordinate number of people heard things from Lady Helena."

"It's not her," Trent said confidently. "At least, not the initial information source. If she had known the day Anthony arrived back in town, she would have come up with some reason to see him."

Griffith nodded. "She's made no secret of her desire to marry you. It's why she turned down Lord Henry last year. She might have known about the opera, but she wasn't watching your house when you arrived."

The three men continued to hold up the ballroom wall, glaring with varying degrees of efficiency at anyone who approached them. Their vantage point from behind the refreshment table gave them an unobstructed view of a large grouping of people, Lady Helena among them.

A nearby servant held a tray of champagne. As Lady Helena passed, the servant tread upon the hem of her ball gown, effectively tripping her. She reached for the arm of a nearby admirer only to find he had turned away to answer another servant's offer of a puffed pastry. With nothing to stop her forward momentum, Lady Helena fell face-first into the punch bowl.

Trent slowly stood up from the wall. "It would appear I was wrong."

"About what?" Griffith and Anthony asked in unison.

Trent shook his head as if to bring himself out of a trance. "Amelia once told me that servant gossip is worse than *ton* gossip because they *know*. They know everything."

"And the servants love our Amelia," Anthony said quietly. He watched as Lady Helena accepted condolences amongst an assortment of poorly hidden laughter.

Then he cursed.

Griffith blinked.

Anthony grimaced. "Apologies. Old habits and all that."

"What do we do now?" Trent asked.

Anthony rubbed a gloved hand over his face. He could think of multiple ways to find vengeance, but none he'd be willing to stand before God and admit. What did they do now? That was a good question.

14

"You should have made her stay home," Anthony grumbled. He, Trent, and Griffith were once more holding up a ballroom wall, trying to decide what to do about the constant tongue wagging. The rumors had moved from truth to ridiculous with no end in sight.

Griffith groaned. "I would hate to see the state of my house if I had a displeased Amelia under my roof. The servants would revolt. No doubt I'd have gruel for dinner, holes in my shirts, and the most foul-smelling tallow candles they could find."

"The footmen rearranged the chairs in the front drawing rooms so that she could sit and watch the people walk by." Trent snickered.

The mental imagery made Anthony smile, but it didn't lighten his mood. "You should have told her not to dance, then."

Griffith and Trent followed Anthony's gaze to the dance floor. "There are worse chaps than Mr. Bentley," Trent said.

"Yes, but other chaps didn't corner me earlier to see if I was finished dallying with Amelia yet."

Griffith winced. "Perhaps I should cut in."

Anthony shook his head. "I'll go. You keep an eye on Lady Helena. I'm likely to hurt her if I stay here."

⁓

"It is a dreadful mess, all this gossip."

Amelia was already regretting accepting the dance with Mr. Oliver

178

Bentley. It had seemed like a fine way to pass the time but now she wasn't sure.

"Despite my low rank, I am quite plump in the pocket."

The bizarre conversation had her longing for a discussion about the possibility of rain. Should she congratulate him on his financial prowess?

"With the scheme uncovered, they'll soon have to let you go. I own a home on the edge of Piccadilly, very circumspect."

The couples around them gasped.

She looked around and was stunned to see Anthony at the edge of the dance floor, fists clenched at his sides. What was he doing? He had been avoiding her all evening.

"Sir," Amelia strained to appear calm even as her heart threatened to break her ribs, "I believe we're delaying the dance." She hated deliberately sounding empty-headed, but the alternative was to spit in this man's face. Amelia wanted to still like herself tomorrow.

But the man continued, "He's flaunted you too publicly to keep you if he wants to take a wife."

The couples to either side of them stopped and stared, mouths agape. The hypocrisy sickened her. They themselves had likely been trashing her reputation earlier in the evening. Since they'd stopped moving, though, the whole dance had stumbled to a halt, leaving Amelia with nowhere to go.

"Well," she said, looking at her dancing companions, "the dance appears to be over. Good-bye."

Desperate to move, she started walking but had no idea where to go. Anthony appeared at her side and took her arm to escort her, not just off the dance floor, but clear out onto the terrace.

As soon as they were free of the ballroom, Amelia released Anthony's arm to lean against the balustrade. "What an insufferable man."

"I am sorry, Amelia," Anthony whispered.

He looked so tortured. Had this gossip brought him such anguish, then? How was that possible? The man had single-handedly fed the gossip mill for years. "Anthony?"

"I should take you back in. All I wanted was to get you away, but out here—"

Amelia cut him off with a shake of her head. "In a moment. I think I need the air. And the space."

He reached out to rest his hands on her shoulders.

Amelia looked down, a slight blush of pleasure on her cheeks.

Anthony gently forced her face up with a knuckle. "You are a wonderful woman. Pure and innocent and gentle and kind. Right now inside that ballroom people are saying hideous things and yet you smile. That man—" Anthony stopped for a moment to gather his composure.

"You would have been well within your rights to give him the cut direct, but you would have finished the dance. I can't understand it. I want to destroy him and everyone else thinking poorly of you.

"But you . . . I've never seen a greater display of God's love in action. I admire you more than I can say, and you deserve the very best man that the world has to offer."

Amelia held her breath. She'd truly never expected to be a part of London society or have a family. Society could go jump in the Thames now that she'd found a family. Perfection would be if the man before her felt the same way about her.

His passionate speech gave her hope. This was it. He was going to reassure her that he loved her despite the hard times ahead.

"I am not the best man that the world has to offer."

Amelia gasped and tears sprang to her eyes. He was supposed to want to protect her, to marry her and spirit her off to his country home. where the rumors couldn't touch them.

"If I were a man like Griffith, well known for being upright and moral and all the things a gentleman should be, this tale would not carry the believability it does. It has brought to light for me that I am not the kind of man you deserve."

Amelia's breath rubbed her throat raw as it jerked in and out of her chest. She shook her head. Anthony's grip tightened on her shoulders until she finally looked up into his face. The pain in his eyes cut her to the bone.

"If I leave you alone," he whispered, "eventually the gossip will die down. With Griffith continuing to support you, you'll find a man that deserves you."

The first tear slid down her cheek. Amelia could do nothing to stop it. His eyes followed it as it fell to the stone. She struggled for words, for composure.

"I am not proud of who I've been, Amelia. I cannot bring that past into a life with you. I am sorry."

"Your past means nothing to me!" The words felt ripped from her chest as he turned to walk away.

Anthony slowly faced her. "It is because of the person they knew me to be"—he jerked his arm, pointing back at the ballroom—"that they have come up with this story! It is my fault that you were so severely insulted just now."

"You are no more responsible for what that man said than I am. You cannot take the blame for another's actions."

Anthony stared at her, unmoving, all the love she could ever want shining behind the hurt in his eyes. She had to make him understand. Then a shutter fell over his gaze. He was blocking her out.

Her hands reached for him, desperate to make him understand. "You have given your life to Jesus. There is no condemnation left for you to claim. I read that, in Romans. You are as pure as I am!"

She gripped his arms with all her strength. "I don't care what you did before. Don't you know that I have heard everything about you? It is not only my name being tossed about in there. That man they talk of is not the man I see in front of me."

Anthony cupped her face in his hands, caressing her cheeks with his thumbs. The shuttered look began to clear. Was he seeing the truth? Was she reaching him?

Without warning, he slid his hand to her neck and leaned in to kiss her. The kiss was fleeting, but she clung to the warm connection. She could taste her own tears on his lips.

Anthony ripped himself away, anguish stamped across his features once more. "I had no decent right to do that. Amelia, I'm so sorry."

He took a step back. "You may not see that man, Amelia, but he still lurks somewhere inside of me. I shall see him in the mirror when I remember this moment." He turned and fled down the stairs into the garden.

⟊

How could he walk away? Amelia stood on the terrace, arms wrapped around her body. She stood there while the tears dried, while the shock faded and anger took its place. If he didn't feel anything for her, she could have accepted his rejection, would have welcomed it even. But using his past as an excuse was unacceptable.

Music drifted on the night air, reminding her of the swirl of people, ambitions, and lies. Why had she wanted that world?

"There you are!" Miranda rushed across the terrace and wrapped Amelia in a hug. She hauled her into a swath of light that shone from an upstairs window.

Her frown was dark, but not enough to make Amelia care how much the tears had ravaged her complexion.

"Come along." Miranda hauled her through a side door and into the retiring room. "What happened?"

"He's gone." Amelia resisted the urge to cry again. "The details are of little consequence. Would it be possible for us to go home?"

"Everyone saw Anthony escort you from the floor. He has not made another appearance so you must."

Miranda handed her a dampened cloth. "Wash your face before we return."

Amelia wiped the crusty tear tracks from her cheeks. "Thank you."

Miranda's silent support wrapped around her. If it came down to it, Amelia knew the other woman would risk her own reputation to stand by Amelia.

She deserved better. Griffith and Trent and Caroline deserved better. Even Mrs. Harris and Fenton deserved better, because who knew what the servants were making of the entire mess.

They didn't try to hide as they entered the ballroom. The more people who saw Miranda and Amelia together, the better. Neither of them counted on one of those people being Lady Helena.

"Embracing your spinsterhood, Lady Miranda?"

Miranda tensed, her grip pinching the bones in Amelia's hand. "I beg your pardon?"

Lady Helena turned her cold glower to Amelia. "Consider it a friendly suggestion from someone who spends a bit more time on the dance floor than you do. The company you keep is important."

"Then I should leave before someone notices this exchange."

Air hissed between Lady Helena's teeth as she stared at Miranda. "Tread lightly, Lady Miranda, for I have the ear of many esteemed young ladies. Your brothers are still unwed? I've warned everyone I could about associating with this . . . well, her." She wrinkled her nose in Amelia's direction. "Perhaps I should warn them of the whole family's character."

Amelia couldn't take it anymore. Anthony was lost to her. She would not lose her family as well.

Visions of the grim looks on Griffith's and Trent's faces when she'd crossed paths with them earlier prodded her onward. She stepped forward, giving Miranda's hand a final squeeze before letting go.

"I do not think we have been properly introduced. Allow me to rectify that. I am Miss Amelia Stalwood, ward to the Duke of Riverton."

Lady Helena scoffed. "I know who you are."

Amelia's eyebrows rose. "My apologies. I assumed you were under the impression that I was a woman of loose morals and wicked character."

"As I said, I know who you are."

By this point someone had noticed the confrontation, and a crowd began to gather around them. The opportunity to share the truth would not come again. *Lord, help me protect my family.*

A calm settled over Amelia. She prayed God would give her the right words. "You have my sympathies."

Amelia blinked, surprised to discover the words were true. She did feel sorry for Lady Helena, who must feel desperate to go to these measures.

Lady Helena's eyes narrowed. "It is not I who will never be able to show my face in London again. I have better sense than to flit about with such a man."

"And yet you wanted to marry him."

A ripple of laughter rolled through the otherwise silent crowd.

"I wanted to be a marchioness."

Those closest to the women gasped.

"Lady Helena." Amelia's voice was quiet, causing everyone in the immediate vicinity to lean forward. "I pity you."

One would think Amelia had just spit on the other woman, the way the crowd drew back in shock.

"What did you say?" Lady Helena's head tilted slightly to the side as she glared at her opponent.

"If this is all you have, I pity you. Your ploys may have hurt the man I love, but that is not all that I have. Even if you succeed in placing these ballrooms beyond my reach, you will never ruin my life. I do not give you that power."

Amelia wasn't sure what her goal had been in this confrontation, certainly not to enter a full-fledged battle of wills. But now that such a volatile cannon had been fired, Amelia could do nothing but wait and see if it would strike true or if a counterattack would be coming her way.

And then she didn't care. She was done with Lady Helena, done kowtowing to the opinions of the *ton*.

Turning her back on Lady Helena, she addressed the avid listeners. "I shall say this once for the benefit of you all. I have never behaved with anyone—man, woman, child, aristocrat, gentry, or servant—in a way that would reflect poorly on my new family."

Amelia stepped toward Lady Helena and lowered her voice, with little hope that what she said would not travel farther than its intended ears. The surrounding listeners were too attuned to the conversation. "Lady Helena, you are as unmarried as I am. For all your schemes and lies, you have yet to obtain your goal. Perhaps it is time to change tactics."

Amelia turned on her heel. "Good evening to you all."

With head held high, Amelia plowed into the crowd, hoping they would give way. They did. All the way to ballroom's exit.

Once she left the room, noise erupted, nearly deafening even out in the hall. How could anyone hear what anyone else was saying? But then again, maybe they didn't care. It seemed more important to be talking than to be heard.

As she put the ballroom behind her, Amelia felt as if she left her courage there as well. She was shaking by the time she made it to the front door.

Then they were there, all of them. Miranda, Griffith, and Trent, even Caroline and Lord Blackstone wrapped their arms around her, whispering words of encouragement, acceptance, and even love.

They piled into their carriages, and even through the darkness caused by Anthony's loss, Amelia saw a faint glimmer of hope about her future.

15

By the next afternoon, Amelia was convinced that everyone in London had lost their mind. From the moment the first matron arrived under the guise of checking after Amelia's health—she had looked quite pale when she left the ball the night before—the drawing room at Hawthorne House saw a constant stream of visitors.

While Amelia had braced herself for a bit of sympathy and a handful of supporters, she never imagined the venomous slander against Lady Helena Bell.

"I have always said that girl would come to no good."

"She set her cap for my son last year, and he made a narrow escape of it, he did."

"Rest assured, she shall not be receiving an invitation to any of my gatherings. I have put it about to my friends that they should strike her off as well."

"I blame her parents, I do. That is what comes of doting so on a child. They become spiteful and hateful."

It was enough to make a girl ill.

The men, who began arriving at a more conventional time, were not any better.

"Lady Helena is all that is bland and lifeless next to your splendid coloring."

"I've written an ode to your spirit and honesty. Would you like to go for a ride and hear it?"

"Will you marry me?"

Griffith had put a cease to the proposal by ushering Mr. Craymore to the door with a friendly but firm hand. "I do not believe that now is the appropriate time for that discussion. I shall let you know when it is an acceptable time to renew your suit."

"Much obliged to you, Your Grace. I am sure you will be anxious to settle her off during her current peak of popularity."

"Pompous man," Caroline said when they heard the front door shut. "Gibson, we will have no more visitors today."

Miranda pointed at Gibson. "Unless it is Anthony." She flopped over the side arm of the sofa. The break in ladylike decorum testifying to the exhausting drama that had played out among the tea cups in the drawing room.

"Anthony will not be visiting today, I can assure you," Amelia whispered. Her vision blurred as tears filled her eyes. "This isn't what I wanted."

Caroline and Miranda both turned to her with looks of inquiry.

"I never sought to hurt her. I wanted . . . I wanted to set things right. This is wrong."

Caroline picked up Amelia's hand and rubbed it between her own. "My dear, in situations with the *ton* there must always be a villain. In every story someone must be the profligate. If you are innocent, then she must be guilty."

"And she is." Miranda shrugged at her mother's exasperated look. "You earned everyone's admiration last night. That forces Lady Helena to be the scoundrel for daring to hurt you."

"How do I stop it?" Amelia smoothed her ribbons across her lap.

Caroline sighed. "Perhaps if Anthony were to return—"

"She declared her love in front of half of London." Miranda punched a needlepoint pillow. "If he doesn't return to her, he's a fool."

Griffith reentered the drawing room and sprawled himself in a wing chair, rubbing his forehead and temples. Amelia knew how he felt. She was trying to hold off a threatening headache herself.

"I wish to go away," Amelia announced.

Griffith dropped his hands and opened his eyes but made no movement otherwise.

"If it is not possible for me to actually leave London, can we tell everyone that I did? I will remain in the house, and no one will be any wiser."

Caroline began to protest, but Griffith held his hand up to stop her. "I have a house outside of London. We have been known to retire there for a breather in the midst of the season. With any luck Lady Helena will go into hiding as well. If neither of you is in Town, the *ton* will find something else to talk about."

Anthony stared at the ceiling, not ready to get out of bed yet. His servants were probably still scrambling from his surprise arrival at his country estate the night before. They hadn't expected him until well after the end of the season.

He rolled over and punched a pillow. "Why, God?" he groaned. Why would God bring Him so far and taunt him with something so precious? How could a loving God bring him to the brink of happiness and then snatch it all away?

The answer materialized, as if the Lord himself had spoken in Anthony's ear. *I didn't take it away. You did.*

Anthony jerked upright in bed, instinctively pulling the covers over his bare chest. Knowing God was always present was different than feeling like He was standing at the foot of the bed.

Then the import of the words sank in. God hadn't taken Amelia away from him. Anthony's own guilt and selfishness had tossed her aside. How could he be so foolish?

"Good morning, my lord." The butler entered with fresh water, preparing to act as Anthony's valet. Harper was probably twisted in knots because Anthony had left him behind.

"Have you ever done something so nonsensical that you were convinced you had mutton for brains?"

The butler froze, casting a look around to see if anyone else was in the room. Anthony laughed at how much Amelia had affected him. He hadn't thought twice about conversing with the butler. The butler was apparently having second, third, and fourth thoughts about answering.

"I beg your pardon, my lord."

Anthony swung his legs over the side of the bed and rubbed his hands over his face. "I did something nonsensical. Did I really think I could save her by abandoning her?"

Chalmers cleared his throat. "Her, my lord?"

Anthony nodded. "I left her standing on that terrace like a coward. Planting Bentley a facer was a bit honorable, but I should have done it at the ball instead of outside his house."

"Er, of course, my lord."

"Why would I do something so cork-brained?" Anthony stabbed his arms into his dressing gown and began to pace as he tied the robe around his middle.

Moments passed. Chalmers looked as if he wanted to bolt, and Anthony couldn't blame him. The butler must think his master had gone mad.

"If I may be so bold, sir, I think you might be looking at this the wrong way."

Anthony gestured for the man to continue.

Chalmers cleared his throat. "It isn't a mental question. There is no logical *why*. I don't know what you've done, my lord, but it sounds as if it's a matter of the heart, not the mind."

Anthony nodded.

"Then focus on truth, not logic. Stop trying to figure out why and look for what is."

Anthony stood in stunned silence. He had a very profound butler. When things settled down he was going to make it a point to have more discussions with the man.

"Logically," Anthony began, pacing the room once more, "I would fall back into my old habits and ways, being the person they thought I was. The truth is that I'm changed."

Chalmers yanked the bellpull and began selecting clothes from the dressing room, nodding that he was still listening to Anthony's ramblings.

"There isn't any sense to it, because it was the work of God, not myself." Anthony strode to the window and looked across his land.

A jacket joined Chalmers clothing selections as he spoke quietly with the footman who'd answered the bell call.

"If God can accept me, then why can't she?"

The voice hammered his ear once more. *She did.*

"She did." Anthony's voice dropped as the truth became clear. He'd been too distraught at the ball to hear it when she voiced it, but his mind had stored it away until he was ready.

"There is no condemnation left for you to claim."

"I am forgiven," he whispered.

He crossed the room and grabbed Chalmers by the shoulders. "I have been given a new life, and she is willing to join me in it. Only a fool leaves a woman like that alone, Chalmers."

"Quite right, my lord."

"I'll need a fresh horse. The one I rode in on can't return to London today. And clothes. I'll need—" Anthony broke off as he noticed the riding breeches and jacket Chalmers had set out.

"The horse is being readied now, my lord." Chalmers pulled out the razor. "Might I suggest a good breakfast before you leave?"

"Yes. Breakfast." Anthony stood dumbfounded. Never had he realized how right Amelia was. People were people, no matter their class. Some were kind, some were smart, and some were mean and petty.

He dressed quickly and when he left the dressing room found a breakfast tray laid out in his room.

Chalmers gathered the dirtied linens and prepared to leave.

"Chalmers," Anthony called. "I have a project for you while I'm away."

"Does she have a favorite color, my lord?"

"Color?"

"Yes, my lord. Does she have a favorite color? If you wish me to see to freshening the mistress's chambers, it would be helpful to know her favorite colors."

Amazing. How had Anthony managed to hire the smartest butler in the country? "Pink," he said, remembering her delight over her first ball gown. "She likes pink."

190

16

The house outside London was peaceful and cozy, though still large by Amelia's standards. Most of the family seemed relieved to leave London behind. Even Trent had joined them on their exodus. Only Georgina seemed bitter about the move.

Where her attitude had been sullen before, she was positively churlish now. Even angry. Amelia had tried to talk to her, determined to do everything she could for this family that had taken her in, but the other girl would only glare and make snide comments.

In an effort to avoid Georgina's anger and Miranda's pity, Amelia tried to take a nap. An hour of staring at the ceiling left her restless. Despite the threat of rain she considered a walk in the garden. Maybe she could interest Trent in a game of piquet.

She strolled down the corridor, taking as much time as possible to get where she was going.

"Amelia! Amelia!"

Her head snapped up. That voice . . . Could it be? She ran for the stairs, heart tripping through her chest, trying to go faster than her feet could carry her. Was she dreaming?

She hit the top of the stairs and saw a figure striding across the front hall.

It was him.

He was more disheveled than she'd ever seen him, breathing hard, running his hands through his hair. Never had he looked more handsome.

She floated down the stairs with no recollection of her feet on the treads.

"Amelia," he breathed as they met at the bottom of the stairs.

He took her in his arms, crushing her and freeing her at the same time. His lips skimmed her cheek as he whispered.

She couldn't make out the words over the roar in her ears, but she knew what they meant. He loved her. He wanted her. He would risk everything for her.

His lips found hers and the warmth shot straight to her heart. She tasted salt. He was crying.

He pulled back, resting his forehead against hers. "I missed you."

She smiled, tears of her own threatening to fall. "I missed you too."

His laughter rang through the hall as he wrapped his arms around her and twirled her through the room. "What a fool I was to think I could walk away from you."

Anthony set her back on the ground but didn't let go. "I came from Hertfordshire. I rode all the way there the morning after I left you on the terrace and I had not been there a day when I realized what a cork-brained idiot I was. I went back to London and Gibson told me you were here. Amelia, I love you. And if a man is blessed enough to find a good woman to love, he does not turn his back on it. I suppose in all propriety I should ask Griffith but I am going to ask you first. Will you marry me?"

"No!"

Amelia turned toward the scream, stunned to find Georgina in the doorway to the parlor, shaking. "You cannot marry *her!* It was supposed to be me. Me!"

"Georgina?" Amelia asked softly. Her gaze swung back and forth between Georgina and Anthony, confusion muddling what few thoughts Anthony's confession had left intact.

Anthony stood there, his mouth slightly open, clearly too shocked to say anything.

Georgina's face contorted with anger. "For two years you have

192

been coming to Riverside Manor, and every time you were there I did everything I could to show you I would make a wonderful marchioness. It was going perfectly until you told Griffith you were ready to take a wife. I begged Mother to let me come out. I begged her because I knew if you could just see me as a woman you would pick me."

"Georgina, I . . ." Anthony stepped away from Amelia but still held her hand in his. His free hand began to reach for Georgina before falling back to his side.

"But they wouldn't let me come out. So I tried to stop you. I told Lady Helena everything. She deserved to know what a mistake you were making, choosing *this* woman. Don't you see how poor a marchioness she would be?" Georgina pointed an accusing finger at Amelia. The visual daggers caused Amelia to wince.

"I knew you would never marry Lady Helena. But you were supposed to abandon your plans to marry Griffith's ward and wait until next year and then I would be there and you would choose me."

"Georgina," he said quietly. "I love Amelia." He dropped Amelia's hand to take another step toward Georgina.

But the young girl must have realized what she'd done, the secrets she'd revealed. She began to shake. Amelia felt pity welling up inside of her.

"Stay away from me! All of you!"

Amelia turned to find that Miranda, Caroline, Trent, and Griffith, and even Lord Blackstone had all been drawn to the front hall by the commotion. Everyone looked uncomfortable with the confession.

Georgina spun on her heel and fled through the parlor and out into the gardens.

Anthony made to go after her but Caroline stopped him. "Let her go. Her pride has been hurt, and a young girl's pride can be massive indeed. You can talk about it when she calms down."

They retired to the parlor to await Georgina's return. Unofficially engaged—Amelia had, after all, not gotten the chance to respond to the proposal—Anthony sat next to Amelia on the settee, holding her hand in his.

He shook his head. "I never knew. I thought she was just your scamp of a little sister. I never saw . . ."

"None of us did," Griffith said.

Anthony gave him a wry smile. "Unfortunately, I have a bit more experience than you do. Looking back I can see several signs that I missed. I am truly sorry."

Amelia leaned forward and took Anthony's face in her hands. "You are very good at taking blame, thinking your past qualifies you to be at fault in every situation. Well, I will have you know that I short-sheeted my governess's bed, placed beetles in the raisin pudding, and lied about anything and everything if I thought it would get my parents' attention. That, sir, is as much of a sin as whatever you did. I sit here forgiven. It is about time you realized that you do too."

Anthony looked into her eyes. Amelia didn't know what he saw there, but it was enough to lift the dark gloom from his face.

"You're right, my love. It is time to forgive myself."

He reached out and smoothed the hair back from her face, leaned forward, and brushed his lips softly against hers.

Miranda sighed.

Griffith cleared his throat.

Caroline sputtered as she swallowed a laugh.

Trent cheered.

Amelia pulled back fanning ineffectively at her flaming cheeks.

Anthony dropped a kiss on her forehead and grinned rakishly.

"Well, I suppose you will have to marry her now," Griffith muttered.

Eventually Caroline went after Georgina. The girl looked young as she joined them in the drawing room. Amelia's offer to make her a bridesmaid caused her eyes to widen. "Why on earth would you do that?"

"Everyone deserves a second chance." Amelia couldn't fault Georgina for trying to create the best future possible for herself, even if her methods were more than a little questionable. A lifetime of watching people get things she thought she wanted made Amelia sympathetic to the young girl. Maybe it could be the start of a new relationship for them.

Amelia would ban her from the proceedings at the first hint of sabotage, though.

Anthony smoothed his thumb across Amelia's knuckles. "I cannot wait until I can call you my wife."

"You'll have to wait until we return to London," Georgina said. "Despite my lapse in judgment, I know how the beau monde works. If you don't want this gossip following you forever, they need to see a happy courtship."

Anthony groaned as Miranda and Caroline agreed with Georgina's claim.

"You'll forget the delay soon enough. We have forever, after all." Amelia smoothed his hair back from his face, marveling at the realization that she now had the right to do that.

"Forever. If the way I feel right now is any indication, we shall live happily ever after."

"At the very least, it will be blessedly ever after," Amelia added. "For if God never grants me anything else in this life, He has given me you, and that is more than I ever dreamed of."

Anthony kissed her gently, ignoring the groans from the rest of the room. "Blessedly ever after has a very nice ring to it."

Acknowledgments

Ah, the acknowledgments section. Possibly the most overlooked portion of any book. Though my name is on the cover and my soul is poured across these pages, it was by no means a solo endeavor. This is a tribute to the people who made it happen, the village to my occasional idiot, the archipelago to my writer's island.

Thank you, God, for the saving gift of Jesus Christ, without whom I would be lost, Amelia would have been alone, and Anthony wouldn't have been redeemed. I also appreciate the months of pregnancy-induced insomnia that allowed me the time to write the first draft of this story. My apologies for all the grumbling and crying about it at the time.

To Jacob, the Hubs, the man who has encouraged and supported me every step of the way, thank you. Thank you for telling me to do something with the story when I finished it. Thank you for pushing me into going to that first writing conference. Thank you for standing with me as I cried in the laundry room and telling me I wasn't allowed to quit. Thank you for being okay with ordering pizza one more night because the words were flowing too well and I didn't want to stop for something as piddling as a trip to the grocery store.

I would also like to thank the pizza delivery man for not commenting on it being your third trip to my house in less than a month.

A shout-out to my kids for willingly eating said pizza without telling their grandparents. Also, thank you for never really understanding what Mommy meant when she asked you to leave her alone and let her write. The reminder that family is important and there is a life to live while my books are being written is invaluable. This gratefulness is going to be known to diminish, however, the closer I get to deadline. Please check the calendar accordingly.

For Amanda, who was the first person aside from Jacob that I allowed to see my work, a huge thank-you. Not only for your honest opinions and encouragement, but also for allowing me to read your collection of inspirational fiction in college. They inspired something in me even as I had to hold them in such a way that I didn't break the binding. I hope you still have the prettiest bookshelf in five counties. I can't wait to be on it.

Everyone should thank Gayle for having the courage to tell me my first version of Anthony was a wuss. After a backbone implant, he's doing just fine.

I have to thank my dad for indirectly providing the inspiration for this story. I'm not going to tell him how. I'm holding that information hostage until he tells us what he wants for Christmas.

To Alana, I can't thank you enough. You've been so much more than a sister-in-law—you've been a friend. Thank you for your time and insight. And for being willing to read my work when my own brother said he's waiting for the movie.

Thank you, Patty Smith Hall, for taking me under your wing. There were days when I wanted to quit, but your encouragement kept me going. Thank you for my magical little bottle of Seekerville sand. Seeing it every morning is very inspiring.

For the rest of my writer family, my Regency Reflections sisters, the group at ACFW North Georgia, and the ever-supportive Georgia Romance Writers, this could not have happened without you. I look forward to giving to others as you have given to me. To the authors whose works have inspired me, my appreciation is limitless—even though you, too, have been a cause for more than one sleepless night.

I want to thank my editors and the rest of the team at Bethany House. The story of Anthony and Amelia has been through so much, and I was almost ready to stick them in a drawer. Thank you so much to Raela and Karen, who labored with me to hone the story into what it is today.

And lastly, I want to thank you, whoever you are, for reading not just the story, but the acknowledgments as well. I especially want to thank those who read it for something other than finding their own name. There are so many people I didn't thank that have been there for me every step of the way. But like an Oscar speech, someone always gets left out. I hope I have thanked you in person, and with any luck I'll remember you next time.

AT YOUR REQUEST

An Apart From the Crowd Novella

JEN TURANO

1

Miss Wilhelmina Radcliff was reluctantly coming to the unfortunate conclusion that there were absolutely no perks to be had when one obtained the unenviable title of wallflower.

Taking a sip of the tepid lemonade she'd actually fetched for herself, she couldn't help but recall the many times in her past when flutes of champagne had shown up in her hand before she'd even proclaimed herself thirsty. Those flutes had been brought to her by her many admirers, admirers who had all but vanished the moment her father's fortune had disappeared—destroyed as so many fortunes were wont to do by a single disastrous investment decision.

Shifting on the uncomfortable chair provided by her hostess, Mrs. William Travers, wife to one of the esteemed New York patriarchs, Wilhelmina paused when the chair gave an ominous groan. Refusing to give in to the urge to heave a sigh—especially since any type of heaving might have the chair giving out underneath her—she remained frozen on the spot, praying that the chair would not collapse, since that would undoubtedly draw unwanted attention.

Attention was not something she actively sought these days, especially because any attention she did garner usually came with a large dollop of pitying looks cast her way by young ladies Wilhelmina had once considered friends.

Blowing out a breath of relief when the legs of the chair continued to hold her hardly slender figure, Wilhelmina took a second to smooth out the folds of her slightly out-of-fashion brocade gown.

Her smoothing came to an abrupt end, however, when the lady sitting two chairs down from her suddenly leaned forward, peered at something in the distance, and then bent her head and began scribbling madly on her dance card. After her scribbling was done, she lifted her head, squinted off into the distance again, and then, to Wilhelmina's surprise, turned and pinned Wilhelmina with eyes that were a very unusual shade of blue.

"I say, Miss Radcliff, given that you are a most sought-after social secretary these days, would you happen to know the name of that gentleman standing over there beside Miss Kasson?" The lady gestured in the direction of one of the refreshment tables. "I took note of him at the Academy of Music earlier this evening, but even though I've been out in society for what seems like ages, I've never seen that particular gentleman before."

With her mouth forming an O of surprise, Wilhelmina responded to the question in the only way she felt capable of responding—she simply took to gawking at the lady. That gawking was undoubtedly caused by the very idea that the lady had *willingly* chosen to break one of the unspoken rules of the wallflowers. That rule, as everyone knew, being that wallflowers did not converse with each other . . . ever.

Wallflowers preferred, or at least she assumed they did, to remain mute, suffering in silence while presenting society with a face of stoic nonchalance. That nonchalance was apparently intended to prove that they were not bothered in the least by the fact they'd been excluded from the fashionable crowd, forced to spend their time twiddling their thumbs while their social superiors waltzed around the dance floor.

Wilhelmina was not a lady who was comfortable with accepting the whole banished-to-the-fringes-of-society notion. Quite honestly, she was fairly certain she'd be far happier not attending society events at all. But, because she did need the funds high-society ladies were willing to pay for her fine penmanship, she found herself included in one society function after another these days. While she attended these functions, it was her duty to take note of all the guests present, observe who seemed to be in highest demand, and then use that information when she compiled the next guest list, making certain those in-demand society members were placed at the very top of the invitation list.

Being required, due to a lack of funds, to take on employment had rankled at first. But with time, and with the realization that her contributions to the meager family coffers actually mattered, Wilhelmina had pushed aside all semblance of pride as she settled into the daunting business of survival.

Because she'd been forced to concern herself with the basic necessities of life, she no longer dwelled on what her future was supposed to have held for her. No longer did she ponder what might have made up her happily-ever-after—especially since she had, at least for a brief moment in time, contemplated allowing Mr. Warren Holland to experience that happily-ever-after with her.

She'd eventually come to realize that she hadn't actually loved Mr. Holland, even if her head had been slightly turned by his handsome face and debonair attitude. Those attributes paled considerably when she discovered he was a complete and utter cad, abandoning her the moment he'd learned about her father's financial setback, while whispering falsehoods in all the right ears that—

"Forgive me, Miss Radcliff. I certainly didn't mean to cause you any distress by asking you what must be a far more difficult question than I knew, given that scowl you now have on your face."

Blinking out of her thoughts, Wilhelmina felt her cheeks warm when she realized she'd been so lost in memories that she'd completely forgotten she'd been asked a question, and a relatively simple question at that.

"I do beg your pardon," Wilhelmina began. "I fear I was so taken aback by your speaking to me that I lost all track of the conversation."

The lady flashed a grin Wilhelmina's way. "Shocking, isn't it, that I'd have the audacity to speak to you?" Tucking her dance card up the sleeve of a very fashionable dark velvet gown, the lady rose to her feet and dropped into the empty seat beside Wilhelmina a moment later.

Without a by-your-leave, she then thrust a gloved hand Wilhelmina's way. "I'm Miss Permilia Griswold."

Having never been presented with another lady's hand before, Wilhelmina hesitated for the briefest of moments before she took the offered hand, discovering as she did so that Miss Griswold possessed a remarkably firm grip. "It's a pleasure to meet you, Miss Griswold, and as you already seem to know, I'm Miss Wilhelmina Radcliff. Although . . ."

Withdrawing her hand, Wilhelmina frowned. "If you've been out in society for what seems like ages—as you just mentioned—why haven't we been formally introduced before?"

Miss Griswold waved that aside with a flick of a gloved wrist. "I don't believe there needs to be much wondering about that, Miss Radcliff. I've never taken within society—not once since I made my debut at the ripe-old age of nineteen, which was . . . goodness . . . six years ago now."

"You've been out for six years?"

"Indeed I have—a situation that my stepmother, the former Ida Webster, contemplates on an almost daily basis." Miss Griswold leaned closer and lowered her voice. "Ida has now come to the conclusion that I've deliberately set society against me in an attempt to annoy her."

Wilhelmina's nose took to wrinkling. "And . . . have you?"

Tapping a finger against her chin, Miss Griswold seemed to consider the question quite thoroughly before she shrugged. "Hard to say. But getting back to the reason you and I have never been formally introduced. . . . I believe it has something to do with me being a wallflower for such an extended period of time. During that time, you, Miss Radcliff, were twirling around the dance floor, one of society's darlings—at least until your . . ." Miss Griswold's voice trailed to nothing as she suddenly began looking quite as if she'd rather be sitting anywhere *except* next to Wilhelmina at this particular moment.

Swallowing a laugh at the look of absolute horror on Miss Griswold's face, Wilhelmina reached over and patted Miss Griswold's arm, an action that surprised not only Miss Griswold, but Wilhelmina as well.

"There's no need to feel remorse for speaking nothing less than the truth, Miss Griswold. I am perfectly aware that I was once a darling of society and am now . . . well, not. Curious as this may sound, I find it rather refreshing that you have no qualms about bringing up my unfortunate fall from the top rungs of the society ladder." Wilhelmina gave a sad shake of her head. "My old friends never acknowledge that I once ruled the ballrooms, acting for all intents and purposes as if my descent from that lofty place might be contagious."

Miss Griswold took to patting Wilhelmina's arm. "I'm sure that must be hard for you, being slighted in such a despicable manner. Although, from the whispers I've heard, your fall from grace had more to do with Mr. Holland implying there was something lacking in your personality than the fact your father lost the family fortune." She let out a small huff. "In my humble opinion, it was hardly fair of society to accept Mr. Holland's explanation so readily—especially since he certainly wasn't behaving in a manner one would expect from a true society gentleman."

"Unfortunately, he was behaving exactly how a gentleman behaves when one needs to marry an heiress, yet discovers that the heiress he had his eye on is no longer flush with funds," Wilhelmina began. "While his behavior was beyond reprehensible, I assumed society would quickly conclude why he was behaving in such a reprehensible manner, and would subsequently readjust their thinking toward me."

"Society isn't known to be reasonable about these matters," Miss Griswold said. "And society ladies are always incredibly keen to see a rival lady suffer a fall from grace. That right there is probably why no one paid much mind to the idea Mr. Holland is a fortune hunter who clearly lacks any sense of honor."

Wilhelmina's enjoyment in the evening suddenly took to improving. "How refreshing to speak with a lady with such a straightforward manner. But enough about my dreary situation. Weren't you inquiring about the identity of someone?"

"I was indeed." Miss Griswold raised a gloved hand and gestured toward some guests gathered around a refreshment table. "I'm curious about the identity of that gentleman over there. The one standing by Miss Kasson."

Wilhelmina leaned to the left and peered through the crowd. "Oh, that's Mr. Asher Rutherford, owner of the new department store that recently opened off of Broadway."

"Not Mr. Rutherford. I know who he is. I was speaking about the gentleman right next to him, the one with the charming smile."

Rising to her feet in order to get a better view, Wilhelmina craned her neck and then lost the ability to breathe when she got her first good glimpse of the gentleman Miss Griswold was inquiring about.

Looking incredibly dashing as he bent his head toward the oh-so-fashionable Miss Kasson was none other than Mr. Edgar Wanamaker —her best friend from childhood, and . . . the very first gentleman to ever offer her a proposal of marriage.

She and Edgar had met when they'd been little more than infants, that circumstance brought about because their parents owned adjacent summer cottages on Long Island. Wilhelmina had spent every childhood summer with Edgar by her side, enjoying the sandy beaches and chilly water of the Atlantic from the moment the sun rose in the morning until it set in the evening.

Even when Edgar had been away at school, being a few years older than Wilhelmina, they'd spent every possible minute they could with each other during the holidays.

He'd even made certain to be in the city the night of her debut ball, waiting for her at the bottom of her family's Park Avenue mansion as she'd descended the grand staircase on her father's arm. As she'd stepped to the highly polished parquet floor, she'd caught his gaze, the intensity of that gaze causing her heart to fill with fondness for her oldest and dearest friend.

That fondness, however, had disappeared a few hours later when Edgar had gone and ruined everything by asking her to marry him.

She'd been all of seventeen years old the night of her debut— seventeen years old with the world spread out at her feet. Add in the notion that the whispers stirring around the ballroom were claiming she was destined to be a diamond of the first water, and the last thing she'd wanted that particular evening was a marriage proposal extended to her from her very best friend.

Edgar, no matter the affection she held for him, was only a second son. Paired with the pesky fact he'd had no idea as to what he'd wanted to do with the rest of his life—except, evidently, to marry her—and she'd been less than impressed by his offer.

What she *had* been impressed with that night, though, was the idea that she'd had very influential gentlemen vying for her attention from the moment her beaded slippers had touched the ballroom floor. Because of that, a second son had not seemed very appealing to her—no matter that Edgar had been her dearest friend forever.

To say she regretted the cavalier manner in which she'd treated Edgar that night was an understatement. She'd wanted more than anything to make matters right between them, especially after she'd matured a bit and realized she'd been a complete ninny where he'd been concerned. However, because Edgar had made himself scarce ever since she'd rejected his offer, she'd never been given the opportunity to beg his pardon.

Dismay suddenly flowed over her as the thought sprang to mind that the very last place she wanted to finally speak with Edgar again was in the midst of a ball, especially a ball where she was sitting in the wallflower section.

Without allowing herself a moment to contemplate the matter further, she surged into motion, scooting around the first row of chairs and plopping to the floor directly behind Miss Griswold and right in between two young ladies, neither of whom Wilhelmina had ever been introduced to.

"Pretend I'm not here," she whispered to a young lady sporting a most unfortunate hairstyle, who looked down at her as if she'd lost her mind.

The young lady blinked right before she smiled. "That might be a little difficult, Miss Radcliff, especially since you're sitting on my feet."

"Goodness, am I really?" Wilhelmina asked, scooting off the feet in question even as she pushed aside a bit of ivory chiffon that made up the young lady's skirt.

"Shall we assume you're hiding from someone?" the young lady pressed.

"Indeed, but . . . don't look over at the refreshment table. That might draw unwanted notice."

Unfortunately, that warning immediately had the young lady craning her neck, while the other young lady sat forward, peering over Miss Griswold's shoulder in an apparent effort to get a better view of the refreshment table.

"Who are you hiding from?" Miss Griswold asked out of the corner of her mouth, having the good sense to keep her attention front and center.

"Mr. Edgar Wanamaker, the gentleman you were inquiring about," Wilhelmina admitted.

"Mr. Wanamaker's here?" the young lady with the unfortunate hairstyle repeated as she actually stood up and edged around Wilhelmina, stepping on Wilhelmina's hand in the process. "Is he the gentleman with the dark hair and . . . goodness . . . very broad shoulders . . . and the one now looking our way? Why, I heard earlier this evening that he's returned to town with a fortune at his disposal—a fortune that, rumor has it, is certain to turn from respectable to impressive in the not too distant future."

"You don't say," Wilhelmina muttered as she tried to tug her hand out from underneath the lady's shoe.

"Miss Cadwalader, you're grinding poor Miss Radcliff's hand into the floor."

Looking up, Wilhelmina stopped her tugging as she met the gaze of the other young lady sitting in the second row of the wallflower section, a lady who was looking somewhat appalled by the fact she'd apparently spoken those words out loud. Without saying another word, the lady rose to her feet, shook out the folds of a gown that was several seasons out of date, whispered something regarding *not wanting to be involved in any shenanigans*, and then dashed straightaway.

"I wasn't aware Miss Flowerdew was even capable of speech," the lady still standing on Wilhelmina's hand said before she suddenly seemed to realize that she was, indeed, grinding Wilhelmina's hand into the ground. Jumping to the left, she sent Wilhelmina a bit of a strained smile. "Do forgive me, Miss Radcliff. I fear with all the intrigue occurring at the moment, paired with hearing Miss Flowerdew string an entire sentence together, well, I evidently quite lost my head and simply didn't notice I was standing on you."

She thrust a hand Wilhelmina's way. "I'm Miss Gertrude Cadwalader, paid companion to Mrs. Davenport. Please do accept my apologies for practically maiming you this evening, although rest assured, it is an unusual event for me to maim a person on a frequent basis."

Taking the offered hand in hers—although she did so rather gingerly since her hand *had* almost been maimed by Miss Cadwalader—Wilhelmina gave it a shake, a circumstance she still found a little peculiar, but resisted when Miss Cadwalader began trying to tug her to her feet.

"How fortunate for Mrs. Davenport that you don't participate in maiming often," she began. "But if you don't mind, I prefer staying down here for the foreseeable future, since I have no desire for Mr. Wanamaker to take notice of me this evening."

"Ah, so we really are in the midst of an intrigue," Miss Cadwalader breathed before she straightened, squeezed her way through the first row of chairs, and then held out her hand to Miss Griswold, who'd been keeping her attention front and center. "We should hide her."

Miss Griswold didn't hesitate. Taking the hand offered her, she rose to her feet, shook out her skirts, sent Wilhelmina the smallest of smiles and turned front and center again. "Perhaps we should engage in conversation, Miss Cadwalader, in order to distract everyone from the idea we're trying to hide someone."

"*That* would most assuredly draw unwanted attention," Miss Cadwalader returned as she shook out her skirts, making them wider in the process. "You know no one is used to seeing wallflowers actually conversing with one an—"

Whatever else Miss Cadwalader had been about to say got lost when she let out a small squeak and motioned with a hand behind her back for Wilhelmina to stay down.

"Good evening, ladies," a deep voice—one that Wilhelmina knew full well belonged, to Mr. Edgar Wanamaker—suddenly said. "I know this is very untoward of me, speaking to you without the benefit of a proper introduction, but I've just learned that the quadrille is about to begin. As I'm sure you're well aware, those particular dances can take quite a bit of time to perform. I'm hoping you'll take pity on a weary gentleman and allow that gentleman, as in me, to join you on those oh-so-delightful-looking chairs as we watch the chosen guests perform their well-rehearsed dance steps."

"Ah . . . well . . . as to that," Miss Cadwalader began. "You see . . . ah . . ."

"Did I mention that I brought treats?" Edgar continued.

"Treats?" Miss Cadwalader repeated. "What type of treats?"

"Miss Cadwalader, you're becoming distracted from the mission at hand," Miss Griswold whispered in a voice that still carried.

"But I'm starving, and you know that it's a rare occasion for a real-live gentleman to bring us treats."

Edgar, Wilhelmina couldn't help but recall, had always possessed a remarkably kind heart, never one to slight a person simply because they weren't acquainted with the right people or possessed of the right fortune. She'd not allowed herself to dwell on his kindness over the last few years—the memory of that particular trait a sore reminder of what she'd so carelessly discarded in her youth.

A sharp ringing of a bell suddenly split the air, signaling that the quadrille was soon to begin. Realizing that the ladies shielding her from view were going to have to take their seats, Wilhelmina began backing as quickly as she could underneath the chair behind her, her only thought being to make an escape as quietly as possible. She'd gotten halfway underneath the chair before her bustle, dratted contraption that it was, snagged on the underside of the chair. Before she could get herself free, a loud clearing of a throat sent a sense of dread flowing through her veins.

Lifting her head, she refused a sigh when her gaze was caught and held by none other than the gentleman she'd been hoping to avoid. Mr. Edgar Wanamaker.

2

"Would you mind holding this platter of treats for me?" Edgar asked of a young lady standing beside him—a young lady who happened to be sporting, curiously enough, a hairstyle that had golden curls springing haphazardly around her head as if someone had lost all control of a hot curling tong.

"Ah, well, yes, of course," the young lady replied, taking the platter he immediately thrust her way. But then, instead of stepping aside or taking her seat, the lady lifted her chin and moved directly between him and his prey—that prey being Miss Wilhelmina Radcliff. "We haven't been introduced," she continued with a hint of stubbornness in her green eyes. "And since our hostess is nowhere to be found, nor I imagine, will she materialize in the wallflower section anytime soon, we'll need to take care of the introduction business in a less-than-proper manner—which is to say, we'll have to do it ourselves. I'm Miss Gertrude Cadwalader."

Edgar's lips took to twitching. "It is a pleasure to meet you, Miss Cadwalader." He extended her a bow. "I'm Mr. Edgar Wanamaker."

Miss Cadwalader dipped into a small curtsy, almost losing the platter of treats in the process, a situation she quickly remedied by pushing the platter into the hands of the lady standing beside her. That lady was dressed to perfection in a dress of the latest style, her perfectly coiffed red hair secured on top of her head with what appeared to be a genuine diamond comb. Her eyes, a lovely shade of blue, were twinkling back at him with what almost seemed to be a large dollop of amusement in them.

"How lovely to meet you, Mr. Wanamaker," Miss Cadwalader continued. "And since you and I have now been introduced—although not properly, I daresay—allow me to present Miss Permilia Griswold."

"I'm delighted to make your acquaintance, Miss Griswold," Edgar said as he sent a bow Miss Griswold's way. "However, before more pleasantries can be exchanged, I have a matter of the utmost importance to attend to—that matter concerning the lady still trying to make what appears to be a less than stealthy attempt at escape." He turned and set his sights on Wilhelmina once again.

Interestingly enough, while he'd been conversing with the ladies who'd evidently been tasked with hiding Wilhelmina from view—the evidence of that notion being that the two ladies had taken to mumbling apologies to her under their breaths—Wilhelmina had obviously been trying to slip farther under the chair. The result of that nasty business, however, had simply led to her now appearing to be well and truly stuck.

Pushing his way through the first row of chairs, he tilted his head and allowed himself the luxury of simply considering Wilhelmina for a long moment. The years they'd been apart hadn't changed her appearance much, except that she was now a more mature lady—being almost twenty-five instead of the near infant she'd been at seventeen. Her brown hair was swept up in a simple style away from her face, and the hint of pink staining her cheeks lent her a charming air, one that suggested she was getting a bit flustered. That idea had his lips curving straight into a smile as he leaned down and caught her eye.

"Honestly, Willie, in all the years we've been apart, I never once considered the idea that when I finally returned to New York society, you'd go to such extremes to avoid me."

Wilhelmina's hazel eyes immediately took to flashing. "I don't like it when you call me Willie. And who said I'm attempting to avoid *you*?"

The flashing, an immediate reminder of Wilhelmina's adorable temper, had his smile turning into a grin. "Since these delightful young ladies were trying their very best to distract me from seeing you—and they were doing a remarkably credible job until I caught sight of the top of that chair you're under moving—I don't understand why you're arguing with me."

Wilhelmina released a dramatic sigh. "Oh, very well. You're right. I was trying to avoid you." She caught his eye, looked incredibly grumpy for all of five seconds, and then released another sigh before the makings of a grin spread over her face. "Since you've clearly caught me in my attempt to escape, and I've somehow managed to get stuck while in the process of that attempt, could I possibly persuade you to be a dear and help me out of this particular pickle I've landed myself in?"

The grin sent him directly back to his youth, where he'd witnessed that particular grin on an almost daily basis, at least during their carefree summer days. Wilhelmina had always been one to appreciate a good laugh or an amusing situation, and over the past few years, he'd almost managed to forget her appealing sense of humor.

He was fairly certain that the reason behind his forgetfulness had something to do with the fact that he'd been wallowing in a rather large vat of self-pity for years, or at least the first year or two after he'd left town.

That wallowing had been a direct result of Wilhelmina—the lady he'd assumed he'd spend the rest of his life with from the time he'd been about ten—turning down his earnest offer of marriage. That rejection had sent him reeling and caused him to try his very best to forget her over the ensuing years.

In hindsight, brought about by time and the wisdom that time brings a person, his offer of marriage to her had been beyond ill-advised and beyond ill-timed.

It was that very hindsight that had him entering New York society again, but only in order to seek Wilhelmina out and finally try to put matters right between them, something he had no idea if she'd even be willing to entertain, or—

"If we could accelerate this whole getting-me-unstuck business, Edgar, I would be forever grateful," Wilhelmina suddenly said, pulling him straight back to the situation at hand. "Especially since we're beginning to draw attention."

Looking over his shoulder, he discovered that was, indeed, the case. Quite a few guests seemed to be edging their way. Turning back to Wilhelmina, he squatted down right next to her. "Do you think the fabric of your skirt snagged on a nail?"

"I'm afraid I'm no longer that type of stuck, Edgar. It's more a case of my, um, parts, not exactly fitting in the small amount of space I tried to squish them into."

It took everything in him to swallow the laugh he longed to release.

Wilhelmina had never been a lady possessed of a waifish figure—a situation that had bothered her no small amount, although he had always, especially as he'd gotten older, found her curves to be rather agreeable. He'd never mentioned that to her, of course. A circumstance he'd been thankful for after she'd broken his heart by rejecting him out of—

"And besides being firmly wedged between the legs of this chair, I think that, what with all the wiggling I've done since I got stuck, my bustle has now become firmly lodged against the seat."

Having never been presented with this specific dilemma before, Edgar couldn't help but feel a touch relieved when Miss Permilia Griswold stepped forward. Tapping her chin with a gloved finger—one that, curiously enough, seemed to be stained with a bit of ink—she tilted her head, then tilted it the other way, before she frowned.

"I'm afraid we're going to have to resort to brute force to release Miss Radcliff from her unfortunate predicament," Miss Griswold said before she turned an unexpectedly bright smile Wilhelmina's way. "The silver lining of this situation, though, can certainly be seen in the fact that bustles have not yet reached the size they're being predicted to reach."

"I'm not certain I see that as a silver lining, but . . ." Wilhelmina's eyes widened. "Did you just say that bustles are expected to get even larger?"

Miss Griswold nodded. "I'm afraid so. According to one of my sources—er . . . friends, I mean—quite a few designers are beginning to contemplate a new silhouette for ladies—one that will require bustles to achieve the size of a large birdcage in order to pull off the look designers are convinced will be complimentary to every lady's figure."

"Who in the world would want to wear a birdcage on their behind?" Miss Cadwalader asked, once again in possession of the platter of treats, treats she immediately began perusing, looking completely delighted.

Miss Griswold reached out, snagged a sugar biscuit, popped it into her mouth, and shrugged even as she swallowed. "I'm sure there are very few ladies who'd appreciate such an appendage attached to them, but evidently the gentlemen in charge of our fashions seem to believe that larger behinds are . . ."

She stopped talking, shot a look to Edgar, turned pink in the face, and immediately returned her attention to Wilhelmina. "Bustles aside, though, we do need to address your predicament, and I'm afraid to say that the only way we're going to be able to free you is by tugging that chair straight off of you." She moved closer and took hold of the back of the chair. "I'm sure this won't hurt too much." Before Wilhelmina could voice even the tiniest of protests, Miss Griswold began tugging on the chair, emitting occasional grunts as she tugged.

"What in the world are you doing, Miss Griswold?" someone demanded from behind them.

Turning, Edgar discovered that Mrs. Travers, their hostess for the evening, had joined them. And unfortunately, she was looking less than pleased.

Miss Griswold let go of the chair, wiped a hand across a brow that seemed to have taken to perspiring, and blew out a breath. "Miss Radcliff is stuck, Mrs. Travers. I'm simply trying to see her released."

Mrs. Travers immediately switched her attention to Wilhelmina. "One would think, given that your presence here tonight is as my social secretary, not as a guest, that you would have taken greater care with the manner in which you comport yourself, Miss Radcliff."

Wilhelmina lifted her chin in a surprisingly regal manner for a woman stuck underneath a chair. "I do apologize, Mrs. Travers, for causing you undue distress. I certainly didn't deliberately set out to get in my current predicament. It simply . . . happened."

"But *how* did it happen?" Mrs. Travers demanded.

"That's a bit difficult to explain," Wilhelmina began. She was spared further response, though, when Miss Cadwalader took that moment to join the conversation.

"She's under there because of the mouse," Miss Cadwalader said in a very loud, very carrying, voice before she took what looked to be some type of cookie from the platter and began nibbling around the edges of it.

"A . . . mouse?" Mrs. Travers repeated slowly.

Miss Cadwalader stopped nibbling and nodded. "Indeed, and it wasn't a little mouse, mind you, but an enormous one, with rather large teeth." She sent what almost seemed to be the smallest of winks Wilhelmina's way. "Miss Radcliff should be commended for being brave enough to take on such a beast, but as she was attempting to lure the creature away, she got stuck underneath that chair." Miss Cadwalader heaved a sigh. "Unfortunately the mouse charged straight through the middle of the ballroom floor."

Edgar could only watch in dumbfounded amazement as chaos immediately took over the ball. The chaos started when one of the ladies who'd been inching ever so casually closer to them let out a shriek, lifted up the hem of her skirt, and was soon standing on top of a chair, joined seconds later by additional ladies, their shrieks about mice being on the loose echoing around the ballroom. In the span of a single minute, all the chairs were occupied with ladies holding their hems up as servants began dashing into the room, all of them carrying brooms.

Edgar heard Wilhelmina toss "That was brilliant" Miss Cadwalader's way as Mrs. Travers seemingly forgot all about Wilhelmina being stuck underneath a chair as she hurried off to join the chaos that was interrupting her ball.

Miss Cadwalader grinned. "I do have my uses."

Wilhelmina returned the grin. "Indeed you do—even though I have to say that, if I had seen a mouse, I'm hardly the type to throw myself on the floor in an attempt to lure it away."

With eyes that had taken to sparkling, Miss Cadwalader's grin widened. "A most excellent point, Miss Radcliff, but quite honestly, I didn't contemplate the mouse explanation very long before it simply burst out of my mouth." Her gaze traveled over the commotion erupting around them. "I certainly had no idea that my explanation would bring about such an exciting twist to the ball."

"I'm afraid your time at the ball may get even more exciting, Miss Cadwalader," Miss Griswold said with a rather significant nod of her head toward a hallway. "I don't mean to be an alarmist, but I do believe I just saw your companion, Mrs. Davenport, scurry out of the room and toward what is probably the private living quarters of the family."

Miss Cadwalader turned rather pale. "You said *scurry*, but should I assume it was more of a *skulk?*"

"I suppose her attitude did have a touch of skulking mixed in with the scurrying," Miss Griswold admitted.

Squaring her shoulders, Miss Cadwalader shook her head. "Honestly, one would think that Mrs. Davenport would have learned her lesson after the last time she went skulking about, but . . . apparently that is not the case." She sent everyone a nod. "Please excuse me. I simply must go and have a little chat with my employer. I do hope no one will mind if I take the treats with me." A bit of pink settled on her cheeks. "They may very well help me entice Mrs. Davenport from . . . Well, no need to get into that." Turning on her heel, Miss Cadwalader hurried away, clutching the platter of treats close, as if she wanted to make certain no one would try to take them away from her.

"That was curious" was all Edgar could think to say when silence, except for all the screaming and shrieking still surrounding them, settled over their small group. Turning to Miss Griswold, the only person left to assist him, he gestured to Wilhelmina, who was still stuck underneath her chair. "I think our best plan of attack, Miss Griswold, would be for you to see if you can get that bustle unstuck. It would hardly be proper for me to attend to that particular task."

"Too right you are, Mr. Wanamaker," Miss Griswold replied before she dropped to her knees beside Wilhelmina. A moment later, after she'd taken to shoving a great deal of the material that made up Wilhelmina's skirt out of the way, Miss Griswold stuck a hand under the chair and set about the tricky business of trying to get Wilhelmina free.

After a great deal of grunting, mutters, and even a yelp or three coming from Wilhelmina, Miss Griswold tipped up her head and caught his gaze.

"I do believe we're almost there, Mr. Wanamaker," Miss Griswold began. "All that's left to do is for me to squeeze Miss Radcliff's, ah . . . gown together—the part that covers her, ah, hips—as tightly as I can in an effort to make her smaller, and when I say ready, you'll need to pull off the chair."

Sending her a nod, even as he tried to hold back a smile over the whole hip-squeezing business, Miss Griswold turned back to Wilhelmina and then said, "Ready," even as Wilhelmina let out another yelp.

Hoping for the best, he took hold of the chair and gave it a good yank, breathing a sigh of relief a second later when it popped free of Wilhelmina, leaving her still on the floor but without a chair attached to her.

Accepting the hand he offered her, Wilhelmina got to her feet and then took to shaking out the folds of her skirt while he helped Miss Griswold up from the floor as well. Beaming a smile his way, and then turning that smile on Miss Griswold, Wilhelmina inclined her head.

"Thank goodness the two of you were able to see me released. Truth be told, I was beginning to think I'd have to return home with a chair stuck to my behind."

"Which would have been a very interesting sight to see," Miss Griswold said. "However, now that we've gotten your dastardly situation under control, I'm afraid I must take my leave of your company as well. I completely forgot that my stepsister, Lucy, is supposed to participate in the quadrille planned for this evening. Since young ladies do seem to be climbing down from their chairs—apparently having come to the conclusion that they won't be getting mauled by a rampaging mouse anytime soon—I'm sure the quadrille is about to begin." She released a bit of a sigh. "Heaven forbid I'm not standing

by my stepmother's side when Lucy glides across the ballroom floor."
Giving Wilhelmina's arm a squeeze, Miss Griswold sent Edgar a small
curtsy and then breezed away.

"She's an unusual lady, isn't she?" he asked.

Wilhelmina pulled her attention away from Miss Griswold's retreating back and settled it on him. "I think she's delightful, but speaking
of unusual—it's rather unusual to discover you in New York, and at
a ball, no less. I don't recall seeing your name on the invitation list."

"Mr. Asher Rutherford secured me a last-minute invitation directly
from Mrs. Travers."

"Was there a specific reason you had Mr. Rutherford do that?"

Edgar smiled. "Curiously enough, there was, and . . . that reason
revolves around you and my need to speak with you about a matter
of great urgency."

Wilhelmina narrowed her eyes. "A matter of great urgency?"

"Indeed," Edgar returned as he took a single step closer to her.
"You see . . . I've decided that it's time for me to consider the idea of
marriage. But, before I proceed further with that decision, I feel it's
imperative that you and I settle matters between us once and for all."

3

"You're getting married?" Wilhelmina somehow managed to get past a throat that had, oddly enough, taken to constricting.

Edgar's brows drew together. "That's not what I said at all. I said I'd decided to get married, but that you and I needed to settle matters between us before I could pursue that decision."

"Have you asked a lady to marry you?" she pressed.

"Why is it that I suddenly feel as if you and I are not sharing the same conversation?" Edgar took a firm grip of her arm and, without asking her permission, began escorting her across the floor at a remarkably fast clip.

Dodging one dancer after another, all of whom were attempting to take their proper places on the ballroom floor, Wilhelmina found her steps faltering ever so slightly when she caught sight of the quadrille leader for that evening, Mr. Dyer. He, unfortunately, was sending a glare her way—brought on no doubt by the fact she and Edgar were disrupting his well-structured dance.

"Where are you trying to take me?" she asked as they passed a group of young ladies, none of whom were making the slightest attempt to hide the fact they were gawking Edgar's way.

"We need to find somewhere private to speak."

"If you've forgotten, we're in the midst of a ball. Privacy is next to impossible to find, unless you want to chance being discovered in what society will assume is a compromising situation. Which," she hurried to say, "is not something I'm willing to do."

Edgar stopped in his tracks. "I would never place you in a compromising situation."

Remorse was swift. Edgar had always been, first and foremost, a gentleman, and implying differently had done him a grave disservice. Inclining her head, Wilhelmina touched his arm. "Do forgive me, Edgar. I didn't mean to question your integrity. Of course you would never place me in a compromising situation."

"Thank you," he said shortly as he prodded her into motion again. Before she knew it, she was standing in front of a pair of French doors.

"I think these might lead outside to the back terrace," she said.

"Which will be the perfect spot for us to have a chat."

Opening her mouth to point out the pesky fact that it was January, in New York of all places, she suddenly found herself unable to speak a single word, because Edgar had gone ahead and opened one of the doors right before he practically pushed her outside and into what could only be described as a blizzard.

"What a lovely night to enjoy a chat outside," she yelled over a howling wind that was tossing snow every which way. "Although I should probably point out that it's not exactly weather a lady wearing a ball gown is usually subjected to, nor . . ."

Before she could finish her complaint, Edgar had shrugged out of his black tailcoat, stuffed her unceremoniously into it, then took hold of her hand and began hauling her forward again.

"Where are we going?" she yelled.

"I overheard a lady remarking about Mrs. Travers having a conservatory back here. It'll be the perfect place for us to have our chat," he called back.

Wilhelmina wrinkled her nose. "Far be it from me to point out the obvious, but since we only recently broached the subject of compromising situations, I feel I really should—"

The rest of her words were cut off when the snow suddenly began whipping around them, stealing the very breath from her. Lowering her head, Wilhelmina didn't bother to protest further, and before she knew it, they'd reached the conservatory in question. Opening the door for her, Edgar ushered her inside and pulled the door firmly shut behind him.

A blast of warm, moist air settled over her.

"See?" he began, brushing snow out of his hair before he brushed it off the sleeves of his starched white shirt and matching silk waistcoat. "I told you it would be the perfect spot, and it's definitely quiet."

"And secluded," she pointed out, shrugging out of his tailcoat and handing it back to him.

Taking the coat, Edgar smiled. "A most excellent point, although given that there is a blizzard raging about outside, I doubt anyone from the warm and toasty confines of the ballroom will feel compelled to follow us. Besides, I doubt anyone even noticed us leaving."

"Didn't you notice that entire gaggle of young ladies perusing you?"

A flash of amusement flickered through Edgar's eyes. "Why, Willie, if I didn't know better, I'd say you sounded a touch jealous just now."

"Don't be ridiculous, and stop calling me Willie."

Instead of looking the least bit contrite, Edgar grinned and took hold of her arm. He steered her along a stone pathway that wound through the many plants surrounding them.

"I am quite capable of walking on my own," she said, ducking underneath the branch of a lush fern that seemed to be thriving in the environment the conservatory provided.

"I don't recall suggesting you weren't, but as I am a gentleman, and the floor of this conservatory does seem to be a little slick, I'd be remiss in my role as that gentleman if I didn't make certain any hazard to your well-being was avoided."

Opening her mouth to apologize once again, she immediately swallowed the apology when she noticed that his lips had taken to twitching at the corners. Tugging her arm free of his, she moved over to a stone bench flanked by some exotic-looking red flowers and took a seat.

She was not amused when he took a seat right beside her, crowding her in the process.

"When did you get so large?" she asked, scooting as casually as she could away from him, not allowing herself to dwell on why his nearness was bothering her.

"When I began working in a steel mill."

Wilhelmina blinked. "You worked in a steel mill?"

Nodding, Edgar smiled. "Surprising, I know, but I'd studied up on the improvements being made in the steel industry while I was attending the university. When I left New York directly after your debut, I decided I needed a distraction. Since steel was becoming in high demand, what with all the bridges and buildings being built in the city, it was the perfect time for me to get some real-life experience within the steel industry."

The casual manner in which Edgar mentioned his need for a distraction didn't fool Wilhelmina in the least. She'd hurt him by rejecting his offer of marriage, and now seemed to be the perfect time to make amends for the hurt she'd dealt him.

Reaching out, she oh-so-casually poked his upper arm, impressed when she felt the hardness underneath his shirt. "While it's obvious you benefited quite notably from your stint in the steel mills, I do want you to know that I'm truly sorry for the pain I put you through when I refused to marry you." She sighed. "It was not well done of me to have treated you in such a cavalier manner, and I have wanted to apologize to you for years."

She caught his gaze. "I did ask your mother about you whenever our paths crossed, but . . . she refused to divulge your whereabouts, and truth be told, I believe she has yet to forgive me for rejecting your proposal."

"Of course she hasn't forgiven you, Wilhelmina. In her mind, you hurt the feelings of her adorable—and need I remind you, charming—son. Which is why she still takes to muttering less-than-pleasant mutters about you under her breath whenever I try to bring you into the conversation."

Edgar gave a sad shake of his head. "She's especially put out with you over the idea that you proclaimed—in front of witnesses, no less—that the very last thing you'd ever want in life was to be known as Wilhelmina Wanamaker for the rest of your days."

Wilhelmina winced. "I completely forgot about that. Do know that I will apologize to your mother about that nasty business, *if* she ever condescends to speak to me again, that is."

"As you should, since Mother always proclaimed that Wilhelmina Wanamaker had a very nice ring to it, a proclamation she's certain you remembered, which has allowed her to believe you were insulting not only me the night of your debut, but her as well."

"Oh . . . dear."

"Oh dear, indeed," Edgar agreed quite cheerfully.

Wilhelmina blew out a breath. "I do hope you know that I didn't deliberately set out to hurt your feelings that particular night, or hurt the feelings of your mother by my careless words. I was simply taken by surprise when you dropped to one knee and proposed to me, in the middle of the ballroom. And because of that, I fear my response was not what anyone could consider kind."

Edgar reached out and took her hand in his. "And that right there, my dear Wilhelmina, is one of the reasons I needed to speak with you. You seem to be under the misimpression that you wronged me the night of your debut, which couldn't be further from the truth. I was the one in the wrong. For that, I am truly sorry, and I hope you'll find it within your heart to accept that apology."

"You returned to the city to apologize to me?" she asked. "I thought you mentioned something about marriage."

"I can't very well move forward with my life while I still have so many issues left unresolved with you."

"So you *are* intending on getting married?"

Edgar frowned. "I'm twenty-eight years old. I certainly can't make the claim that the thought of marriage hasn't flashed to mind more and more often as time goes ticking on by at a remarkable faster and faster clip."

Wilhelmina's brows drew together. "And you have a specific lady in mind to do this settling down with?"

With his brows drawing together as well, Edgar took to considering her for a long moment, something interesting taking up residence in his eyes. "I would imagine that I do have a lady in mind, although . . .

I'm not certain she returns my interest." The look in his eyes intensi-
fied. "Tell me this, Wilhelmina. . . . Why do you sound so disgruntled
by the idea of me settling down?"

Swallowing the denial that had been on the very tip of her tongue,
Wilhelmina considered the question, realizing a mere second later that
she *was* disgruntled. The reasoning behind that disgruntlement, curiously enough, seemed to revolve around the idea that the very thought
of him marrying another woman set her teeth on edge.

Drawing in a sharp breath over that revelation, she then completely
forgot all about releasing the breath when truth reared up and smacked
her firmly over the head.

Edgar Wanamaker—no matter that she'd rejected him out of hand
and hadn't set eyes on him for years—was a gentleman she could
easily picture herself growing old with, sharing children with, and
. . . loving . . . forever.

That she hadn't even realized any of that until this very moment,
with him sitting right beside her no less, had her feeling distinctly
light-headed, although that might have been because she'd been holding her breath and . . .

"On my word, Willie, you've taken to looking rather queasy—what
with your face turning that somewhat disturbing shade of green. Are
you all right?"

Having no idea how to respond to that since she was certainly
not all right—especially since the world as she knew it had suddenly
taken a turn for the concerning—Wilhelmina pulled her hand from
Edgar's and rose to her feet. "I'm afraid the heat in this conservatory
has begun taking a toll on me, which means we really should return
to the ball."

Rising to his feet as well, Edgar took hold of her arm, pulled her
directly over to a door that led to the back of the conservatory, pushed
it open, and pulled her outside with him.

A blast of freezing air settled over her, followed by snow. Blinking
flakes out of her lashes and feeling anything but overly warm, she
lifted her head and caught his eye. "This wasn't exactly what I had
in mind when I said the heat had gotten to me."

Edgar smiled. "But I imagine it did the trick, though, didn't it? You're looking far less queasy now, and . . . we'll be able to finish our conversation without being surrounded by curious guests."

Not caring to hear more about his marriage plans, Wilhelmina lifted her chin. "I'm not certain we have much more to discuss."

Taking hold of her hand, Edgar pulled her back inside the conservatory and hustled her straight back to their bench. Lowering himself down beside her, he pulled her hand back into his.

"Now then, where were we?" he asked pleasantly.

"How is it possible that I'd forgotten how stubborn you can be?" she asked.

"I'm sure I have no idea, since I've been told that stubbornness is part of my charm."

"I'm not certain I'd call it charming, but . . ." She felt her lips begin to curve. "I have, curiously enough, missed your incredibly stubborn self over the last few years."

"And I've missed your incredibly delightful habit of contradicting me at every turn."

"I'm sure I don't contradict you at *every* turn," she said as he quirked a brow her way.

"I'm sure you do, but before we find ourselves at sixes and sevens with each other, tell me what you've been doing over the years I've been gone."

Having no wish to speak about the mundane path her life had traveled of late, she shook her head. "I'd much rather hear about you, specifically about that stint in a steel mill you mentioned."

"I still work in the steel industry," Edgar began. "Although I work in my own mills instead of working for someone else these days."

"Which does explain why someone mentioned you've returned to town with a respectable fortune at your disposal."

"I don't know if I'd consider my fortune as being at the respectable level as of yet, but I do have high hopes for the future if my Pittsburgh mills keep performing as well as they have been of late."

Wilhelmina wrinkled her nose. "You live in Pittsburgh?"

"Why do I get the distinct feeling that I've just said something that's gotten me into trouble?"

228

"Because Pittsburgh isn't that far away from New York City, and yet, you've stayed remarkably absent from New York these past seven years."

Edgar's brows drew together. "Who said I haven't visited New York over the past seven years?"

For a second, she found herself speechless, but only for a second. "Are you saying that you've come home often but have never, as in ever, stopped in to see me?"

"Surely, given that you were once very familiar with my mother, you couldn't have thought that she'd be willing to accept the idea that I'd not visit her for occasions such as her birthday and other holidays, could you?"

"You've been back *numerous* times?"

Edgar had the audacity to laugh. "I must admit that your indignation is doing wonders for that wounded pride I've been living with for years."

"I highly doubt your pride was wounded for years," she said with her best attempt at a sniff, an attempt she obviously didn't pull off well since he laughed again.

Giving her hand a bit of a pat, Edgar leaned closer. "My pride was wounded long enough, thank you very much, especially since I'd never considered the idea that you'd turn down my marriage proposal."

"Your proposal took me by complete surprise."

Edgar nodded. "I realized that almost as soon as it popped out of my mouth and you turned a concerning shade of white. But, in my defense, it never crossed my mind that you hadn't come to the same conclusion I had—that conclusion being that we'd spend our lives together. We were the closest of friends."

Her shoulders took to drooping. "I know we were, but in *my* defense, I was young, selfish, and somewhat self-absorbed the night of my debut." She released a tiny sigh. "Quite honestly, it wasn't as if the thought had *never* crossed my mind that you and I might very well see ourselves married at some point in the future—the very distant future. However, on that particular evening, my only clear objective was to be admired and fawned over as I made what I hoped was going to be a most spectacular debut."

Edgar brought her hand up to his lips and pressed a quick kiss on it. "You were absolutely beautiful that night, deserved to bask in all the attention you were receiving, and . . ." He smiled and lowered her hand. "If it makes you feel less guilty, do know that I've come to believe that your rejection was one of the best things that could have ever happened to me."

4

"You're *thankful* I rejected your offer?" Wilhelmina all but sputtered.

To her extreme annoyance, Edgar didn't hesitate to nod. "But of course. To refresh your memory, I was quite aimless before you rejected me. My older brother, if you'll recall, was responsible for taking over the family business while I was left to do whatever I pleased." His smile dimmed. "While you and I know many second sons who embrace a frivolous lifestyle, I was beginning to find that frivolous life quite boring, and was counting on my marriage to you to change that."

"May I assume you decided that you would have grown bored with me as well?" The indignation bubbling up inside her was making it a little difficult to think.

He winced. "That didn't come out nearly the way I intended, and I fear I may very well be making a muddle of this."

"Too right you are."

He sent her one of his most charming of smiles, the one he'd always brought out whenever he'd done something to annoy her in the past. The sight of it had her stomach feeling as if an entire flock of butterflies had begun fluttering through it, a feeling she didn't appreciate in the least—especially considering how annoyed she was with the gentleman at the moment.

"Now that we've gotten that out of the way," he continued, although Wilhelmina wasn't exactly certain what they'd gotten out of the way, "I'd like to offer you a sincere apology for the distress I caused you all those years ago."

She waved his apology aside. "You've already apologized, Edgar. And again, I was more at fault than you that night."

"I ruined what should have been one of your most memorable nights."

"You didn't ruin anything."

"You *weren't* upset that I called you a brat and told you that you'd be sorry for years and years to come that I'd never again be in your life?"

"Well, when you remind of those particular memories, yes, I was upset with you, but . . ." She smiled. "After you stormed away from my father's house, there were quite a few gentlemen who seemed very keen to try and cheer me up."

He narrowed his eyes. "You're still a bit of a brat, aren't you."

Getting up from the bench, she sent him a grin before she began wandering down one of the aisles, not surprised when he joined her. Stopping beside an unusual purple flower, she leaned forward to give it a sniff. "While I freely admit that I once fit the description of a brat to perfection, I'm afraid I have far too many responsibilities these days to indulge myself with that particular attitude."

Edgar reached out and traced a finger down the curve of her cheek, his touch lodging the breath in her throat. "I've heard from my mother that your father does not seem to be well these days. In fact, according to her, he's not seen out and about in the city at all."

Resisting the urge to sigh when he stopped touching her cheek, Wilhelmina took hold of the arm Edgar offered her and started down the path. "He never leaves the house," she admitted. "And what I'm about to tell you is not well-known information. You see, when Father learned he'd lost the majority of his fortune in a shipping deal gone bad two years ago, he became embroiled in an argument with Mr. Jonathon Melville, the man he'd trusted to see the deal through. While Father was engaged in that heated argument, he, unfortunately, suffered an apoplectic fit. He lost his ability to speak for three months, and while he has made some improvements recovering his speech and mobility, he's turned morose over losing his fortune, and quite honestly, I believe he's given up all interest in living."

Edgar pulled her to a stop. "Your father lost everything?"

Wilhelmina nodded. "I'm afraid he did, or almost everything. He'd overextended himself you see, or so the bankers have told me, to cover the shipping investment. When the entire fleet of ships went down while crossing the ocean, most of my father's money went down with them."

"The entire fleet went down?"

"I'm afraid so."

"And this Mr. Melville—he suffered a great loss as well?"

"We haven't see Mr. Melville since he dashed out of our old house on Park Avenue—leaving Father writhing about on the ground, no less."

Edgar's dark brows drew together. "You said your *old* house on Park Avenue. May I assume you were forced to move out of it due to lack of funds?"

"We were forced to sell all but one of our homes, including the cottage on Long Island." She summoned up a smile when she realized Edgar had taken to looking downright horrified. "However, we were able to retain that little house my mother's aunt left her years ago, the one that's located on the less-than-fashionable side of Gramercy Park, so it's not as if we were cast out into the streets."

Lifting her gloved hand, Edgar placed a kiss on it. "Why didn't you simply marry well in order to avoid having to sell all of your father's property? From what I've been told, you spent quite a few seasons fending off one proposal after another."

Ignoring the shivers that had started inching up her arm the moment his lips touched her gloved hand, Wilhelmina tilted her head. "Keeping an eye on me over the years, were you?"

Edgar smiled. "My mother, while remarkably stingy with news of you, did see fit to write to me about your many conquests." He shook his head. "In all honesty, I think she passed those tidbits along as a way of discouraging me from continual wallowing over the years in regard to you and your rejection."

"I'm surprised your mother didn't write to tell you about my fall from grace," Wilhelmina muttered, earning another smile from Edgar in the process.

"Given the extent of your fall, and the fact that you've apparently taken up a position that has you working as a social secretary, or so Miss Kasson told me, I'm surprised as well. Although . . ." Edgar tilted his head. "Now that I think about it, it's not really so surprising that Mother never mentioned how dire your situation had turned."

"It's not?"

"Not when I take into account how upset she's been with you over the years for not becoming her daughter-in-law—a relationship I believe she'd been looking forward to embracing. Because of that, I can certainly see her withholding information that might have sent me racing off to your rescue."

Unexpected tears took that moment to cloud Wilhelmina's vision. Dashing a hand over her eyes, she plopped down on the nearby bench and released a bit of a watery-sounding snort. "I wouldn't have expected you to race to my rescue, Edgar, especially not given the abhorrent manner in which I'd treated you."

As he sat beside her, Edgar captured a tear she'd missed with his finger. "We may have parted on less than amicable terms, Wilhelmina, but you were my dearest friend throughout my childhood, and a bit beyond. Because of that, you should have known that I was a person you could always count on."

Wilhelmina struggled to hold additional tears at bay. "Did your mother ever mention anything to you about a gentleman by the name of Mr. Holland?"

"Of course she did, although she didn't go into any particulars except to tell me he was one of your many admirers. But even if this Mr. Holland was a gentleman you cared deeply about, I would have still offered you my assistance if you had need of it."

A single tear leaked out of her eye, one she hid by dipping her head and pretending an interest in a somewhat ordinary yellow flower. "I never cared deeply about Mr. Holland, Edgar. He was very diligent as he went about the whole business of courting me, but a part of me knew that something simply wasn't right with him. He was always too well-dressed, too charming, and paid too much attention to me."

"You took issue with him because he paid too much attention to you?"

"I did because it was a deliberate attention, although I didn't realize that at the time. But then, when he ended his courtship of me because he needed to marry a woman of fortune, well . . . everything became crystal clear. In all honesty, I was somewhat relieved to have him out of my life, but then he went and started the most dreadful rumors about me, implying there was something wrong with me. That right there is what set society against me and saw me banished to the wallflower section."

"There's nothing wrong with you," Edgar began before he suddenly took to cracking his knuckles. "But tell me, where is Mr. Holland now?"

With her spirits lifting the moment she heard him crack his knuckles, Wilhelmina pulled her attention away from the yellow flower and smiled. "It's very sweet of you to adopt such a protective attitude on my behalf, Edgar. But sad as I am to tell you this, I'm afraid Mr. Holland is no longer in the city. He's sailing about the world on a yacht his new wife bought for him, a wife who had quite the impressive fortune, and a fortune she was apparently all too willing to share with Mr. Holland if he agreed to marry her."

She shook her head somewhat sadly. "I'm afraid the current Mrs. Holland was under the impression Mr. Holland was a bit of a prize."

"Perhaps by now, she'd appreciate me teaching Mr. Holland some manners then."

"Since she's not sailing on that yacht around the world with him, Edgar, you probably have a most excellent point, but again, he's not in New York."

Edgar cracked his knuckles one more time. "Very well, I won't be able to deal with him just yet. But mark my words, Mr. Holland will be made to pay for his abuse of you. It's simply a question of when."

Unable to help but wonder how in the world she'd been so ridiculous back in the day to let this very honorable, and incredibly sweet, gentleman get away from her, Wilhelmina forced a smile. "Goodness, Edgar, there's no need for you to turn all threatening on my behalf. That nasty business with Mr. Holland happened ages ago, and I assure you, I'm quite over it."

"If you were quite over the embarrassment of Mr. Holland's abandonment, and then your subsequent tumble down the society ladder, you wouldn't have bothered to try and hide from me earlier."

Not quite knowing what to do with the idea that Edgar still seemed to understand her far too well, Wilhelmina gave a bit of a shrug. "Perhaps I was simply trying to hide from you because I didn't know what to say to you after all these years."

He narrowed his eyes on her. "That excuse would have been more believable if you'd been at a loss for words for more than a second since I've been in your company."

Narrowing her eyes right back at him, Wilhelmina found herself caught in his gaze, the intensity having her breath catching in her throat. Knowing he was not going to be distracted from the subject at hand, she allowed her shoulders to sag ever so slightly. "Oh, very well. You're right. I was embarrassed and didn't want you to see how far I've fallen in the world."

Both of her hands were suddenly taken in his. "You, my darling friend, are not, and could never be, defined by the position you hold within society."

"I'm fairly certain I've been defined by society as nothing more than a wallflower these days."

Drawing her closer, he tipped her chin up and met her gaze. "You may be known as a wallflower to society, Wilhelmina, but I'll always think of you as the most extraordinary woman I've ever known."

With that, and before she could do more than let out the tiniest of sighs, he leaned closer to her, his breath warm against her face right before he claimed her lips with his own.

Just when her entire body began tingling in a most delicious fashion, a blast of cold air swirled around them, the unexpectedness of it having her pulling her lips from Edgar's.

Swiveling around on the bench, every tingle she'd been feeling disappeared as dread settled over her when she caught sight of Mrs. Travers marching her way.

To Wilhelmina's concern, the lady was not alone but was accompanied by two ladies, both of whom were dusted with snow and one of whom turned out to be Miss Permilia Griswold.

Miss Griswold, Wilhelmina couldn't help but notice, was in the process of sending looks of extreme annoyance to the other young lady, that annoyance, for some odd reason, calming a bit of the dread that had taken to sinking into Wilhelmina's very bones.

Coming to a stop a few feet away from where Wilhelmina was sitting, Mrs. Travers lifted her chin and folded her arms over her chest.

"I was hoping Miss Lucy Webster," Mrs. Travers began, nodding to the young lady standing beside her, a young lady Wilhelmina realized must be Miss Griswold's stepsister, "was mistaken when she sought me out and whispered that she'd seen you disappear with Mr. Wanamaker, but . . . clearly that is not the case. So . . . explain yourself, Miss Radcliff."

"Ah . . . well, you see . . ."

"I'll take it from here, darling," Edgar said, moving a step away from the bench he'd risen from the moment Mrs. Travers had marched into the room. Presenting Mrs. Travers with a bow, he straightened. "Allow me to assure you, Mrs. Travers, that there is absolutely nothing untoward transpiring at the moment. In fact, it is my great pleasure to disclose to you that, right in the midst of your delightful ball, Miss Wilhelmina Radcliff has finally agreed to become . . . my wife."

5

"Ah, darling, how wonderful that you've finally decided to grace me with your delightful presence. One would have thought you might have considered seeking me out earlier, what with all the questions you left me with after our little talk we shared late last night."

Handing his heavy greatcoat to Mr. Hodges, the family butler, Edgar lifted his head and set his sights on his mother, Nora Wanamaker.

Curiously enough, he found her sitting smack-dab in the middle of the entranceway with a shawl wrapped around her shoulders. The chair she was sitting in was one that normally resided in the drawing room, as was the small table that was right beside the chair, and the fact that her slipper-clad feet were resting on a small pouf of a footstool had him struggling to swallow a laugh.

"I do beg your pardon, Mother," he began, wiping his feet on the entranceway mat before walking in her direction. "I'm afraid the weather is beyond dreadful today, so it took me longer than expected to take care of business around the city this morning. However, foul weather aside, you haven't been sitting here long, have you?" he asked, leaning down to place a kiss on his mother's upturned cheek.

After he straightened, Nora immediately took to consulting a small watch pinned to the underside of her sleeve. "I've been waiting here for exactly two hours and forty-seven minutes."

"Why in the world wouldn't you have simply waited for me in the drawing room, where I'm sure there's a roaring fire in the fireplace and a lovely view of the snow-covered trees from the windows?"

"And chance missing you again?" Nora folded her hands primly in her lap. "I think not. After returning home from the ball, you, my dear boy, were unsatisfactorily vague about where matters stood with Wilhelmina. Because of that, I'm sorry to say that I eventually came to the conclusion that you might very well try your hand at avoidance tactics—your goal with that being, of course, to avoid *me*."

A scraping noise distracted Edgar from the slightly concerning conversation he was sharing with his mother. Turning, he discovered Mr. Hodges dragging a chair—one that matched the chair his mother was sitting in—across the entranceway. Angling it exactly so, Mr. Hodges gestured Edgar toward it.

Not caring to disappoint the butler who'd taken to moping his brow with a handkerchief—the exertion from the dragging apparently having been a bit much for the man—Edgar settled into the chair and accepted the cup of tea his mother poured for him from a silver pot resting on her small table. Taking a sip, he regarded his mother and Mr. Hodges, refusing to sigh when they took to watching him in what could only be described as an anticipatory way.

"What do you think?" Nora asked when he lowered the cup.

"About your suspicious nature, or . . . something else?"

"The tea, dear," she said with a sniff. "I don't possess a suspicious nature."

"Of course you don't, especially given the unusual occurrence of you taking up a position in the entranceway."

He thought he heard his mother mutter something about "Daunting circumstances call for unusual methods" before she tugged the shawl more snuggly around herself. "The entranceway suits me this morning." She lifted her nose in the air. "But returning to the tea . . . ?"

Taking another sip of tea, he smiled. "It's excellent as I'm certain you already know."

Nora picked up her own cup and saluted him with it. "Your friend Mr. Asher Rutherford sent the tea to me the other day, seeking my opinion about the blend before he makes a firm decision on whether or not to stock it in his charming shop." Her eyes turned rather distant. "Asher is such a dear, sweet boy, one whom I have to imagine never gives his mother a second of trouble."

It took a concerted effort to avoid releasing the snort he longed to release. "I've known Asher Rutherford since my school days, Mother, and believe me, he is no angel—no matter that he seems especially proficient at convincing the mothers of his closest friends he is."

Nora pursed her lips. "Any gentleman who has been able to create such an inviting atmosphere for ladies to shop in has to be possessed of a most considerate nature, darling. Why, he has actually decorated the designer room in shades of pale pink, giving clear testimony to what I can only describe as his sensitive side."

Seeing little point in arguing with his mother, or disappointing her by explaining that Asher had only chosen the pink because he'd discovered that particular color seemed to increase spending in his store, Edgar crossed one ankle over the other and sent his mother a smile. "I'll be sure to tell Asher that you're impressed with how sensitive he is. But really, Mother, I must admit I take issue with the direction of this conversation. I have rarely caused you any trouble, something your earlier statement seems to suggest you've forgotten."

"You don't think the current state of affairs with Wilhelmina constitutes a troubling situation?"

"Since I haven't seen Wilhelmina since we parted ways at the ball last night, I can't say with any certainty just yet if she and I *are* involved in anything that could be considered troubling."

Nora leaned toward Edgar. "She did actually agree to marry you this time, though, didn't she? I'm afraid that is something you didn't explain to satisfaction last night."

"When you say agree, do you mean *verbally* agree?" Edgar asked slowly.

Nora took a hefty gulp of her tea, set down the cup, and exchanged a rather meaningful look with Mr. Hodges. "Didn't I tell you, Mr. Hodges, that I had a feeling Edgar hadn't settled matters properly with Wilhelmina?"

"You did, Mrs. Wanamaker, and once again, it appears you were quite right."

Edgar pretended he hadn't heard that bit of nonsense. "The only reason Wilhelmina and I didn't completely settle matters between us was because we were forced to contend with a blizzard."

"What does that have to do with you being unable to settle matters properly with Wilhelmina?" Nora demanded.

"I'm getting to that," Edgar said even as he caught his mother and Mr. Hodges exchange yet another significant glance.

"You're not getting to it very quickly," his mother muttered.

"It's not a very complicated story, Mother," Edgar returned. "Right after I announced to Mrs. Travers that Wilhelmina and I were getting married, the walls of the conservatory we were in began shaking quite fiercely, lending credence to the idea that the blizzard was increasing in intensity. Because of that, I, along with Wilhelmina, Mrs. Travers, Miss Permilia Griswold, and a lady I believe was named Miss Lucy Webster, deemed it prudent to make our way back to the ball before the courtyard became impassable."

"Why didn't you settle matters once you returned to the ball?" Nora pressed.

"Because all the guests decided directly after we returned that it would be in their best interests to leave while they still could. However, since most of the carriages had already become buried in snow, I, along with a good many other gentlemen, were pressed into service to help get those carriages unburied."

He held up his hand when Nora opened her mouth again. "And before you inquire as to why I didn't settle matters with Wilhelmina after I finished my task, allow me to tell you that she'd accepted a ride home with Miss Griswold, a practical young lady who'd had the foresight to arrive at the ball in a sleigh."

Nora leaned forward. "Wilhelmina departing in such a cloak-and-dagger fashion seems to me to be a most ominous sign."

"There was nothing cloak and dagger about it, Mother. In fact, I was the one who encouraged her to accept Miss Griswold's offer, knowing there was little chance my carriage would be up for the task of getting Wilhelmina all the way to Gramercy Park—the area of the city where she and her family are now living."

He took a sip of his tea and regarded his mother over the rim of the cup. "I considered making my way to Wilhelmina's home after I finished seeing everyone safely off in their carriages, but by the time I got into my own carriage, the roads were almost impassable."

Nora narrowed her eyes on him. "While I must admit that does make a great deal of sense, I would have thought you'd have gone out bright and early this morning to get matters firmed up between the two of you once and for all."

"I had to meet with Asher this morning."

"Whatever for?"

"He has a useful contact in the shipping industry, a gentleman we then sought out down on 28th Street, although that seeking took far longer than I expected, given the abysmal state of the streets today."

Nora arched a brow. "Don't you believe your time would have been better spent seeking out an audience with Wilhelmina instead of visiting some shipping gentleman on 28th Street?"

"That visit is directly tied to my current situation with Wilhelmina, Mother. Although, I can't say much more on the subject just yet, since I don't know what the outcome will be from meeting with Mr. Harrison Sinclair, Asher's friend in the shipping industry."

With eyes that now held a distinct trace of annoyance, Nora let out a huff. "That is a less-than-sufficient explanation, as I'm sure you're well aware. But I'm afraid you don't have the luxury of time to finalize affairs with Wilhelmina, especially given the rumors that are already swirling around the city about the two of you. Such rumors will not aid Wilhelmina's reputation if they're not put to rest quickly."

"What rumors?" Edgar asked slowly.

"Ones that center on the idea that you and Wilhelmina were discovered alone together in Mrs. Travers' conservatory." Nora caught Edgar's eye. "The only reason the poor girl's reputation isn't in complete tatters is because rumors are also flying about that the two of you are the most romantic couple of the season—childhood sweethearts who were kept apart in your youth but who have finally been reunited."

Edgar set aside his teacup. "How, pray tell, is it even possible that rumors are swirling around the city? As I mentioned before, everyone left the ball before Mrs. Travers would have had an opportunity to do more than bid everyone a good evening. Add in the notion that the conditions outside on the streets today are less than ideal, and I would have thought that any and all rumors would have been put on hold for the foreseeable future."

Nora's forehead took to furrowing. "Surely you haven't been away from society so long that you've forgotten that there is little, even a blizzard, that can stop a good story from making the rounds." She reached over the side of her chair and snatched up a newspaper, which she immediately took to snapping open.

"Surely you're not about to tell me that Wilhelmina and I made the newspapers, are you?" Edgar asked rather weakly as Nora began thumbing through the pages.

Nora nodded. "I'm afraid you did, dear—and not a mere mention, mind you, but almost an entire column dedicated to you and Wilhelmina, a column that was penned by the illustrious and oh-so-mysterious Miss Quill."

"Miss . . . Quill?"

"She's the darling of the society columns these days, writing about the current fashions that are being worn to all the balls and operas. She's even been known to include descriptions of the interiors of the houses owned by society members, a circumstance that has had society in an uproar ever since her first column appeared two years ago."

Nora peered at him over the top of the newspaper. "Our family has endeavored to keep our business out of the public eye, but you and Wilhelmina somehow attracted Miss Quill's notice."

"How is that possible? As I said, few people even knew that Wilhelmina and I had stepped away from the crowds in order to have a private conversation."

"Far be it from me to point out the foolishness of the two of you choosing a secluded conservatory to have that conversation in, dear, but . . . you did choose it, you were discovered, and Miss Quill—bless her far too observant heart—found out about it."

Edgar sat forward. "You mentioned something about Wilhelmina and me being touted as the romance story of the season, but how in the world did that come about? Believe me, there was nothing romantic at all regarding the manner in which I announced to Mrs. Travers that there was soon to be a wedding."

"I would hope there was *something* romantic about your announcement."

"I'm afraid not."

Edgar wasn't certain, but it seemed as if his mother actually took to exchanging a rolling of the eyes with Mr. Hodges this time.

"I can only thank the good Lord above," she began after she turned back to him and Mr. Hodges assumed his usual stoic demeanor, "that your father and brother are away on business at the moment, because, well, I'm sure they'd have quite a bit to say regarding your current circumstance."

She released the tiniest of sighs. "Honestly, Edgar, one would have thought, considering you failed so spectacularly to win Wilhelmina's hand the first time you proposed to her, that you would have tried a little more diligently to pull off a romantic moment the second time around."

"And one would have thought, considering how put out you've been at Wilhelmina over her rejecting my proposal all those years ago, that you would be trying to figure out a way to get me out of marrying her rather than marrying her."

"I've always adored Wilhelmina," Nora said with a rattle of the paper she was still holding. "And while I'm sure I did lend the impression of being put out with her, that was mostly for your benefit, dear."

Edgar's mouth dropped open. "Do not tell me that you've been holding out hope all these years for something like this to happen."

"I must admit that I have, and . . . now it would seem as if that hope was not misplaced if a wedding does indeed occur between the two of you in the foreseeable future."

Reaching for his tea again, Edgar drained the cup and set it aside. "I'm hesitantly optimistic that a wedding may soon take place, espe-

244

cially since I have come to realize that I still love Wilhelmina. I find her to be a most enchanting creature, and I would be a lucky gentleman indeed if she would truly agree to become my wife."

Nora frowned. "I'm afraid I don't understand why you're only *hesitantly optimistic* about marrying Wilhelmina. You've mentioned a time or two now that you told Mrs. Travers you were to be married, and while I know you've been away from society for quite some time, surely you haven't forgotten that, as a gentleman, you have no choice but to go through with the wedding. And, as a lady, Wilhelmina can't refute your declaration, not if she wants to keep her reputation, and . . . she can forget about continuing on as a social secretary if she doesn't go through with the marriage because she'll be looked at forevermore as a woman of loose moral values."

She rattled the paper again. "Add in the article Miss Quill published, and I can say with all certainty that there *will* be a wedding to plan, whether Wilhelmina has doubts or not."

Turning his attention to the newspaper in his mother's hand, Edgar felt a trace of trepidation begin to run through him. Wilhelmina, he well remembered, was not a lady who ever did the expected. If she came to the conclusion they were being forced to marry because of Mrs. Travers and now an article penned by some mysterious Miss Quill person, there was absolutely no telling how she might react.

Reaching out, he nodded to the paper his mother was holding. "Perhaps I should take a gander at that article."

"Too right you should, dear, especially since I would have to imagine Wilhelmina has already seen Miss Quill's piece." Nora handed the paper to Edgar. "It's the article in the second column."

Scanning the page, Edgar's attention was captured by a headline he wasn't used to seeing in a reputable paper.

The Quality Corner
A Column by Miss Quill
The Most Charming Romance of the Season

"What a curious way to phrase a headline," he said.

"Miss Quill is nothing if not curious," Nora returned. "But, you'd best keep reading, dear. Prepare yourself for a bit of a . . . shock."

Finding that less than encouraging, Edgar settled his attention to the words printed on the page.

> Dear Reader,
>
> Given the dreadful weather you've woken up to today, I felt it necessary to provide you with a story that is certain to warm you all the way to your toes. Last night, in the midst of a most delightful ball, held by Mrs. T., a swoon-worthy love story took place, one that deserves an entire book written about it, but will need to settle, at least for the here and now, for my humble column.
>
> This love story, gentle reader, started when Mr. W. and Miss R. were but mere children. I've been told by a most credible source that they shared a special bond throughout their childhood, but when they reached an age where they might have married, circumstances beyond their control kept them apart.

Edgar raised his head. "What in the world is this Miss Quill going on about? 'Circumstances beyond their control'? Wilhelmina rejected me out of hand, which certainly suggests she, at least, had a rather large measure of control over the event."

"I don't believe it's in your best interest to stop and ponder each paragraph, dear. Perhaps you'll get the full meaning of the article once you've gotten through the entire piece."

Knowing full well he was hardly likely to get the full meaning of a piece that already made little sense, but knowing there was nothing to do *but* continue onward, he dropped his head, found his place, and took to reading again.

> These childhood sweethearts were finally reunited last evening after being parted from each other for years. I am thrilled to report that their reunion was a most happy event, with our delightful hero and heroine proclaiming their very great affection for each other. The evening then culminated with a marriage proposal, one that I've been told was delivered by Mr. W. with a most romantic turn of phrase.

Miss R., I'm happy to report, was so overjoyed that tears cascaded down her beautiful face. And while society will surely miss her charming presence at their events, Pittsburgh, where I've been told Mr. W. now resides, has gained a most lovely addition to their social circles. More details to follow as they become known, but do feel free to extend this happy, happy couple your warmest wishes if you happen upon them somewhere in the city.

Lifting his head, Edgar's brows drew together. "Didn't you say this Miss Quill normally restricts her writing to fashion and decorating habits of the society set?"

"She's apparently decided to branch out," Nora said with a breezy wave of her hand. "But to give Miss Quill her due, her article may have very well saved Wilhelmina's reputation, as well as your own."

"And you're fairly confident that Wilhelmina would have already seen this piece?" Edgar asked as a sense of foreboding began replacing the trepidation he'd recently been feeling.

"I imagine she has, or if she hasn't read the article, I would think some helpful soul has paid a call on her to bring her up to date on the rumors swirling around the city about the two of you." Nora nodded to Mr. Hodges. "Poor Mr. Hodges had to stay directly inside the door today throughout calling hours, given that so many ladies wanted to pay a call on us in an attempt to find out all the pertinent details regarding your situation."

"Ladies were out and about during calling hours *today?*"

Mr. Hodges moved to a small rectangular table that stood beside the front door, picking up a silver platter. That platter was completely filled with calling cards. The sheer volume of cards left Edgar shaking his head even as his mother smiled and shook her head back at him.

"A little snow is not enough to deter determined ladies from searching out the truth regarding the most charming romance of the season, Edgar. I will say that none of them were so determined to pursue the matter, though, that they actually got out of their sleighs to personally deliver their calling cards. They had their drivers do that, knowing that I'll be required to acknowledge their call with either a call of my own or an invitation to dine with me for lunch sometime in the next week or so."

She smiled. "Hopefully I'll have good news to share with them by then or I might actually consider taking a trip out of the city for a few weeks."

Edgar returned her smile. "I don't think you'll be forced to leave the city, Mother, although I have to say it's becoming quite clear that society is growing more peculiar by the minute. Why, I can't imagine what these ladies were thinking, braving the elements in order to learn more about the so-called romance of the season, an event that just happens to be a complete fabrication on the part of what is clearly a delusional columnist. In all honesty, there was absolutely nothing of a romantic nature to be witnessed last night, unless you count the part where I kissed Wilhelmina, but no one was even around to witness that event."

"You never mentioned a thing about kissing Wilhelmina."

"And as a gentleman, I shouldn't have mentioned it now. So in order to maintain my position as a gentleman, while avoiding questions I know you're about to pose, I'll bid you good afternoon for now. Hopefully, I'll have encouraging news to share with you after I've spoken with Wilhelmina."

Mr. Hodges, who'd taken up his usual position by the door, took that moment to clear his throat. "If I may make a suggestion, sir? I would look in Central Park for Miss Radcliff first before traveling on to Gramercy Park. Quite a few of the drivers saw fit to tell me there are plans for society to gather in the park this afternoon, plans that include ice-skating, if I'm not mistaken."

Edgar frowned as he got to his feet. "Won't the ice at the lake in Central Park be buried under too much snow for skating?"

Mr. Hodges returned the frown. "Surely, sir, you haven't forgotten that something as trivial as a blizzard will have little to no impact on society and their pursuit of frivolities."

"I suppose I have, but I do thank you for the suggestion. It may very well save me some time in tracking her down."

Giving his mother a kiss on her cheek, Edgar turned and accepted

248

the greatcoat Mr. Hodges was holding out to him. Slipping his arms into the sleeves, he buttoned it up, stepped through the door Mr. Hodges was holding open, and found himself considering a sky that was beginning to look threatening once again. Flipping up his collar, he strode down the snow-covered sidewalk, unable to help but wonder if he might actually be fortunate enough to win Wilhelmina's hand once and for all before this day was through.

6

"I simply cannot apologize to you enough, Miss Radcliff, for the truly deplorable behavior of my stepsister, Lucy, last night," Miss Griswold said as she steered the well-appointed sleigh down the surprisingly busy snow-covered street.

Tucking a strand of hair that had escaped its pins back underneath her hat, Wilhelmina smiled as she turned to her new friend. "You really must not consider the matter another minute, Miss Griswold. I'm sure your stepsister didn't notify Mrs. Travers about seeing me and Mr. Wanamaker disappear through the French doors out of any sense of malice. As I've mentioned, the blizzard struck right around the time Edgar and I were foolish enough to venture outside, so I'm sure your stepsister was simply concerned for our welfare."

Miss Griswold suddenly seemed to forget she was responsible for controlling the magnificent beast that was pulling the sleigh, because she oh- so-casually dropped the reins into her lap even as she turned to catch Wilhelmina's eye. "I do wish I could agree with you, Miss Radcliff, but my stepsister has been cosseted outrageously throughout her nineteen years on this earth. That cosseting only increased when her father died five years back. While she doesn't possess a truly vindictive nature, she does possess a self-indulgent one, and that right there is why she alerted Mrs. Travers to your disappearance."

"I'm afraid I'm not following you," Wilhelmina admitted, keeping an eye on the horse that, surprisingly enough, didn't seem to need a guiding hand as it pulled them ever closer to Central Park.

"Mr. Wanamaker is an extremely handsome gentleman, Miss Radcliff. Add in the rumors regarding that respectable fortune he's apparently in possession of, and I'm afraid he's just become of great interest to all the eligible society ladies in the city. Lucy, I'm sad to say, is no exception to that and apparently decided she wanted your Mr. Wanamaker for herself. That, my dear, is exactly why you were discovered in the conservatory."

"He's not actually my Mr. Wanamaker quite yet" was all Wilhelmina could think to respond—a response that Miss Griswold completely ignored as she smiled somewhat grimly and continued on as if Wilhelmina had not even spoken.

"In all honesty, I don't believe Lucy thought the matter through properly, although the whole thinking business is always questionable when it concerns my stepsister. Lucy evidently didn't consider the potential consequences of you and Mr. Wanamaker being discovered alone together. I certainly don't believe she expected him to immediately declare his intention to marry you. That intention, amusingly enough, has caused my stepsister to take to her bed today. She's armed with a cool cloth and a bottle of smelling salts, moaning ever so often as her mother, my stepmother, sits by her side, wringing her hands and pondering whether or not a doctor should be summoned."

Wilhelmina fought a smile. "You do have a way of painting a scene with your words, Miss Griswold. But if you'll recall our conversation of last night, as you so kindly drove me home, I'm not entirely convinced it would be fair of me to take Edgar up on his offer."

"Mr. Wanamaker, from what I've observed of him so far, is a gentleman," Miss Griswold countered. "Because of that, you have no option but to take him up on his offer, or else he'll be forever plagued with feelings of guilt and . . . he will most certainly sink into a deep and life-altering melancholy."

"Edgar has never been prone to melancholy."

Miss Griswold pursed her lips. "He'll more than likely become prone to it if you don't accept his offer, especially after Mrs. Travers makes certain your reputation is destroyed. That will then see you out of your job as a social secretary, and the next thing you know, you'll be seen wandering through the city in rags, holding out your hand for a scrap of bread from anyone who passes you by."

Wilhelmina tilted her head. "Have you ever considered dabbling a bit with writing? I daresay you'd do well penning a gothic novel, what with the knack you seem to have for imagery."

Waving that observation aside, Miss Griswold plowed on with her argument as if Wilhelmina hadn't just voiced a brilliant suggestion. "Truth be told, I'm not exactly certain why you're dithering about accepting Mr. Wanamaker's proposal of marriage—especially since I'm convinced you truly care about the gentleman." She gave a rather knowing nod of her head. "You probably have never realized this, but when you speak of the man, your voice takes on a distinctly sappy tone."

Opening her mouth to dismiss that idea, Wilhelmina suddenly pressed her lips together when the thought struck that there just might be a grain of truth to Miss Griswold's observation.

"I fear you may be right about that, Miss Griswold," she finally admitted. "And truth be told, I have recently come to the conclusion that I care about Edgar far more than I'd realized. Having said that, I'm simply not comfortable with the marriage idea, given that he made his offer under what can only be described as extenuating circumstances."

"Wasn't it his idea to go to the conservatory in the first place?"

"Well, yes, but considering nothing untoward happened between us, I'm not comfortable holding him responsible for us being found out, nor am I comfortable holding him to his offer of marriage, especially after I rejected him all those years ago."

The sting of tears caught her by surprise. Turning her head, she brushed them away, but when she returned her attention to Miss Griswold, she found that lady considering her with far too much understanding resting in her unusual eyes.

Clearing her throat, Wilhelmina summoned up a smile. "The good news about that long ago rejection, though, at least according to

Edgar, is that he claims it helped turn him into a man—a role he fills rather nicely."

"He does indeed," Miss Griswold agreed.

Wilhelmina's smile widened. "Do you know that one of the reasons I turned down his proposal all those years ago was because I didn't think he was measuring up very well against the older gentlemen who were seeking my favor?"

Her smile faded straightaway as the truth of what she'd actually done that night settled into her very soul. "I was so foolish, you see, having my head turned by those other gentlemen, all of whom were certainly more sophisticated than Edgar, but none of whom, in hindsight, were prepared to give me what I truly needed—affection of the most genuine sort, something Edgar had always made available to me from the time we were mere children."

Miss Griswold immediately took to clucking. "From what you told me last night, you, my dear Miss Radcliff, were all of seventeen years old. Most young ladies are complete idiots at that age and make ridiculous choices on a frequent basis."

"Did you make ridiculous choices when you were seventeen?"

Miss Griswold tilted her head and adjusted the reins on her lap. "None that I can think of. But . . . I've always been a somewhat unusual sort, a circumstance that practically guaranteed my admittance into the wallflower set instead of the fashionable one when my father and I moved to New York."

"My tumble down the society ladder and into the wallflower set is yet another reason why I'm uncomfortable marrying Edgar. I'm afraid he'll eventually come to the conclusion that I only accepted his offer in order to escape the difficulties of my life."

"I don't think you're giving the gentleman enough credit. If you ask me, I think he returned to the city in order to discern whether or not you still held any affection for him—because he obviously still holds a great deal of affection for you." She gave a short bob of her head. "I could see it in his eyes last night whenever he looked at you. He adores you."

"Which is an encouraging idea. Although . . ." Looking up, the rest of Wilhelmina's words died on her tongue when she took note of a delivery wagon sliding its way through the street. Unfortunately, that wagon seemed to be sliding in their direction, a circumstance Miss Griswold had yet to notice. "I don't mean to be an alarmist, Miss Griswold, but it might be a sensible choice to retake the reins at this particular moment. If we don't remove ourselves from that wagon's path, I'm fairly certain it is soon to crash into us, leaving your sleigh—along with us, I must add—a mess of tangled parts."

Miss Griswold glanced at the wagon in question, and then returned her attention to Wilhelmina. "Mr. Merriweather doesn't need me to hold on to the reins. He's very good at getting us around the city on his own, as well as dodging any and all obstacles that might appear in our way."

"You named your horse Mr. Merriweather?" Wilhelmina couldn't resist asking, even with certain danger and death sliding ever closer their way.

"I did. I actually wanted to name him Charlie, but he simply refused to answer to that name."

Holding her breath as the wagon drew ever nearer *and* Miss Griswold did not pick up the reins, Wilhelmina felt herself going a bit dizzy from lack of air . . . but then sucked in a large breath a mere moment later, when Mr. Merriweather pulled the sleigh over to the very farthest corner of the road, giving the wagon a wide berth.

Sending Wilhelmina a rather smug smile, Miss Griswold picked up the reins, although she held them in a hand that, to Wilhelmina's eye, was merely for show.

"Do you and Mr. Merriweather spend much time traveling around the city?" she asked as the horse took that moment to pick up his pace, almost as if he wanted to prove to Wilhelmina that he was in complete control of their situation.

"We travel to Central Park nearly every day to watch society take their afternoon strolls or drives. We also travel to the shops on the Ladies' Mile as well as the shops located in the seedier parts of the city, because I simply can't resist searching out a good bargain."

Wilhelmina's nose took to wrinkling. "Isn't your father one of the wealthiest men in America these days?"

"I don't know if he's one of the wealthiest, but he does have a rather impressive fortune. I, however, have always possessed a frugal nature—thus the reason for shopping with an eye toward thrift."

Before Wilhelmina could ask why Miss Griswold would spend every afternoon watching society stroll around Central Park when she was probably never invited to stroll with any of the society members gathered there, Miss Griswold suddenly pulled back on the reins. Unsurprisingly, Mr. Merriweather tossed his head in clear protest, though he immediately slowed his pace.

"There seems to be some type of commotion up ahead, right by the entrance to Central Park, but . . ." Miss Griswold leaned forward, squinting at something in the distance. "On my word, I do believe that Mr. Asher Rutherford might be responsible for the congestion. Although . . ." She leaned further forward. "I'm sure I must be much mistaken about this, but it almost appears as if Mr. Rutherford has taken to hawking some manner of goods in the entranceway to Central Park."

With that, Miss Griswold clicked her tongue and steered Mr. Merriweather off to the side of the road, pulling on the brake when the horse came to a smart stop. Turning to Wilhelmina, she nodded. "Shall we nip over by Mr. Rutherford and investigate?"

"Investigate what, exactly?"

"What Mr. Rutherford is truly up to, of course. Surely you must find it just as curious as I do that the owner of one of the most prestigious stores in the city seems to be personally peddling wares."

Seeing no reason to balk over what seemed like a reasonable request, Wilhelmina climbed down from the sleigh, smiling when Miss Griswold moved directly to her side and linked their arms together. Giving their entwined arms a good pat, Miss Griswold immediately took to grinning.

"It's ever so lovely to have friends, isn't it?"

Unable to help but return the grin, even as she found herself wondering how it was possible that a charming lady like Miss Griswold had apparently spent her life bereft of many friends, Wilhelmina nodded. "It is indeed, Miss Griswold, and I feel I owe you an apology for neglecting to make a point of getting acquainted with you sooner."

"Since we're now on our way to becoming fast friends, you simply must call me Permilia, and I will, of course, call you Wilhelmina, even when you marry your Mr. Wanamaker and become Mrs. Wanamaker to the world at large."

"I don't recall stating for certain that I'm going to accept his offer, not that he, now that I consider the matter, did any offering. It was more on the lines of a statement."

"Only a ninny would cast Mr. Edgar Wanamaker aside, and you, my dear, don't strike me as a ninny," Permilia said before she prodded Wilhelmina into motion.

Slipping their way into Central Park , they didn't stop until they reached a stack of rectangular boxes coated in a glossy pink finish. Mr. Asher Rutherford, owner of Rutherford & Company—a store known for its fine goods—stood directly beside those boxes.

"Ladies," Mr. Rutherford exclaimed as he slid money into a cash register set up on what appeared to be an old crate. "Have you come to purchase a pair of skates? I have the very latest in ice skates available, and still have a nice selection of styles to choose from."

Stepping forward with an air that could only be described as confident, Permilia opened a box and stuck her hand inside, peeling away the tissue paper that cushioned the skates inside. "How much are you charging for these?" she asked.

"Five dollars, seventy-seven cents," Mr. Rutherford said with a smile, the smile fading straightaway when Permilia withdrew her hand from the box and closed the lid.

"That's flat-out robbery, that is," Permilia said, apparently not impressed in the least by the idea she was conversing with a gentleman who was considered one of the most eligible gentlemen in the city.

Mr. Rutherford narrowed his eyes. "It most certainly is not."

"Bloomingdales has skates for under four dollars," Permilia proclaimed.

"For roller skates, and low quality roller skates, at that," Mr. Rutherford countered.

Permilia's lips pursed for a moment before she surprised Wilhelmina by nodding. "You might be right about that."

"There's no *might* about it," Mr. Rutherford returned. "I know exactly what Bloomingdales charges for the majority of their items, along with what every other store in the city charges as well. What I'm asking for these skates—the convenience of which you'll be able to enjoy at no extra charge today—is more than fair."

"I'll give you six dollars and thirty-two cents for two pairs of ladies' skates," Permilia said.

"Did you just pull that figure out of thin air?"

"Of course not. I noted that you purchased your supply—at least the skate I saw in that box—from Dame, Stoddard, and Kendal out of Boston, and they charge around two dollars a pair if you purchase from them directly. However, since you have incurred the cost of having that company send you the skates, as well as the cost of employees you hire to manage your stock, and have included those lovely pink boxes with the purchase of the skates as well, I'm willing to add a bit more to the final cost."

"I don't need a pair of skates," Wilhelmina said before Mr. Rutherford could take to arguing with Permilia, something his expression clearly suggested he longed to do. "I only brought a few coins with me, so even at the discounted price, well, I'm afraid I don't have enough to cover my share of the bill."

"I wouldn't expect you to pay anything," Permilia said. "They'd be my gift to you—my new and delightful friend."

Before Wilhelmina could insist that she wasn't comfortable accepting charity, Mr. Rutherford stepped around his makeshift cash register and sent her a most charming smile—one that he'd certainly not been bestowing on Permilia a second before.

"Miss Radcliff, how delightful to see you this fine afternoon. I must beg your pardon for not recognizing you straightaway." He sent a narrowing of his eyes toward Permilia, as if he blamed her for that unfortunate happenstance. When Permilia calmly began inspecting the stormy skies, Mr. Rutherford's lips curved just a smidgen at the corners before he returned his attention to Wilhelmina. "Mr. Wanamaker arrived in Central Park about thirty minutes ago, looking for you, of course. But before you go off to find him, do allow me to extend to you my warmest congratulations. Edgar is one of my closest friends from my school days, and I couldn't be happier for the two of you." He beamed a charming smile Wilhelmina's way, the beaming bringing two dimples popping out on either side of his mouth. "What size are those boots you're wearing?"

"You want to know my boot size?" she asked somewhat weakly, even as she stuck a boot out from underneath the hem of her skirt to peruse it.

"Ah, that looks to be around a size six. So . . ." Mr. Rutherford turned from her, pulled out a glossy pink box, opened the lid, checked the skates inside, then turned and handed her the box. "These should fit just fine."

Wilhelmina tried to give the box back to the gentleman, but he stuck his hands behind his back and simply wouldn't take it.

"I'm not comfortable accepting these," she said.

He smiled another charming smile. "Nonsense, there's absolutely no reason for you to be uncomfortable about accepting a pair of skates from me. Especially since"—his smile, impossible as it seemed, turned even more charming—"Edgar already compensated me for those on the chance that you'd show up here at the park without a pair of skates. He wanted to make certain that you'd be able to enjoy a day on the ice."

Wilhelmina's eyes immediately filled with pesky tears once again, their appearance having Mr. Rutherford whipping a handkerchief from his pocket and pressing it into her hand. Snuffling into it, she managed to get out a word of thanks as Mr. Rutherford took to beaming back at her.

"I'm delighted to discover that Edgar has found himself such a sensitive young lady," Mr. Rutherford said after Wilhelmina finished her snuffling. "And being a sensitive sort, I'm sure you're anxious to seek Edgar out so the two of you might share a special moment over his considerate gesture. You'll be able to make immediate use of the skates he provided for you since he's currently to be found out on the ice, testing a new style of skates for me."

Wilhelmina blinked. "I've never known Edgar to be what anyone could call proficient on the ice."

"Which is why I've given him skates that sport two blades instead of one—a style that should see him finding more enjoyment in the whole skating business, since he shouldn't spend as much time losing his balance."

"I wouldn't be so certain about that."

Mr. Rutherford tilted his head and seemed to consider that for a long moment. "You might have a point. But do know that I didn't send him off on the ice all by himself. He's in the company of Mr. Harrison Sinclair, a gentleman possessed of a brawny figure and enough muscles to get Edgar pulled off the ice if he does have some difficulties with his skating."

"I'm afraid I'm not familiar with a Mr. Sinclair. Is he new to the city?"

Curiously enough, Mr. Rutherford suddenly took to looking rather shifty. "Do forgive me, Miss Radcliff. I neglected to remember that the subject of Mr. Sinclair is a somewhat delicate one, especially since I'm not exactly certain what Edgar wants you to know about that particular man just yet."

7

Having no idea what she could possibly say to that, Wilhelmina found herself spared any response at all when Permilia suddenly appeared by her side. She was clutching one of the pink boxes to her chest but seemed to forget all about that box as she launched herself into the midst of Wilhelmina's conversation.

"Honestly, Mr. Rutherford, don't you realize that by speaking to Miss Radcliff in such a cryptic fashion, you've piqued her curiosity and probably left her believing the very worst about Mr. Sinclair."

Permilia turned to Wilhelmina. "Mr. Sinclair, from what I've been told, is a shipping magnate who has increased the family fortune exponentially over the past decade. He rarely travels in the highest realms of society, though, given that his fortune is not the three-generations-old that Mrs. Astor claims makes one acceptable."

Wilhelmina wrinkled her nose. "Is Mr. Sinclair known for shady business dealings?"

"Of course not," Permilia returned. "He's from a well-respected family—although I don't believe they're originally from New York—and his family members, besides being wealthy, are known to possess remarkably good looks. But that has nothing to do with the subject at hand." She set her sights on Mr. Rutherford. "What business would Mr. Wanamaker possibly have with a shipping magnate?"

Mr. Rutherford crossed his arms over his chest. "As I said before,

Edgar's business with Mr. Sinclair is his business, and I'm not at liberty to divulge the particulars to you."

"Fine," Permilia began with a lift of her chin. "We'll go track him down and get our answers straight from the source." She thrust the pink box she was holding into Mr. Rutherford's hands before she opened up her reticule and pulled out a fistful of coins. Counting them out very precisely, she stopped counting when she reached three dollars, sixty-two cents. Handing Mr. Rutherford the coins, she then took back the pink box, completely ignoring the scowl Mr. Rutherford was now sending her.

"This is not the amount of money I quoted you for the skates, Miss . . . ?"

"Miss Griswold," Permilia supplied as she opened up the box and began rummaging through the thin paper that covered her skates.

Mr. Rutherford's brows drew together. "Surely you're not related to Mr. George Griswold, are you?"

"He's my father," Permilia returned before she frowned and lifted out what appeared to be some type of printed form, one that had a small pencil attached to it with a maroon ribbon. "What is this?"

Mr. Rutherford returned the frown, looking as if he wanted to discuss something besides the form Permilia was now waving his way, but he finally relented—although he did so with a somewhat heavy sigh. "It's a survey, and I would be ever so grateful if you and Miss Radcliff would take a few moments to fill it out, returning it after you're done to a member of my staff, many of whom can be found offering hot chocolate for a mere five cents at a stand we've erected by the side of the lake. I'm trying to determine which styles of skates my customers prefer, and after I'm armed with that information, I'll be better prepared to stock my store next year with the best possible products."

"Far be it from me to point out the obvious, Mr. Rutherford, but one has to wonder about your audacity," Permilia said. "It's confounding to me that you're so successful in business, especially since not only are you overcharging your customers for the skates today, you also expect those very customers to extend you a service by taking time out of their day to fill out a survey for you. And then, to top matters off nicely, instead of extending those customers a free cup of hot chocolate for their time and effort, you're charging them for that as well."

"I'm a businessman, Miss Griswold—as is your father, if I need remind you. I'm sure he'd understand exactly what my strategy is here today, as well as agree with that strategy."

Permilia stuck her nose into the air. "You may very well be right, Mr. Rutherford, but . . ." She thrust the box back into his hands. "Since I'm unwilling to pay more than I've already given you for these skates, I'll take my money back, if you please."

"Don't be ridiculous," Mr. Rutherford said, thrusting the box right back at Permilia. "Now, if the two of you will excuse me, I have other customers to attend to." With that, he sent Wilhelmina a nod, scowled at Permilia, and strode through the snow back to his cash register. He immediately took to smiling a charming smile at the line of young ladies who'd gathered around the pink boxes, none of them appearing to be perturbed in the least by the price Mr. Rutherford had set for the skates, especially since most of them were already waving money his way.

Taking hold of Permilia's arm, Wilhelmina couldn't help but grin when she saw the sparkle in her new friend's eyes. "You're a little frightening. You realize that, don't you?"

"I've always enjoyed a rousing barter, but I must admit that I didn't truly know whether or not I'd win this round in the end." Permilia smiled and nodded to an empty bench by the side of the ice. "Shall we see if Mr. Rutherford's skates are worth the exorbitant price he's asking for them?"

"You didn't pay what he was asking for them, and I, well, I didn't pay anything at all, since Edgar purchased the skates for me in advance," Wilhelmina pointed out.

"Which speaks volumes about Mr. Wanamaker's character." Reaching the bench, Permilia took a seat, Wilhelmina joining her a moment later. Before either one of them could begin getting their skates on over their buttoned boots, though, two young men from Rutherford & Company appeared out of nowhere and began assisting them.

"Perhaps Mr. Rutherford does know a thing or two about what he's doing after all," Permilia said as the two young men sent them nods and hurried away to help other ladies with their skates.

Rising from the bench, Wilhelmina took the arm Permilia offered her, and together the two ladies made their way through the snow and onto the ice.

Smiling as ladies and gentlemen glided past them with cheeks rosy from the cold air, Wilhelmina moved into motion, keeping to the very edge of the lake until she found her balance. Increasing her speed as her confidence improved, she linked her arm with Permilia, and with their glides matching, they moved toward the center of the lake. Enjoying the breeze flowing over her, she searched the crowd, slowing to an immediate stop when a curious sight met her eyes.

Sitting on the ice in the very middle of the lake was none other than Edgar, his legs stretched out in front of him while a large gentleman Wilhelmina assumed was the mysterious Mr. Sinclair lounged on the ice next to him.

Shaking her head, she tugged Permilia in Edgar's direction, frowning when Permilia brought them to a stop a mere second later and unlinked their arms.

"It may be for the best for you to do this on your own," Permilia said.

"You don't want to see how this ends?"

Biting her lip, Permilia shook her head. "I don't have the gift of conversing well with gentlemen I don't know, and . . . I don't want to make this situation any more difficult for you than it already is."

"Last night you had no difficulty conversing with Edgar, whom I know for fact you'd never met before, and . . . you certainly had no difficulty conversing with poor Mr. Rutherford."

Frowning, Permilia wrinkled her nose. "That is a most excellent point. I suppose I didn't have much difficulty speaking with your Mr. Wanamaker last night because I was at first tasked with the mission of keeping you out of sight, which must have distracted me from my usual discomfort."

"What about Mr. Rutherford, then?"

Permilia tilted her head. "I have no idea why I can speak so easily, or rather argue so easily, with him, but . . . now is hardly the moment for us to ponder that matter. You have a gentleman intent on marriage to deal with, so . . . off you go." With that, Permilia sent Wilhelmina a grin and glided away.

Squaring her shoulders after Permilia disappeared into the crowd, Wilhelmina began skating in Edgar's direction. Coming to a stop a few feet away from him, she smiled when he looked up. That smile, unfortunately, turned to a wince a mere second later, when he tried to get to his feet and immediately took to flailing about. Before she could do more than blink, he was sprawled facedown on the ice.

Skating up next to him, she bent over. "Are you all right?"

"I'm fine—well, except for my bruised pride," he said, rolling over before he struggled to a sitting position. "One would think that since I'm testing skates with two blades, I'd have an easier time of staying upright. But . . . I'm afraid that has not been the case." He caught her eye again and smiled. "But enough about that. I'm delighted you showed up at the park today, although I was planning on seeking you out at your house if you didn't arrive here soon." He nodded to the gentleman who'd risen to his feet and was now smiling Wilhelmina's way as well. "I'd like you to meet a new friend of mine, Mr. Harrison Sinclair. Mr. Sinclair, this is my very good friend, Miss Wilhelmina Radcliff."

Taking her gloved hand in his, Mr. Sinclair raised it to his lips in a practiced move and kissed it. "It's a pleasure to meet you, Miss Radcliff."

"It's a pleasure to meet you as well, Mr. Sinclair."

"Mr. Sinclair has just disclosed some information that I believe you're going to find quite interesting, Wilhelmina." Edgar struggled to get to his feet, not hesitating for even a second when Mr. Sinclair offered him a hand and pulled him upright. "Thank you," he said.

"You're welcome," Mr. Sinclair returned before he nodded to Wilhelmina. "And, because I can see the curiosity in your eyes, allow me to disclose that the information Edgar just mentioned pertains to your father and the financial setback he suffered."

Wilhelmina frowned. "I'm not certain losing the majority of the family fortune on a risky investment can actually be considered a *financial setback*, Mr. Sinclair. *Complete and utter disaster* springs to mind, but *setback* . . . I don't think that term sufficiently describes what happened."

Mr. Sinclair inclined his head. "That's a fair point, Miss Radcliff, and do know that I'm sorry for the trials your family has obviously suffered. I understand the reason for the loss of your family fortune was due to an entire fleet of ships going down as they were crossing the Atlantic Ocean."

"That is exactly what happened, Mr. Sinclair. A circumstance that Mr. Melville, my father's partner in this particular venture, claimed was a most unusual happenstance, one that is rarely, if ever, seen."

"I would have to agree with this Mr. Melville on that, because entire fleets rarely go down." Mr. Sinclair shook his head. "A ship might capsize due to a wave, or take on water that has it sinking, but it's a rare occurrence for all the ships in a fleet to sink. One ship usually manages to float its way back into port at some point in time, even if it has sustained heavy damages."

Edgar reached out and took Wilhelmina's hand in his. "That right there is why I sought out Mr. Sinclair today in order to get his perspective on your situation."

"You sought him out because of me?"

Edgar smiled at her, the warmth of that smile sending little flutters through her stomach. "I just had this feeling that in order for you and me to be able to move on successfully together, we'd be more capable of reaching that success if you had a bit of closure regarding the nasty business surrounding the loss of your father's fortune. And . . ." he continued before she could pose a single argument to that, "I also thought, if there was a small chance of regaining some of that fortune, it would allow you to feel more secure in any relationship you and I may decide to pursue."

His smile widened. "I wouldn't want you to worry that I'd come to question why you'd want to embrace the idea of a future with me after you'd rejected me all of those years ago."

Her flutters immediately took to increasing, probably due to the idea that Edgar truly did still understand her—had always understood her—and had taken that knowledge and used it to try and create a feeling of equality between them. Although . . .

With her brows knitting together, Wilhelmina tilted her head. "I'm not certain about this, but I truly don't believe there's a way to create an equality between us in regard to finances, unless, of course, you're about to tell me that Mr. Sinclair just happened to have found the fleet of ships that we were told sunk."

"That's exactly what Mr. Wanamaker is trying to tell you," Mr. Sinclair said, his words having Wilhelmina's knees going so weak that she had no choice but to take a seat directly on the hard ice.

"I don't understand," she whispered.

Joining her on the ice—although that seemed to be more because his feet slipped out from underneath him again rather than his deliberately deciding to take a seat next to her—Edgar pulled her hand into his. "I was curious, you see, about what you'd disclosed to me about this Mr. Melville. He sounded like a somewhat suspicious sort, especially after you told me he completely disappeared after your father suffered his apoplexy."

Edgar lifted her hand and pressed a kiss to her gloved fingers. "I was very concerned that Mr. Melville might have taken advantage of your father's descent into poor health, and . . . I was right."

"You were right . . . how?"

Edgar turned his gaze on Mr. Sinclair. "Perhaps it would be best for you to explain the situation, Mr. Sinclair, since you're the one who was able to discover the facts so quickly."

Nodding, Mr. Sinclair crouched beside Wilhelmina. "My family, Miss Radcliff, has been in shipping in one form or another for generations. I've grown up around docks all over the world, and because of that upbringing, I'm very familiar with how rampant rumors are around a shipyard. Having said that, when my friend, Asher Rutherford, came to my office today—in the company of your Mr. Wanamaker, of course—and inquired about the missing fleet your father invested in, I couldn't recall a single rumor regarding such a happenstance in recent history."

He shook his head. "In order to make certain I hadn't missed hearing about the fleet, we proceeded to the docks to track down a few of my friends and associates, and not a single one of them could recall news about an entire fleet being lost at sea."

"Some of Mr. Sinclair's friends *did* remember a fleet being blown off course, and that the fleet was originally believed to be lost at sea for a good month or so," Edgar added.

Wilhelmina's heart accelerated to an almost painful rate. "Are you saying . . . ?"

Edgar kissed her hand again even as he nodded. "I am. The fleet that your father invested the majority of his money in did go missing. And to give Mr. Melville the benefit of the doubt, I believe that when he went to speak to your father, it was still missing and was presumed at that time to be lost at sea."

"But it eventually showed up?" Wilhelmina pressed.

"It did," Mr. Sinclair said. "Although, I do feel it necessary to tell you that some of the goods didn't pull into the harbor with the fleet, having been damaged or lost overboard when the storm hit. However, having said that, there was a tidy profit made—a tidy profit, I'm sorry to report, that Mr. Melville decided to keep for himself."

Wilhelmina's mouth dropped open. "He stole my father's portion of the profits?"

"He did, and moved off to Georgia with them."

"How do you know that?"

"I have many associates involved in the shipping industry, Miss Radcliff, and those associates have a network of other associates, a wonderful system if one is looking for certain information. I simply put out the word today that I was looking for a Mr. Melville, and a captain from a ship currently stuck in the harbor due to the weather, knew exactly where to find the man. You'll be happy to learn that a telegram has already been sent off to the proper authorities, and . . . I'm certain Mr. Melville will soon be apprehended."

Wilhelmina blinked rapidly in order to hold at bay the tears that had suddenly sprung to her eyes. "This seems so . . . well . . . astonishing."

Mr. Sinclair smiled, pushed himself to his feet, and caught her gaze as he looked down at her. "Mr. Wanamaker has proclaimed more than once that he finds you to be quite remarkable. Because of that, I do believe he was rather determined to do whatever it took to make matters right for your family." He sent her a wink. "Make certain to remember that when he goes about the business of extending to you a proper proposal. Although . . . I wasn't supposed to say anything about that." Sending her another wink, Mr. Sinclair set off across the lake, vanishing into the crowd a second later.

Turning back to Edgar, Wilhelmina arched a brow. "Did I hear correctly about something regarding a proper proposal?"

Edgar smiled a little sheepishly. "This wasn't exactly how I pictured it, me sitting on a frozen lake of incredibly cold ice with seemingly half of New York society skating around us."

Disappointment was swift and evidently showed on her face, because the next thing she knew, Edgar was leaning closer to her, his eyes suddenly holding that certain something she'd seen the night before at the ball, something that had her toes curling.

"Would it be completely untoward of me to voice a proposal this very minute?" he asked.

"Are you going to do so simply because a marriage between us is now expected, given that Mrs. Travers discovered us alone together?" Wilhelmina asked in voice that had turned slightly breathless.

"Absolutely not."

"Then why are you so determined to marry me?" She couldn't resist asking, even though she was beginning to come to her own conclusion regarding that, a conclusion that left her feeling distinctly light-headed.

"I believe it might have something to do with the fact I love you, and . . . something to do with the fact that I know you're the only woman I've ever loved, and will ever love, so . . ." Edgar paused and sent her a small smile. "Please put me out of my misery and finally agree to become my wife."

For a second, as her breath got caught in her throat, she could only stare at the gentleman who'd always been her very dearest friend, and evidently wanted to become an even dearer friend—albeit one known as her husband—for the rest of her days. Leaning in toward him, she smiled. "You do realize that I would have agreed to marry you even if you hadn't solved the mystery of the missing fleet, don't you?"

He traced a lazy finger down her cheek as his smile turned into a grin. "I would have investigated the matter even if I thought you wouldn't accept my proposal, but . . ." He suddenly stopped smiling. "Wait a minute. Did you just agree to marry me?"

"I did, although . . . I do have some . . . conditions."

"You have . . . conditions?"

She couldn't help but grin at the incredulous look crossing his face. "They're not difficult conditions, Edgar, and in all honesty, there's only one."

"And . . . ?"

"I think we should enjoy a long engagement, especially because it's been seven years since you've been in my company for any significant amount of time. It could turn out that you don't care for me as much as you think you do, and . . . while I don't care to dwell on how miserable that would make me, it still needs to be a consideration."

"I distinctly remember professing my love for you just a few short minutes ago," Edgar said slowly.

"And while I distinctly remember you *professing* your love for me, something I assure you I'll never forget, it wouldn't hurt to enjoy a long engagement. Although . . ." Her eyes widened. "Good heavens, Edgar, I do beg your pardon. I've just now recalled that I have yet to profess my feelings for you, although I would imagine you've already figured out that I love you as well."

"You . . . love me?" Edgar asked.

Wilhelmina smiled. "I readily admit that I do, although it certainly took me long enough to realize that what I've always felt for you is love of the deepest sort."

"At least you finally did."

"Indeed."

Edgar leaned closer to her. "Very well, I will agree to your condition, but only if you'll clarify what you consider to be a reasonable amount of time to get to know each other again, and if I agree that it's not too long."

"Hmm . . ." Wilhelmina began. "What about six months?"

"What about three?"

Without the least little hesitation, she nodded. "Done." And then, before he could negotiate further, and even with the throngs of skaters circling them, Wilhelmina leaned forward, placed her lips on his, and found herself more than content with the idea that she'd be free to kiss his lips anytime she wanted to for the rest of their lives.

Epilogue

"I'm simply thrilled you permitted me the honor, my dear Wilhelmina, of hosting the ball that will formally allow society to know you've accepted Edgar's proposal of marriage."

Smiling, Wilhelmina turned to Nora Wanamaker, unable to resist the urge to lean in and kiss her soon to be mother-in-law's cheek.

"I wouldn't have had it any other way," Wilhelmina said. "And allow me to say, while you and I are waiting for additional guests to arrive, that I'm delighted you're no longer put out with me, and . . . delighted to learn that you've been secretly holding out hope that Edgar and I would someday find our way back to each other."

"I've spent a good deal of time at church, praying over that particular hope," Nora said with a smile of her own before she nodded to where Wilhelmina's father was standing at the end of the receiving line. "It's wonderful to see your father out and about. I was afraid he wouldn't be well enough to join the festivities tonight."

Wilhelmina turned her attention to her father, who was still forced to use a cane, although the air of moroseness that had been settled around him for the past two years was nowhere to be found.

Switching her gaze to her mother, who was standing directly beside her father, Wilhelmina smiled over the fact that her mother no longer looked as if she carried the weight of the world on her

271

slender shoulders. That look had disappeared almost the moment she'd learned that Wilhelmina was marrying Edgar and learned that her days of being a pauper were over.

"My parents did not do well with the whole being-poor notion," Wilhelmina said right as Edgar touched her sleeve, drawing her attention. Her smile immediately turned into a grin when she found Permilia standing beside Edgar.

"I'm so delighted you could make it," Wilhelmina said, leaning forward to accept Permilia's kiss on her cheek.

"Of course I made it," Permilia returned before she lowered her voice to a mere whisper. "And while I would normally make the claim that this is certain to be the event of the season, I've recently learned that Alva Vanderbilt has let it be known she's going to host a spectacular costume ball in that new mansion of hers on Fifth Avenue—a ball in March, no less, after the season is officially over." She let out a bit of a sigh. "Since I'm very much afraid Alva is going to do her very best to make sure her ball will be spoken about a hundred years from now, I do hope you won't be disappointed when everyone discontinues talking about this ball."

"That won't bother me in the least, since I'm more concerned with marrying Edgar than making an impression on society, but . . ." Wilhelmina leaned closer and dropped her voice to a whisper quite like Permilia had only recently done. "How did you learn about Alva Vanderbilt's ball?"

"I have my ways," Permilia said rather mysteriously. "Now then, since I don't want to monopolize your time, I'll leave you to your other guests, but do make certain to come find me when you're done with the receiving line." She winked. "I'll be one of the ladies lounging in the wallflower section."

Before Wilhelmina could respond, Permilia glided away, leaving Wilhelmina to face Miss Lucy Webster, Permilia's stepsister and the young lady who'd been responsible for Edgar proposing in the first place. Swallowing a laugh when Miss Webster took to gushing about what a lovely couple Wilhelmina and Edgar made, Wilhelmina threw herself back into the process of extending the proper pleasantries to the guests who followed after Miss Webster.

Blowing out a satisfied breath an hour later, when she finished greeting the last guest, she turned to Edgar again.

"Do you mind if I go off to speak with Permilia and the rest of the wallflowers for a bit?" she asked.

Edgar smiled, kissed her cheek, and shooed her away, saying something about searching out Mr. Rutherford to enjoy a celebratory toast.

Making her way through the crowded house, Wilhelmina discovered that she wasn't in the least upset to be leaving the social world of New York City behind. She and Edgar had agreed that with his mills being where they were, it would make more sense to live in Pittsburgh. Even though society had wholeheartedly accepted her with open arms after it had become known her father's fortune was being restored, and that she was soon to become Mrs. Edgar Wanamaker, Wilhelmina had discovered that the New York social world no longer appealed to her as it once had done.

Coming to a stop when she reached the back wall of the ballroom, she simply stood there for a moment, watching Permilia, Miss Gertrude Cadwalader, Miss Temperance Flowerdew, and a few other young ladies she didn't know well, chat with each other—although Miss Flowerdew seemed content with merely listening.

The mere idea that the wallflowers were engaged with each other was an enormous change from just a few weeks before, and that warmed Wilhelmina all the way down to the tips of her toes.

Lifting her chin, she moved to join the group, knowing without a shadow of a doubt that these wallflowers, all of whom society had relegated to the sidelines, were soon to break free from those sidelines and hopefully claim their happily-ever-after just as she'd been able to do.

She couldn't wait to see how they went about accomplishing exactly that.

About the Authors

Mary Connealy writes "romantic comedies with cowboys" and is celebrated for her fun, zany, action-packed style. She has more than half a million books in print. She is the author of the popular series WILD AT HEART, KINCAID BRIDES, TROUBLE IN TEXAS, LASSOED IN TEXAS, SOPHIE'S DAUGHTERS, and many other books. Mary lives on a ranch in eastern Nebraska with her very own romantic cowboy hero. Learn more at www.maryconnealy.com.

∾

Kristi Ann Hunter graduated from Georgia Tech with a degree in computer science but always knew she wanted to write. Kristi is an RWA Rita® Award–winning author and a finalist for the Christy Award and the Georgia Romance Writers Maggie Award for Excellence. She lives with her husband and three children in Georgia. Find her online at www.kristiannhunter.com.

∾

Jen Turano, a *USA Today* bestselling author, is a graduate of the University of Akron with a degree in clothing and textiles. She is a member of ACFW and RWA. She lives in a suburb of Denver, Colorado. Visit her website at www.jenturano.com.

Books by Mary Connealy

From Bethany House Publishers

THE KINCAID BRIDES

Out of Control
In Too Deep
Over the Edge

TROUBLE IN TEXAS

Swept Away
Fired Up
Stuck Together

WILD AT HEART

Tried & True
Now & Forever
Fire & Ice

THE CIMARRON LEGACY

No Way Up
Long Time Gone
Too Far Down

HIGH SIERRA SWEETHEARTS

The Accidental Guardian

A Match Made in Texas: A Novella Collection*
With This Ring? A Novella Collection of Proposals Gone Awry*
Hearts Entwined: A Historical Romance Novella Collection*
All for Love: Three Historical Romance Novellas of Love and Laughter*

*Connealy contributed to this collection.

Books by Kristi Ann Hunter

HAWTHORNE HOUSE

A Lady of Esteem (novella)
A Noble Masquerade
An Elegant Façade
An Uncommon Courtship
An Inconvenient Beauty

HAVEN MANOR

A Search for Refuge (novella)
A Defense of Honor

Books by Jen Turano

Sign Up for the Authors' Newsletters!

Keep up to date with latest news on book releases
and events by signing up for their email lists at:

maryconnealy.com

kristiannhunter.com

jenturano.com

◊ BETHANYHOUSE

 Stay up to date on your favorite books and authors with our free e-newsletters.
Sign up today at bethanyhouse.com.

 Find us on Facebook. facebook.com/bethanyhousepublishers

 Free exclusive resources for your book group! bethanyhouse.com/anopenbook

anopenbook

More from the Authors

After Chance Boden is wounded in an avalanche, he demands that the conditions of his will go into effect: His children must either live and work at home for one year or forfeit the ranch. He trusts Heath Kincaid to see it done. But when Heath begins to suspect the accident was due to foul play, he finds his desire to protect Chance's daughter goes way beyond duty.

No Way Up by Mary Connealy
THE CIMARRON LEGACY #1
maryconnealy.com

Entering her fourth season, Lady Miranda Hawthorne secretly longs to be bold. But she is mortified when her brother's handsome new valet accidentally mails her private thoughts to a duke she's never met—until he responds. As she tries to sort out her growing feelings for two men, it becomes clear that Miranda's heart is not the only thing at risk for the Hawthorne family.

A Noble Masquerade by Kristi Ann Hunter
HAWTHORNE HOUSE
kristiannhunter.com

When paid companion Gertrude Cadwalader is caught returning items pilfered by her employer, her friend Harrison's mother jumps to the wrong conclusion. But Harrison quickly comes to Gertrude's defense— and initiates an outlandish plan to turn their friendship into a romance.

Out of the Ordinary by Jen Turano
APART FROM THE CROWD
jenturano.com